TIGHT CASE

TIGHT CASE

EDWARD J. HOGAN

EAST CHICAGO PUBLIC LIBRARY
EAST CHICAGO, INDIANA

MACMILLAN PUBLISHING COMPANY • NEW YORK

ML /87 4223

Copyright © 1987 by Edward J. Hogan

All rights reserved. No part of this book may be reproduced or transmitted in any form or by any means, electronic or mechanical, including photocopying, recording or by any information storage and retrieval system, without permission in writing from the Publisher.

Macmillan Publishing Company
866 Third Avenue, New York, N.Y. 10022
Collier Macmillan Canada, Inc.

Library of Congress Cataloging-in-Publication Data
Hogan, Edward J.
Tight case.
I. Title.
PS3558.034724T5 1987   813'.54   87-15217
ISBN 0-02-553330-4

10 9 8 7 6 5 4 3 2 1

Designed by Jack Meserole

PRINTED IN THE UNITED STATES OF AMERICA

This novel is a work of fiction. Names, characters, places, and incidents are either the products of the author's imagination or are used fictitiously. Any resemblance to actual persons, living or dead, events, or locales is entirely coincidental.

TIGHT CASE

F
H7131t

CHAPTER 1

THIS is horseshit," Ed Fleming said as he stared at the tiny spitmarks of snow blowing onto the windshield. "Two white guys parked in the middle of Harlem. We might as well put up a fucking sign—'NARCS'—in big red letters." He shifted his long legs into a new uncomfortable position. That was another thing about stakeouts. If you were tall, there was no way to stretch out.

A bunch of street kids came up the nearly deserted block, dressed in their finest threads. "Whatchoo want, you dumb nigger?" one shouted, slapping playfully at a friend. When they saw the sedan with two antennas, the kids

I

strutted right by, seeming to ignore the car—and the two men inside . . . except for the sidelong glances and grins among themselves.

Fleming shook his head. "See what I mean?"

His partner, Jack Ross, turned in the driver's seat. "We don't need a sign, Ed. The natives can read the smoke signals." He jerked a thumb over his shoulder. In the cold air, the car's exhaust was rising like a big white cloud behind them. "And don't even suggest turning off the engine. You wanna freeze your balls off, just step outside. After sixteen years on the job, I stay where it's nice and warm." He rapped his fist on the dashboard. "Not that this heater is so fucking great."

Fleming went back to looking out the window. Not that there was much to see—the hulking figure of their undercover man, Grover Alston, on the block ahead of them, and a junkie on the next corner. The guy was dressed for summer in the middle of a snowstorm, and kept dancing around to keep off the cold. Just watching him made Fleming feel colder.

Ross must have felt cold, too. He reached into his coat for a flask of blackberry brandy and took a swig. That made his nineteenth since they'd parked the car.

"How can you keep drinking that piss?"

Ross grinned. He was short, maybe five-nine, and skinny—booze being a poor substitute for food. He looked every one of his forty-five years. "Keeps me warm. And after sixteen years . . ."

"Jesus, will you knock off that seniority crap? You've got one year on me in the Agency!" Fleming burst out.

They lapsed into silence. *Both of us have been on the job too long,* Fleming thought. *We're beginning to sound like an old married couple.* Although from his experience, old married couples didn't squabble. They just coldly ignored each other. He remembered those last few months with Meg—like living in a graveyard. Then the divorce, the custody fight . . . could it really be four years since he saw the kids?

"Hey, where's Grover?"

Ross's words shook Fleming free from his thoughts. He roused himself in the seat. "Weren't you watching him? Goddammit, he's carrying money." They stared anxiously out the windshield.

As suddenly as Grover had disappeared, he reappeared, talking with his supposed coke connection . . . a young black guy in torn jeans, sneakers, and a ragged army coat that hung at least two sizes too big on him. As the connection walked beside Grover, he almost fell into a dance step.

Fleming shook his head. "Look at this guy—his ass is coming out his pants, and he's doing the junkie trot. If he has goods to sell, why isn't he using any? This is some big fucking connection to give up Christmas for." He'd rushed out that morning with just a few minutes to exchange presents with Joan. Her eyes went big when she saw the antique pin she'd lusted after back in August. Buying it and hiding it may have been silly—but that's the kind of thing you did when you were married just a year and a half.

Joan had thrown herself into his arms with a hot thank-you kiss that promised a lot more. But no, he had to run—for this.

Ross was talking. "Oh, fuck that growling, Fleming. Dealing today makes the spook feel safe. Remember what Grover said?" He went into his jive imitation. "We goan do de deal on *Chris*-muss, 'cause de Man be at home, unwrapping presents wif de kids."

"Yeah, Christmas. That's why that scumbag over there wore his best suit. You gonna tell me he felt he had to dress for the part? Or maybe . . ." Fleming began to smile. "Maybe he's a city narc."

That got a laugh out of Ross. "Probably. And he's got six guys for backup, since he never saw such a mean-looking motherfucker as Grover Alston. Shit! If the regular cops came by, they would pinch Alston and let the junkie go."

Grover Alston had exactly the right credentials for an undercover narcotics agent—he was big, black, and ugly. His huge head seemed to grow right out of his shoulders with no neck in between, and his face looked like a gorilla's. It was always surprising that when Grover wasn't putting on his mean-mother act, he had one of the gentlest voices Fleming had ever heard.

"Only bad thing about Grover is that he's *too* convincing," Fleming said. "A couple of years ago, Grover made some buys from this guy who pushes for an Italian family. We wanted him to stool on the guineas so bad that after the bust, I told him Alston was an agent. The guy wouldn't fucking believe me—even after I showed him Grover's badge and papers."

"And?"

"The case finally goes to trial, and the guy pleads not guilty. Grover was our first witness. They swore him in, he identified himself as a Special Agent of the DEA, and the guy ups and changes his plea to guilty. Tells the judge he just wanted to hear Grover swear to it in court."

Down the block, Alston and the junkie were arguing. The junkie was shaking his head and throwing his arms around. Alston began to look pissed off.

"C'mon, Grover, don't fuck up the deal," Fleming muttered as he watched. "We don't need the buy of the century on nose candy. We need evidence. Even a few grams of shit with traces in it. We need a case." Fleming's last decent bust had been more than three months ago. *I'm spending my Christmas in Harlem. Christ, that's just how hard up I've gotten for a good collar.*

"They always screw around over the price. Grover will get the stuff. Then we nail this guy." Ross was trying hard to sound optimistic. He'd been *four* months without a case.

Both agents jumped as the two-way radio, quiet all morning, crackled to life. "I thought we were the only car out," Ross said. "What do they want with us?"

The voice of the base operator blared from the speaker. "Call the office."

As Ross lowered the volume, Fleming grabbed the radio mike. "This is a bad time. We've got something going down."

"Fleming, this is important. Very important."

"Give me a hint," Fleming said.

"Larry has been busted," the operator replied.

"What the fuck?" Fleming shouted in disbelief. He tried to think, to figure out what to say, but his thumb was already pressing the "Send" button on the mike. "Larry . . . my snitch, Larry?" Even as he spoke, Fleming was regretting those words. No way was an agent supposed to talk about that kind of stuff on the air. But Fleming found he couldn't help himself. "Who got him, and how?"

But the operator wasn't giving anything away. "Call the office," she repeated.

Fleming rammed the door open. "Keep an eye on Alston," he told Ross. "I'll find a phone down the other way."

It took him a moment to get his big, heavy frame free of the car—Ross always pulled the seats too far up. He groaned and stretched. *Got to do something about that belly,* he thought. Then he was hurrying through the gray drizzling snowfall.

The raw wind made his ruddy face even pinker, bringing out what his mom used to call "choirboy cheeks." Choirboy cheeks with a beak of a nose and eyes as gray as the leaden skies above. Fleming glanced at the wet snow falling down as he walked. *Instant slush,* he thought. *Just enough will fall to cover the shit in the streets. You won't know what you're stepping into.* He carefully skirted a lump in the snow cover. *Especially up here.*

The phone booth on the corner had all the glass knocked out, leaving the thin metal frame open to the wind. Fleming was amazed that "Hector 152" had taken the time to redecorate all the two-inch-wide metal trim with his spray can. Then he wound up cursing Hector and all his friends when the phone took his quarter and didn't give a dial tone.

Fleming stepped back into the snow. He'd left his overcoat in the car, and his jacket didn't keep away the cold or the wetness. Pulling up his collar, he headed for the next corner.

"Hey, mister, you want to buy some black pussy?" The hooker must have been about sixteen years old, shivering in a barred-up doorway. "C'mon, you know what they say—get yourself a piece of black ass, and you change your luck."

Fleming walked past her without a word. *Change my luck. Just what I need. Fifteen years of playing cops and robbers—sixty Feds against 10,000 pushers and half a million users. No cases. And now my best snitch pinched . . .*

The phones on the next corner were broken, too. It took

6

four blocks and six phones before Fleming found one that worked. No glass broken, the door closed—but it smelled like the whole neighborhood used it for a community urinal. The stench actually brought tears to Fleming's eyes. He opened the door and got an icy blast of wind, but the cold seemed better than the odor. Fleming was shivering as he dialed.

Answering the phone, the operator cut Fleming short as soon as he identified himself. "Mr. Powers will speak with you." Fleming grunted as he was put on hold. *So, Powers did it. Could be worse. Dick's still my friend, and I don't think he'd give a raw deal to an old partner.* He shuffled his feet, trying to keep warm, and finally closed the door. Smelling piss was better than growing icicles.

Across the street, a crowd had gathered in front of Sherman's Bar-B-Q—the kind that usually gathers at car accidents. They were staring through the window at something happening inside the store, blocking Fleming's view. He was curious. What would catch the attention of the people who lived in this neighborhood? It would have to be a real winner.

"Hey, Eddie-boy, you're a busy man, working Christmas." Dick Powers's voice came over the receiver. "They pulled me out of the house for this little ruction." His mellow, put-on Irish brogue grated on Fleming's nerves.

"Don't try to blow smoke up my ass, Dick," he snapped. "What do you think you're doing, pinching my snitch?"

"Eddie, Eddie, calm down, boyo. I don't have to take this, you know. Larry could be out of our hands before you get down here. Right now, he's in the can. I'm keeping him there so you can talk to him."

Fleming paused for a moment. What was going on

7

here? He pulled back on his anger. Right now, he needed information. "Come on, you can understand why I'm pissed. Tell me what happened."

"That would take a lot of quarters on a public phone," Powers said. "Why don't you come down to the office? We can explain it all to you then . . ."

" 'We'? And just who the fuck is 'we'? " Fleming's patience was completely gone. "Do 'we' have new rules now? Do 'we' bust other people's snitches? You know Larry. How did you let this happen? Why did . . ."

Powers cut in. "This isn't something we can talk about on the phone. Come on in. It wasn't just us. The City is involved."

"Fuck the City!" Fleming's voice was loud, but it was all bluster. He could taste the bile in the back of his throat. City cops meant trouble—maybe big trouble. "Who?" he asked, holding his breath.

"Peretti."

"That mother—" Fleming broke off. "How could you let him do this?"

"Goddammit, no more talking on the phone. You don't know who could be listening." Before Fleming could say more, Powers had hung up.

Fleming slammed his receiver down so hard it broke. He kicked the door open and stormed across the street. The crowd parted to let him up to the window, black faces studiously blank, making room for the obvious white cop.

A rack of spareribs hung in the display window, three feet above the floor. Two rats jumped up to the ribs, hanging onto the meat until their weight pulled a hunk free. They'd fall to the floor, gorge, then jump again. Fleming turned away. In another hour, the owner would be in there, open for business.

8

He got back to the car to find Ross taking another nip of blackberry brandy, and Grover Alston standing alone in the street. Fleming pulled on his coat and signaled Grover over. "So what have we got here?" he asked.

Alston was so cold he could hardly speak. "The guy's gone to get the stuff. He's late, but I think he lives in that building."

Fleming's impatience flared. "Then where is he? You sure this is legit?"

"I think so. He sounds real." But Alston sounded more hopeful than sure.

"We can't wait, Grover. I've gotta get to the office right away."

"He's only a half-hour late," Alston pleaded. "Suppose he shows."

"We get him next time," Fleming said.

"We've gotta get him now," Alston's voice rose. "I fronted the money!"

Both Ross and Fleming stared. "You what?"

"I . . . I gave him six hundred bucks." Alston's voice cracked. "Look, man, I need this case."

"We all need this case," Fleming said. They stood in silence, looking at one another. Fleming glanced at his watch, shook his head, and finally grinned. "So what we do is go back to the office, take an ounce out of my locker, bless it, and John Doe, Suspect, becomes John Doe, Defendant. We all saw the delivery being made. Understand?"

He leaned forward, staring at the other two agents. They could get away with it. Three Federal narcs against one broken-down junkie—a guy who would surely have a record. "Understand?" he repeated. "We lie." Time was passing. He had to get this sewn up. "Say something. You've got to express yourselves, gentlemen."

9

From the look on Jack Ross's face, all he wanted to do was get back inside the car. "He's just a fucking nig—" He glanced at Alston. "Junkie," he amended. "Let's do it."

Grover Alston stood still, the snow blowing into his face.

Fleming shook his head. Grover was a young guy, new in the trenches. Still young enough to be idealistic about the job.

"Look, Grover. This guy just took your money and promised to sell you cocaine. Does he sound like an innocent to you?"

"No . . . It's . . ."

Fleming's voice fell. "You've been standing out here, freezing your ass off. You freeze your brain, too? This guy isn't going to show. And you're about to lose your backup. This guy is dirty. We can't wait for him. Do you want to send him an invitation?"

Grover Alston loomed over him. "This isn't funny, Fleming. You sound good with these instant decisions, but if something goes wrong, we're all fucked." He hesitated for a second. "How do we write this up?"

"From scratch." Fleming grinned. "We make the entire thing up. If you like, we'll start it 'Once upon a time.' "

Ross laughed, but Alston was silent. "You pretend like this is all a big joke, but . . ."

Fleming cut him off. "You want to explain to the boss that you fronted the dough? That you gave away six hundred bucks of government money? Fine with me. But don't expect me to chip in anything to make it good."

Alston's voice was quiet, and very tight. "Okay."

Fleming looked at the black man's troubled face. *It's a hell of a time to lose your cherry, but I don't have time to dick around.* "Cheer up, Grover," he said, "this will be a cinch. Remember, there's no defense against perjury."

They split up, Fleming and Ross going to the car, Alston heading back down the block. "And Grover," Fleming called.

Alston stopped and turned around.

"Merry Christmas."

CHAPTER 2

MONICA, watch the gravy, not the street,"
said Felicia Castelli to her daughter-in-law, who absently
stirred a simmering pot while staring out the window to
the street below.

"I'm sorry, Mamma Castelli. I'm just wondering where
Joey is."

"So am I. He's two hours late. Where did he say he was
going?"

Monica paled and nibbled on her lower lip. "We don't
talk very much, Mamma. You know that."

Felicia threw up her hands as though warding off evil

spirits. "Don't tell me any more. Your problems with my son are your own and private."

"Can you talk to him? Please."

"What can I say to a grown man? He has a mind of his own. Be patient with him. He's just a little confused."

"What's to be confused about? We're husband and wife. Yet you'd never know we were married the way he carries on."

"You must be patient with him."

"He's sleeping with Connie Buttafari. How much patience am I supposed to have?"

Felicia gasped and made the sign of the cross. "You know how men are. Sometimes one woman is not enough."

"I'm enough when he's in our bed. But he's been playing the alley cat since the first month we were married."

"Why are you telling me these things, Monica?" Felicia bit her knuckles and closed her eyes while mumbling prayers to the Virgin Mary.

"Because I still love him. And I want him back. Help me to save my marriage."

Felicia brushed some lint from her black dress and fussed over a pot of boiling water. She was short and plump. Never a beauty, at fifty-five she looked ten years older. She believed that a man's business was not to be questioned and could not understand why Monica talked so freely about her disintegrating marriage.

"Your problems are between you and your husband. It is not my place to tell you how to live your life. Sit down with Joey and talk to him. Maybe you could smooth things out." She looked at Monica pleadingly. "Be understanding. He's a man. You know how they are."

She's real old-world, Monica thought. *The women are slaves to the whims of their men. She won't help me. She'll*

*just wring her hands and make a few novenas. And that
bastard will still run around on me. My sister said that I
could live with her if things don't get better. Maybe I'll
take her up on her offer after the holidays.*

Monica dipped a wooden spoon into the bubbling pot of
gravy and gingerly sipped it. "Hey, Mamma, it tastes
pretty good. What do you think?"

Anxious to change the subject, Felicia pounced on the
spoon like a lion downing a prey. "It's just right. Go get
Jean, it's time to set the table."

"But Joey's not here yet," said Monica.

"Uncle Angelo is due in ten minutes and he's never late.
I just hope he understands Joey's absence. Go."

Billy Castelli drifted into the kitchen as the women set
the table. He hugged his mother and laughed as their bellies got in the way.

"Hey, Ma, it's time to knock off the pasta. I'm getting too
big for my clothes."

Felicia pinched his cheeks with both hands and pulled
him down so she could kiss him on the forehead. *My
son. Thirty-nine and losing his hair already. Look at
his bald spot. Like a monk's cap. But he's strong. Like a
Tartagliano.* "That's why women sew. Your clothes get too
tight, bring them to Mamma. I fix them for you."

"So where's the kid, Ma?"

"He should be here any minute."

"But not before Uncle Angelo. What's the matter with
him? Don't he have any respect anymore?"

"He's your brother, Billy. Why don't you talk to him?"

"I have. He don't listen. He's thickheaded, Ma. It's
gonna get him in trouble one day."

Billy reached for a fork, plucked a meatball from the
gravy, and nestled it in a slice of Italian bread. He topped

it with a dab of gravy and a sprinkling of parmesan cheese. He popped it in his mouth and sighed with pleasure. "Nobody makes meatballs like you, Ma. Delicious. And the house looks great. You decorated the tree real nice, too."

"Mamma, Billy, Uncle Angelo is here. I just saw his car pull up."

Billy and Felicia walked to the window and stared down at the long black limousine that sat idling in the street below. Achille Aspermonte got out first and carefully scanned the street. He liked homburg hats and expensive suits but the handsome thirty-year-old was a cold-blooded killer.

Rocco Mazzi stepped from the driver's side and moved to open the rear door of the car. He was whipcord lean, and was sloppy about his appearance. But then, he didn't have the face of a snappy dresser. A mass of chicken-pox scars covered his cheeks. The tip of his nose had been bitten off in a fight, and his ever-present tinted sunglasses hid his reptilian eyes. He had killed seventeen men for Angelo Tartagliano.

Two men left the limousine and rushed into the building, using Mazzi and Aspermonte to shield them. But today there was no danger. It was Christmas, and families met to celebrate the birth of the Saviour.

Felicia opened the door and the men came into the apartment. Rocco and Achille stayed outside, making sure their master was safe.

"Merry Christmas, sister," said Angelo Tartagliano as he stepped into the living room to greet the rest of the family, who deferred to him respectfully.

His brother Frankie came in next and gripped Felicia in a warm embrace. He was thirty-eight and was short like his brother. His middle was turning to fat. When he smiled, his face came alive, giving his eyes an impish cast. "Merry Christmas, sis. Thanks for having us." He eyed the apartment and nodded approvingly at the table setting and the eight-foot pine heavy with ornaments, blinking lights, and silver tinsel. "The house looks great."

"Thanks, Frank. I try. Come, let me take your coat. Angelo, give me your coat. Billy, make your uncles a drink."

Billy kissed Angelo on the cheek and patted him gently on the shoulder. "Merry Christmas, uncle. You're looking good today."

Angelo grunted. *Something's not right here. Somebody's missing.* "Where's your brother?"

"He's pickin' up somethin' at Ferrara's."

"I didn't see him on the street. Hey, Frankie, you see Joey near Ferrara's?"

"I wasn't looking for him, Angelo."

"Don't be a wise guy." Angelo was short and stocky with massive arms and hands and an eighteen-inch neck. The stumpy fingers on his right hand glistened with a diamond pinkie ring and a gold signet ring. His left hand sported a garnet ring and an emerald pinkie ring. A hand-crafted watch made from a solid gold coin adorned his right wrist. His thousand-dollar suit was immaculately tailored. He liked expensive cigars and homemade wine. But the look on his face made Billy shiver. "Didn't Joey know I was coming?" he asked quietly.

"Maybe he got caught in traffic," Felicia said.

"It's Christmas, Felicia. There's no traffic out there."

"Uncle Angelo," cried Billy's two boys as they mobbed their uncle. Momentarily distracted, he crushed them in a hard embrace and ruffled their hair. He put them down on the floor and they stared at him expectantly.

16

"Rocco, go down to the car and bring up the presents."
He chucked young Vincent under the chin and pinched
Angelo's cheeks. "Who's your favorite uncle?"

"You are," they cried in unison.

"We play a game. Stay here and don't peek." Angelo
turned his back to the boys and reached his hands into his
pockets. He faced the boys and held out his closed fists to
them. "Pick a hand, Angelo."

The youngster hesitated, then picked the right one.

"You sure?" Angelo asked.

The boy nodded.

"You win." Angelo unfurled a crisp five-dollar bill and
gave it to him. He next turned to Vincent. "Keep your eye
on my hand." He held up a quarter in his left hand between his thumb and forefinger. He grabbed it with the
thumb and forefinger of his right hand and quickly closed
both hands in a lightning-fast move.

"Which hand is it in, Vincent?"

Vincent bit on his knuckle and hesitantly pointed to the
left hand. Uncle Angelo unfolded the fist and nestled in the
palm was a shiny quarter. He flipped it to his nephew.

"Thank you, Uncle Angelo," said the boy as he smiled
and jammed the coin in his pocket. He turned away and
went back to his toys.

"Hey, Vincent, come here," said Angelo. The youngster
peered up at his uncle, who picked him up under the arms.
He kissed Vincent on the cheek. It was a wet sloppy kiss
that made Vincent grimace. But he didn't wipe it off.
"You're a good boy, Vincent. You never complain. Here!"
He handed him a five-dollar bill every bit as new as the
one he had given to young Angelo.

Vincent's face beamed with pleasure and he hugged
his uncle. "Can I go play now?" he asked.

"Go. Have fun. Be a kid." Angelo watched Vincent scamper off. *One day, little Vincent. This family will be yours. You're tough and strong. And you never beg. Just like me.*

Rocco returned with an armload of gifts that were spread under the tree. Angelo and Frankie relaxed in the living room and sipped Scotch while talking with Monica, Jean, and Billy.

Angelo glanced at his watch. *Two o'clock. And still no Joey. This is the respect I get after all I've done for him. Where is he?*

"Hey, Mario, Merry Christmas, you fuck. How ya been."

"For cryin' out loud, Joey, it's Christmas. Do you have to curse?"

"Don't be so touchy. I'm sorry. I gotta pick up the pastry I ordered. Is it ready yet?"

"I'll check." Mario ducked behind the glass counter at Ferrara's and checked the order slips. "Yeah, I see the slip. I'll get it for you."

"Thanks, Mario." Joey eyed the pastry shop and tried flirting with the cute cashier. But she ignored Joey as though he were a speck of lint. *Bitch,* he thought. *Actin' so high and mighty. If you knew who I was you'd be creaming all over yourself to get to know me better. And I got ten grand in my pocket. With five more on the way. What a sweet deal. That dumb shit spade didn't even check the shit I gave him. I coulda given him scouring powder and he woulda bought it.*

"Here it is, Joey."

"Thanks a lot. But let me see it first."

"It's pastry, for crying out loud. You've seen it before.

There's cannoli, baba, pignioli, sfogliatelle, cream puffs. Besides, I already wrapped the box."

"You don't show me, you can shove it up your ass. It's for my family and my Uncle Angelo will be there. And I don't think ya put the powdered sugar on it. Eh, the kids are over, too. They like that."

Mario paled and hastily snipped the cake-box cord. He opened the box. Joey looked quickly and jumped up, slapping Mario on the side of the head. "Look at this. A rum cake. I order pastry and you give me rum cake. I look like a fool in front of my family because you can't keep the order straight. What the hell's the matter with you?"

"Gimme a break, Joey, huh? I been workin' all mornin'. Everybody makes mistakes."

"I'll break your fuckin' head if you don't give me what I ordered."

"Is there a problem here?" asked a manager.

"Yeah, there's a problem. Your name's Phil, right?"

"Yes. I'm going to have to ask you to lower your voice. You're disturbing the other customers."

Joey was about to lash out at the young man when he remembered the ten thousand dollars that he had in his pockets. *Bright, asshole. You're gonna make a scene and get arrested. How are you gonna explain the money? Be cool. Act like your uncle.*

"I'm sorry. It's just that I've been waiting a long time and my order doesn't come out right. My family's been doing business with you for a lot of years and I've never received such lousy service before."

The manager glared at Mario. "What did this gentleman order?"

"Assorted pastries."

"What did you give him?"

"A rum cake. But . . ."

"Let me see the order slip." He snatched the paper from Mario's hand and quickly scanned it. "I'm very sorry, Mr. Castelli. Fill up a new box of fresh pastry and give it to Mr. Castelli. And no charge."

Bein' a fuckin' gentleman is all right. Smart move, Joey. Getting a box of pastry for free. Hey, Joey Castelli don't take handouts from no one. "Thanks for the offer, but I always pay my way." Joey pulled out his wallet. "How much do I owe you?"

"Nothing. We made the mistake. If you didn't open the box you would have paid for an order you didn't receive. I insist."

"Okay. Thanks again." He peeked at Mario. "Don't forget the powdered sugar."

Joey sauntered out of the shop, snapping his fingers. He felt good about himself. Earlier in the day he had sold fifteen thousand dollars worth of cocaine to a new buyer and he had the down payment in his pocket. He was five thousand dollars light and it annoyed him that the buyer hadn't brought all the money because he didn't anticipate the size of the delivery. Ever the accommodating supplier, he agreed to advance him a delivery until he came up with the cash.

Won't my uncle shit? Dumb Joey just made a big score. With more to come. And not even quality junk. I'm so fuckin' cool. Now he'll give me the support I deserve.

He bent over and stared at his reflection in the side mirror of a new Cadillac. His brown wavy hair was combed haphazardly. A gust of wind fluffed it out. He saw a blackhead on his chin and squeezed it with his thumbnails. The eruption popped, leaving a blood bubble. He dabbed it away with his handkerchief. Not a handsome man, his best feature was his nose. It was well-shaped, and Joey liked the profile it gave him. He splayed his fleshy lips with his forefinger and thumb and ran his tongue over his yellowing teeth. Satisfied with the results, he continued on his way.

As he turned onto Hester Street, he saw a black limousine. *Shit! Uncle Angelo's here already. Dammit.* He ran to his mother's apartment. At the foot of the stairs, he deliberately made as much noise as he could going up. He didn't want either Mazzi or Aspermonte to think him a threat.

When he reached the top step he was met by a smiling Achille Aspermonte. Only recently arrived from Sicily, Aspermonte spoke no English. He wished Joey a Merry Christmas in Italian. To his right, with his hand inside his overcoat, was a bored Rocco Mazzi. *Look at that fuck,* thought Joey, *wearin' those damn shades inside.*

"You're late, Joey," Rocco taunted. "Uncle Angelo won't like it."

"Fuck you, creep. Mind your own business."

Rocco grinned but remained calm. "One day you *will* be my business, Joey. Then we'll see how tough you really are."

"Get fucked." Joey entered his mother's apartment.

Monica met him at the door. "Where were you?" she hissed as she took the pastry box.

"Out. I told you. Stop asking me so many damn questions." He eyed his wife. Her blond hair hung shoulder length. She wore a cream-colored blouse with a long brown skirt and knee-high calfskin boots. Around her neck was a simple strand of white pearls. Her well-formed breasts pushed gently on her blouse. Joey brushed her breasts with the back of his hand and imagined Monica's large brown nipples hardening as he sucked on them. "You look beautiful, baby," he said, nuzzling her neck.

"Stop it," she snapped. "Go say hello to your uncle. He's been asking where you were."

Joey walked into the living room, smiling.

"So you finally come," said Angelo. "Where were you?"

"They gave me the wrong order. I had to wait . . ."

Angelo stopped him with a withering look that made Joey nauseated. "No lies."

"I had business, uncle. It went great . . ."

"Stop!" Angelo commanded and Joey instantly obeyed. "What kind of business is more important than your family on Christmas Day?"

"It's hot, uncle, I . . ."

"Later," snapped Angelo. "First we eat. Later we talk. Then you tell me all about your business."

"Joey," said Felicia as she came into the room, "Merry Christmas."

He kissed his mother. "Merry Christmas, Mamma. How'd you like the pastries?"

"They look nice. I'm sure we'll enjoy them. It's time to eat."

The men tramped into the dining room and took their places around the table. The women sat only after making sure that the men were fed. Since the gathering was small, the boys sat on either side of Uncle Angelo, who sat at the head of the table. Frankie sat opposite him.

Felicia was proud of her home cooking and had spent the better part of two days preparing the Christmas meal. Her chicken soup with tiny meatballs and thin noodles was Joey's favorite. Next came the homemade lasagna and the meat platter with sausages, meatballs, braciola, and pork. The meat was tender and hot since it had been cooked in the gravy. Roast chicken breasts, artichokes, stuffed baked mushrooms, and a tossed salad topped off the meal. It was washed down with homemade red wine and water. The kids drank soda.

Felicia stared at her brother with mounting concern as he ate his meal in silence. Angelo normally talked and joked when he ate with his family. His odd behavior today frightened his sister.

Angelo sat back in his chair, a stern expression on his face. "In all my years," he said, "I never thought I'd say this." He put his knife and fork in his plate. "Take this dish away from me."

Felicia's heart fluttered. Her fingers nervously twisted the cloth napkin. "I worked so hard. Didn't you like it?"

"I loved it, sis," said Angelo, a smile spreading across his face. "If I ate any more, I'm afraid I'd explode." He burst out laughing, much to the delight of the family, who joined in happily.

"I just hope you saved room for dessert," said Felicia, as she put out trays of fruit and nuts, along with Joey's pastries.

Billy's kids were excused to watch television. The women cleared the table. The men discussed business, knowing that they would not be disturbed.

"I have news," said Uncle Angelo. "And it ain't good. The Senate hearings got everybody all hot and bothered. The politicians take our money and give us construction contracts. The cops take our drugs and our money, then close their eyes to our other activities. But in election years everything is different. Now our friendly politicians don't know us. And the cops arrest us."

"Bastards," said Billy.

Angelo smiled and continued. "With all the newspaper

stories about drugs, even the people are getting crazy and they want the cops to crack down. So the Feds have to give them someone to hang. Let it be the spics and the niggers. Not us. We make no deals unless you know the guy twenty years. Only one mistake and this whole business, the family business, comes down. Understand?" He scanned the table. There were no dissenters, but Joey was frowning.

"Why the face, Joey?"

"I got things on my mind."

"You always got things on your mind. Show some respect for once in your worthless life. Look at me when I'm talking to you, not at the table. Where were you so that I had to be kept waiting for you to show up? You said you had business. What business?"

Joey grinned lewdly and rolled his eyes. "You know, uncle, sometimes a man gets desires . . ."

"So you got your pipes cleaned. Is that what you're telling us?" questioned Frankie. "On Christmas Day?"

"Sure. Why not? Pussy is pussy . . ."

"Shut your filthy mouth," ordered Angelo. "The women may hear. You insult them with your talk. And what about your wife? She's beautiful. Why do you need a *putana?*"

"She doesn't do certain things . . ."

"Joey, do you think I was born yesterday?" Angelo said quietly. His tone prickled Joey's neck hairs, making him squirm in his seat. "Your *putana* went to her family in New Jersey two days ago."

"I didn't say it was her," whined Joey.

Angelo pounded his fist on the table, spilling a glass of wine. "The truth, Joey. Now!" His eyes flared like hot lumps of coal.

"I did some business."

"What kind?"

"I made a sale. Quarter of a key."

"Who?"

"A guy I know."

"What guy?" asked Angelo. "What's his name? How long you know him?"

"Jesus, uncle, he's just a guy I met. He wanted to deal. So I sold him what I had. Don't worry. The shit was cut so much that I just about stole his money."

"How much?"

"Fifteen thousand. He gave me ten. And he'll give me five more in a couple of days. He wasn't expecting so much shit." Joey smiled, pleased with himself.

"Are you crazy?" snapped Billy. "Don't you ever think? The Feds have been sniffin' at our asses for weeks now. Nobody's dealin'. And you set up this penny-ante shit. Why?"

"Why not? I saw a chance and I took it. What's the big deal anyway?"

"Who is this guy?" asked Angelo.

"Just a guy. His name's Larry."

"What is he?"

"He's black. So what?"

"How long do you know him?"

"A couple of weeks . . ."

Billy exploded. "He could be a cop or a Fed, you asshole."

"He's no cop. If he was, he woulda busted me today when I gave him the shit."

"Where's the money?" asked Angelo.

"I got it right here." Joey smiled, reached into his pants pocket, pulled out the wad of bills, and tossed them on the table. He was very pleased with himself and didn't notice the shocked looks around the table.

25

"Imbecile! Get this money out of here. Now!" roared Angelo. "Felicia!"

Felicia and the other women ran into the dining room. Angelo stood up, knocking over his chair. "Give me your apron," said Angelo. He spread the apron on the table and threw the cash into it. He tied it in a loose bundle and ran into the kitchen.

Joey trailed behind him. "What are you doing?" he cried.

"The money could be marked. It could lead the Feds right to me." Angelo pulled out a baking pan, throwing the money inside while dousing it with olive oil. He lit a match and ignited the soggy mass of money.

"No!" yelled Joey as he tried to stop his uncle, but Angelo swatted him away like a pesky fly. He opened the oven, turned it on and threw in the burning pan. The pan smoked as the bills were turned to ashes.

Joey went pale as Angelo stared at him, the rage plain and terrifying in his weathered face. "You bring this money here? You sell to a *mulignan*?" He slapped Joey hard enough to bring tears to his nephew's eyes. "Do you forget how the *mulignans* sold us out? You and Billy went to jail. Do you forget already? And you come straight from the deal to this house. Your mother's house. Where are your brains? He could be a snitch. The Feds could have followed you. They could be listening right now."

Angelo turned on the kitchen radio and turned the volume up high. He calmed himself by pacing, clenching and unclenching his fists. After a few moments he shut off the radio.

Joey rubbed his cheek, which still stung from the slap. "I'm sorry, uncle."

"You're always sorry. I don't want you to see this Larry

again. Do you understand? No deals. Of any kind. You *capische*?"

"Yes."

"You'd better. Where did you meet this Larry?"

"At Zebra's, in the Village."

"We'll check him out," said Angelo as he left the kitchen.

Joey bit his thumbnail and stared at his uncle's retreating back. *Sonofabitch. Burnin' my money. You're just trying to keep me down, you old fart. Now what am I gonna do? I got no money and I still owe Larry more shit. Fuck it. I'll finish up this deal. Then no more.*

CHAPTER 3

HAIL was rattling down with the snow as Fleming drove the Agency car downtown. Drug Enforcement had the tenth floor of an old post office building in the Wall Street area. Usually, the streets would be jammed. But today, Fleming was able to park right in front. The streets were deserted. *Merry fucking Christmas,* Fleming thought.

He'd already dropped Ross off. If anything was going to be salvaged, it would be between him and Powers. Fleming walked into the building, past the dozing guard.

The guy stirred. "Hey, you got to sign in."

Fleming scrawled his name in the logbook.

"Tenth floor, huh?" said the guard. It was easier than checking for identification.

"Yeah." Fleming walked into the elevator. As he rode up, he remembered the night he and Powers had brought Rodriguez in. Iron Man Rodriguez? No, Candy Man Rodriguez. Fleming shook his head. Too many Rodriguezes. They'd brought this pusher in, and both of them were half in the bag. The elevator reached ten and they got off, but Rodriguez stayed on. They'd raced down ten flights of stairs, panting and cursing. But the Candy Man was gone.

Yeah, the guard remembered him signing out. He still had handcuffs on. "Why?" the guy had asked. "Was it important?"

Then came the desperate search of the area, the dash uptown to check Rodriguez's house. He never turned up again. So Powers decided to unarrest the guy. They destroyed all records of Rodriguez ever existing, not to mention being arrested.

Fleming smiled. He and Powers had thought it a great joke—Rodriguez hiding under a bed, crapping himself whenever a cop looked at him. And he was a free man.

Those had been the days. They'd been the unbeatable partners, the happy headhunters. Every case was a win. They'd laughed a lot. Keeping a sense of humor about yourself—that was how you survived the job. As long as you could see the funny side, it made things . . . bearable. Then came the problems with Meg, and he'd gotten by on anger, punching pushers' heads and kicking junkies' asses.

He'd been able to laugh again with Joan, for a while. But things were different. Powers was a supervisor now.

They'd still go out and have a drink, but the laughter was forced. Politics got in the way. Fleming's smile had disappeared by the time the doors opened on the tenth floor.

He'd never seen the office so deserted. The prisoner lockup was dark and empty. He could just get a shadowy impression of the long hallway. An open doorway at the far end threw a shaft of harsh light, illuminating a stretch of dingy wall and turning the bulletin boards a dirty gray. Powers's office.

Fleming walked down the hall, hearing a loud voice. "So this big Polack linebacker, he say, 'Run, nigger, run. 'Cause if I catch you, you gonna have to crawl.' " Laughter came from the office as he stopped at the doorway.

Larry stood in the middle of the office, acting out a tale of his past football glory.

"Did he catch you, Larry?" Powers asked.

"Broke my fucking leg," Larry answered. "But it was worth it. When he came down on me, I had my knee in his balls. I didn't walk for three months. But he didn't fuck for two years."

Powers and Peretti were laughing again. But Peretti stopped when he saw Fleming. He got to his feet, taking the brace of a man who expects a fight—a fight he expects to win.

"Just us?" Fleming asked, trying to keep cool.

"Come on, Ed. It's Christmas, boyo." Powers gave Fleming his "trust me" smile. Fleming's gut chilled. He knew that look. The face that sank a thousand junkies.

Fleming purposely ignored Peretti as he looked from Larry to the bag of junk on the table. The only response he got was a slight shrug of the shoulders. But that told him the whole story.

"That's a quarter of a kilo. Heavily cut Colombian."

Peretti had a tight, intense face, the face of a tough cop. Fleming didn't like cops. DEA and NYPD's Special Services Division worked together—especially when the City boys needed a wiretap. But Fleming didn't trust cops. They always sold out.

Peretti went on. "For some reason, we missed the connection."

Dick Powers laughed, trying to ease the moment.

Peretti turned to Larry. "You. Wait outside."

"*I* tell him what to do. He's my snitch." The words were out of Fleming's mouth almost before he realized what he was saying.

"Not anymore. His ass is mine now. He'll be working for me tomorrow." Peretti had great control. Even in an argument, he chose his words. He didn't say "snitching." He used "working for"—the polite term for when an informant was present. Otherwise, he'd be referred to as "the scum."

"Easy, gentlemen, easy." Powers sounded like the Great White Father as he pushed his way in. "Larry, wait outside."

Fleming glared as his boss ordered his snitch outside. Larry gave him a grin and left the room, closing the door.

Powers gave Fleming another smile. "It was a tap, Ed. Not on Larry, but on one of his customers. He identified Larry as his source, and mentioned that he would score today. We lost him in the city, but nabbed him when he came back to his crib. We didn't know who it was until it was too late."

"Bullshit," said Fleming. Powers gave his story all too glibly. He'd rehearsed it, which didn't surprise Fleming a bit. He knew Powers. That phony Irish prick would lie about what he had for lunch, just for practice. "You think

I'm gonna swallow this wiretap shit? You got him from a snitch!"

"Okay, he was set up." Peretti still was cool, but Fleming knew he'd scored points. "The snitch got snitched on. What difference does it make?"

Fleming completely lost it. "The difference is, he's the best in the city—I've made fifty cases out of him—and he's *my fucking snitch!"*

Peretti lost his temper, too. "Look, Fleming. Maybe talking loud and saying 'fuck' scares the shit out of the junkies on the street. But it doesn't impress me."

"And bullshit doesn't impress me," Fleming shouted. "It just hides the truth. You knew who Larry was long before today." He jabbed his finger at Peretti. "And if you knew, *he* knew."

He looked at Powers. "You should have told me, Dick—warned me, for Chrissake. You're a Fed first. You should have called me."

Powers shook his head. "You'd have told him, Ed." He looked at Peretti. "Can we step away for a moment? Have a bit of a chat by ourselves?"

They stepped over to the glass partition in the office. Larry sat on the other side, looking like a man without a care in the world. *Two hundred pounds of black bastard,* Fleming thought. *Four years in school on a football scholarship, with a major in recreational drugs. Three years of pro ball, where his whole salary went up his nose. Then the injury list, the end of the gravy train, dealing—until I busted him.*

Larry turned around to grin through the glass, his head looking tiny on his bull neck, his eyes bulging slightly. He had complete confidence that Fleming would work things out. *Like I've always done before,* Fleming thought.

Powers followed Fleming's eyes. He smiled at Larry, then turned around. "You're making a major mistake with him, Ed. Snitches have the life expectancy of a cockroach. Use them, then step on them. I don't know why you're coddling this big jig."

"He produces cases for me, Dick." Fleming didn't add that Larry had produced for him during the lean months when he really needed cases.

"He's nailed lots of guys for you. If you took your three best busts and turned those guys, you'd have a new snitch now—maybe more." Powers shook his head. "You had him for a long time. But you'll have to give him up. The Agency has fences to mend with the local authorities."

"So you give them my best snitch!"

"I thought I could depend on you, Eddie-boy. My old partner. We had good times . . ."

Fleming turned away. "I stopped being your partner four years ago. Remember the big bust? Five pushers— and Harrelson. We busted an innocent guy. But to save the case, you made him dirty. You faked evidence, railroaded him. It was a really good job. They promoted you to section chief, gave you a gold badge."

"That's a long time ago, bucko," Powers said. "If you wanted to complain, you should have done it then."

"Not so long ago. Harrelson died in October. In the joint. Or didn't you know?"

Powers was quiet for a moment. "What do you want, Ed?"

"Are you fucking deaf or something?" Fleming hissed. "I want my snitch."

"No can do, Ed." Powers sighed. "The best you can do is make a deal. I'll back you—as far as I can."

"That should be a lot of help," Fleming muttered as

they went back to Peretti. "Okay. What can we do here?"

Peretti's response was immediate. "I get the case. You get the connection. You drop the old case on Larry. I get Larry."

Fleming was impressed by Peretti's directness. It made a refreshing change from Powers's ridiculous wiretap story. "That's the best I can expect, huh?" He grinned as Powers gave him a warning look. "Okay. But you've got to stay out until I nail the connection. And not a word to Larry until then."

Peretti shrugged. "Okay with me. You can tell him to go home. I already got the D.A.'s blessing."

"So, what did he tell us about his connection?" Fleming asked.

"Nothing," Powers said.

Fleming smiled. "Good. I trained that boy right." He opened the door. "Okay, Larry," he called. "Time to go home."

"My *man!*" said Larry. "Better than a fucking lawyer." He stopped by the door. "Now we back in business. But I need my goods. I owe the man on my last deal. I need the goods to keep it going."

Peretti looked at the two Federal agents for a second, then shrugged. He opened the plastic envelope of cocaine, and removed about an ounce. Silently, he pushed the remainder back across the table.

Larry hastily pocketed it, like a kid afraid that somebody was going to take his candy away. Fleming thought of the saying on the streets—"In the hand is good, in the pocket is better, in the stash is best." Larry would be off right away.

But Larry still hesitated. "And my money? My three thousand bucks?"

"There was no money," Powers said quickly. A little *too* quickly. Still the same—best arrest record and stickiest fingers in the Agency.

"Outside," Fleming said quietly. Larry left. Peretti turned his back, finding something very interesting to look at in the ceiling panels.

Before Fleming could even say a word, Powers handed him ten hundred-dollar bills. A thousand bucks, already counted out. Ready to be given away—if necessary.

Fleming pocketed the money, then called out the door, "You made a mistake, Larry. There was no money."

Larry was no fool. "What money, man?" Fleming took him to his desk as Powers and Peretti left.

Fleming turned to his snitch. "You are some piece of work, fucking up my Christmas. So who is this guy you're doing business with?"

He glanced at his watch. Two hours ago, he was supposed to be back with Joan. Better get this wrapped up and get out of here.

Larry didn't answer.

Fleming began to get angry. "Who is this guy? Gimme a fucking name."

"Joey," Larry said quickly. "I don't know his last name. I met him in a bar in the Village—he was trying to pick up this piece of ass, but she wasn't interested. Then he starts talking to Bumpy Morgan . . ."

"You know Bumpy?"

Larry shrugged. "To talk to, but not to deal with. I met him through this lady we both know. Anyway, he's talking with this guy, and then I'm talking, too, you know? We have a couple of drinks—Joey tries to line up a little pussy—then he starts talking shit. I didn't bring it up at all."

35

"You holding out on me?" Fleming said. He knew Larry's M.O. Deal with a guy, get a line of credit, deal for a big amount of goods, then burn the connection—turn him in. "Tell me more about this guy. Joey, was it? A guinea?"

"Yeah, he's Italian."

"And you don't know his last name." Fleming was getting more and more interested. Joan would be madder than hell, but he had to find out about this new connection. "Siddown." He pulled an old file from his cabinet—the ten-year-old Panella case, a Shining Moment for the Agency—and a *Who's Who* of the Italian underworld. Panella, Tartagliano, Genovese, Mazilla . . . and one black guy—Bumpy Morgan.

As Larry looked through the defendants' photos, Fleming dragged impatiently on a cigarette. It was a long shot—these were all big-leaguers . . .

"Here's my man," said Larry. "That's Joey."

Fleming grabbed the photo from his hands, glanced at it, then turned it over. JOSEPH G. CASTELLI
DOB: 2/14/49
NY: S 9791

He thumbed through the case file, knowing from long practice where to look. The more he read, the more excited Fleming became.

NAME:	JOSEPH GIOVANNI CASTELLI
ALIAS:	@Joey Castle @Peter Pecker
POLICE AGENCY FILES:	Drug Enforcement Agency NY:S 9791 NYPD B#6917271, FBI #548970

LAST KNOWN ADDRESS: 7207 Kappock Street
Yonkers, NY, Apt 4-C

PREVIOUS ADDRESS: 475 Hester Street, NYC

PHYSICAL DESCRIPTION: 68″, 150 lbs., medium build, dark
hair, brown eyes, olive
complexion

DISTINGUISHING MARKS: ½″ scar on right wrist
5″ appendectomy scar

DOB: February 14, 1949 (37)
St. Vincent's Hospital, NYC

MILITARY STATUS: Drafted April 6, 1967, U.S. Army
P.I. #649 572 613
Dishonorably discharged May 2,
1967

RELATIVES: Monica Castelli née de Fabrizio
 (Wife)
Felicia Castelli née Tartagliano
 (Mother)
Vincent Castelli
 (Father—Deceased)
William Castelli (Brother)
 Subject DEA file NY:S 9791
Angelo Tartagliano (Uncle)
 Subject DEA file NY:S 9791
Francis Tartagliano (Uncle)
 Subject DEA File NY:S 9791

KNOWN ACCOMPLICES: His brother, William Castelli
His uncles Angelo and
Frank Tartagliano
Benny Mancuso @Cockeye Benny
Vinny Mauro @Cheech
Ellsworth Morgan @Bumpy

CRIMINAL RECORD:	1979: Arrested assault w/deadly weapon—charges dropped
	1977: Served 5 years Danbury Federal Prison for violation Federal Narcotics Laws (Refer NY:S 9791)
	1969: Arrest bookmaking— charges dropped
	1967: Arrested statutory rape, re: Monica de Fabrizio—case dismissed, charges dropped
MODUS OPERANDI:	With his brother William @ Billy, he is believed to be the major customer of his uncles Angelo and Frank Tartagliano's drug distribution operation. The Tartagliano brothers have many major Italian customers, who in turn distribute drugs to Negro organizations in Harlem and the Bronx.
SOURCE OF SUPPLY:	The Tartaglianos have heroin connections from Marseilles, France, and are arranging Colombian connections for cocaine.
SOCIAL SECURITY:	068-30-4506

Fleming could hardly believe what he was reading. *Joey Castelli. Angelo Tartagliano's nephew Joey. Tartagliano, the head man. And Larry has just delivered his nephew.*

He turned to Larry, crushing down his excitement. "Larry, not a word about this. Don't talk about this guy. Don't mention his name. Not to anyone. How do you get in touch with him?"

"I don't," said Larry. "He calls me."

Fleming hid his disappointment. "You think he'll call?"

"No sweat," said Larry with a confident smile. "I cut him short on the deal. I owe him five grand. He call me."

CHAPTER 4

THE SNOW was finally starting to accumulate as Fleming slogged his way up the BQE. After the stakeout and the argument at the office, he should have felt wiped out. Instead, he was pounding on the dashboard, trying to move as fast as the traffic would allow—almost supercharged.

It had been a long time since a case made him feel like this. *Just when I thought the glory days were over.* He grinned to himself, then shook his head. No, it wasn't just the happy headhunter feeling he got when he was out with Powers. This was a *case,* a shot at the Tartagliano crime family, maybe even a chance to nail Angelo Tartagliano himself.

After two years of piss-ant nickel-and-dimers, he could make a bust that would make a difference. *I'm not burnt out yet . . .*

Fleming threw the door of the apartment open, stomping to get the snow off his shoes. "Hey, Joan!" he called. At a time like this, he wished he had a bottle of wine in his hand. But of course the liquor stores weren't open. He stopped when he saw Joan sitting on the couch.

Joan Fleming was wearing her long blond hair softly around her face. She wore a loose black sweater and a pair of gray tweed slacks. A red jacket lay beside her on the couch. One look at her big hazel eyes, and Fleming didn't have to check his watch. By now he had to be three hours late for dinner—a dinner with Joan's folks.

"Hey, I'm sorry," Fleming said. "The job . . ."

"I guessed that much," Joan said. "That's what I told Mom and Dad. 'Ed's on a case,' I told them. 'Looks like he's going to run late. Very late.' " She glared at him. "I lied to my parents, Ed, because I didn't know where the hell you were. Didn't you ever hear of a telephone? Couldn't you have called me? I've been sitting here like an idiot for hours."

Fleming felt an old weight settling in his gut. Not even two years together, and it was already turning into a replay of his first marriage. "And a Merry Christmas to you, too," he said. "I really feel bad about all this. Do you want to go now? Or should we set something up for tomorrow?"

"Now?" The color crept up her high cheekbones. "We should be just in time to help them finish the washing up. Mom's been working since yesterday on that dinner. And tomorrow? God knows where you'll be tomorrow!"

"It's not a job you can just turn off," Fleming said.

"Oh, I know, I know!" Joan said. "When I started going out with you it was exciting. It was like dating James Bond. If you had to leave early, or cut a date, it was part of the adventure. But now I've lived with you, and your job." Her face was grim. "Lately, all I've been living with is your job. It's eating you up, Ed. And it's leaving me out."

"It's not like that." Fleming paused. If this had been a case, he'd probably have a facile line. But he'd promised himself: *no bullshit with Joan.* So how could he explain that she was important to him—precisely *because* she had nothing to do with the job? "What do you expect me to do?" he finally said. "Take you along with me? Let you meet the scum?"

"Oh, I know, you never tell me how it really is. You keep it strictly light—funny things, silly things. But I've been living with you, even if you don't notice sometimes. I know the way you act. And I know that when you act like a real bastard, it's always something to do with your job."

Fleming had no answer to that. It was true.

Joan silently got up from the couch, passed Fleming, and walked into the bedroom.

Fleming watched her go. Where was his silver tongue when he needed it? He moved to the liquor cabinet, opened it, then slammed it closed. He'd been taking that route too often lately.

He walked down the hall, toward the closed bedroom door. Through it he could hear muffled singing, some kind of holiday special on the television. He stopped at the spare closet, opened it, and rummaged around. From the top shelf, he pulled out a box—his old Marine footlocker, securely padlocked.

Back out in the living room, he poured himself a drink

after all. Then he opened the box, and looked at memories—not exactly pleasant memories, but he could handle that.

Jumbled in the box was a pile of hardware—at first glance, useless junk. But in the right hands, the junk could be deadly.

Fleming pulled out what looked like a Bic pen. He pulled loose the cap to reveal, not a pen nib, but a shaft of metal. Pulling it all the way out revealed a length of knitting needle glued to the pen cap.

Fleming grinned. The junkie who owned that rig didn't have the right hands. He'd fumbled with the pen, giving Fleming the chance to ram a fist into his gut. And the chance to add a concealed-weapons charge to the half-kilo the guy was holding.

And the rolled-up belt—Fleming held it up, looking at the buckle. It looked like a regulation USMC seal. Fleming gave it a tug—to reveal the three-inch knife blade. He remembered this one very well. It was the start of his collection—and the previous owner had very good hands.

This dated back to the early seventies, to Fleming's second hitch in the Marines. His college degree had gotten him into the Military Police—CID. In two hitches, he never made it to Nam. The closest he came was Guam—investigating a drug ring in Camp Hansen. A dirty case—guys smuggling the stuff out in body bags—but he'd cracked it. It was the first time he'd worked with people from the DEA.

They'd nailed the ring, but one guy—a private named Drake—made a run for it. Fleming chased him, cornering him against a chain-link fence. Drake was halfway up the fence, then jumped back down as Fleming came up. His hand went to his belt, then flashed at Fleming's face.

43

Fleming took off his shirt and looked at his right arm. From his palm to his elbow snaked a ridge of scar tissue— the only wound he'd taken in the line of duty. He nearly beat Drake to death. And after the court-martial was over, he'd taken the belt knife.

Since then, whenever a perp tried to pull a weapon, he'd taken it after the trial. Kind of a superstition, he supposed. Warding off evil. He had no proof that it kept his skin whole—except for an otherwise unmarked hide. And it had certainly filled his footlocker. Knives that looked like pens, innocent-looking items with spring-activated blades, even a couple of one-shot guns disguised as pipes and keychains. Sleazy weapons, for sleazy people. The kind you meet in a sleazy job.

He tossed everything back in the box, locking it shut. Back down the hallway, with a brief stop to shove the footlocker back in the closet. Then on to the bedroom door.

At least it wasn't locked.

Joan sat on the bed, watching TV. Fleming had to grin when he saw her. Joan was not one for sexy negligees. When she went to bed, she dressed for warmth. In this case, adult-size Dr. Denton's.

"You're right, you know," Fleming said. "It's a shitty job. And when you work in shit, some of it sticks to you. But somebody's got to do it. And wouldn't you know? I do it pretty well."

"Maybe," Joan said warily. "But each of those cases takes a piece out of you."

"This case is different," Fleming assured her. "I can crack a major distribution ring. The last time we did this, it took them a long time to recover. It—it's important." He looked at her for a long moment. "Let's not turn it into something to fight about."

Joan looked back at him. "Where did you leave your shirt?"

"On the couch. What's that go to do . . ."

"It leads into the next question." She grinned. "Where will you be leaving your pants?"

Fleming kicked off his shoes and shucked off his pants. Then he got into bed. Joan leaned over and they kissed. "Friends again?" Fleming asked as they came up for air.

"Friends." Joan snuggled into his arms. "So what's the story?"

Fleming shook his head. Joan was the most anti-cop cop buff he'd ever seen. "I don't know if I should tell you," he said. "Remember Tony's Delicatessen."

They both laughed. It had happened right after the honeymoon. Fleming had left their new number with Larry for a special operation. He'd warned Joan that there might be phone calls coming from a stranger. She should take a message.

Joan had agreed, expecting all sorts of cloak-and-dagger stuff. And then it had happened! A stranger's voice on the line! "Is this Tony's?"

"Yes," she'd answered.

"Can you deliver an order?"

Now she was sure. "I'll take it," she said, reaching for a pencil.

"Great," said the voice. "A pound of butter, a dozen eggs, a six-pack of Bud, two rolls of toilet paper . . ."

Too late, Joan realized her mistake.

Only Fleming's arrival had saved the day. "Sorry, pal," he'd said, "my wife is a sick woman. Some days she thinks she's a delicatessen. Only thing is, she doesn't deliver."

They'd laughed all night over the episode. In between bouts of Joan showing that she could "deliver."

45

Fleming began explaining about the case—for about two minutes. Joan squirmed as his arms tightened. "You know what the problem is with you?" he said. "You always take my mind off business." He kissed her again, hard.

His hand went to the neck of her Doctor Denton's. He undid the snap there, and the next two, down the front of the pajamas. Then, as he looked into her eyes, he slid his hand in to capture her right breast.

Joan's eyes were large, a soft hazel that had caught his attention the first time they'd met. That, and her laugh. It was—uninhibited. Somehow, it made him wonder how she'd sound in bed.

He'd joked with her in the travel agency where she worked, just to hear that laugh. They'd ended up planning the goddamnedest trip. And he'd asked her out. Part of it was to find out if the body under those classy clothes was as good as he was imagining. But it was that laugh . . .

The same laugh he was hearing now as Joan's nipple hardened against his palm and she lifted her lips to his.

Fleming opened more of the snaps, until the suit was opened halfway down her belly.

Joan moved over him for a moment, while he pulled the flannel down from around her shoulders. She slipped her arms out, and her breasts came free. Fleming licked along the underside of one breast, just enjoying the taste of her.

"What kind of aim is that?" Joan teased, drawing her nipple past his lips.

"I'll show you aim," Fleming said. His big hand traced its way along her soft belly flesh, tearing open the rest of the snaps while delicately caressing her.

His fingers slid lower, and Joan gave a little shuddery breath. She rose on her haunches as his hand pushed aside to run over her hipbone. The modest Dr. Denton's were now gathered around her knees. She worked to pull Fleming's undershirt off, while kicking her own legs to free them.

Fleming's hand moved inward, following the soft crease of her groin, where her upper thigh met her lower body. "Still a little off . . ." she whispered. Then, "Oooh . . ." as his thumb traced its way through her pubic curls to the soft, damp lips.

Joan's body swayed, her flesh glowing in the semi-darkness. Fleming gasped as her fingers groped for his shorts, pulling them open, reaching inside to flutter along the length of him.

Fleming got to his knees, letting his last garment fall. His hand never left the junction of her thighs. Her fingers fisted around him. He kissed Joan's mouth, dueling with her tongue, then worked along the cords of her neck, to her shoulder. She leaned hungrily into him. He ran his free hand down the suppleness of her back.

She hunched once, twice, letting his fingers breach her more deeply. "I don't know about the right or the left," she breathed. "But I believe we're ready on the firing line."

They sank together to the mattress.

CHAPTER 5

LIFE'S a bitch, Joey thought. *Monica was one sweet woman when we met. Tits so high and firm that I'd get off just by squeezing her nipples. And what a pussy! So warm and wet and tight. When I was in her I never wanted to get out. We fucked all the time. He sighed. Then we got married. Now I'm lucky if I get it once a month. Her tits are sagging and her pussy is drier than the desert. But what's a guy going to do? She's my wife, dammit. And she still gets me hot.*

He reached down and massaged his throbbing member. Beside him, Monica snored gently, then rolled over on her side, brushing her buttocks against his arm. Joey grunted and rolled over, pressing his erection between the cheeks of Monica's ass. The friction felt good and he began pumping back and forth.

"Oh, baby," he whispered, "yeah, do it to me. That's it." He moaned as waves of pleasure washed over his body. *I'm doin' it, baby. Feels good,* he thought. *Almost there . . .*

"What the hell's the matter with you, you pig! Can't I get any sleep around here?" Monica slapped him hard in the face, stunning him.

Joey sat up, holding his stinging cheek in his hand. "You bitch, I oughta knock you out for doing that."

"Oh, yeah? Go ahead, Joey. Hit me." She thrust her jaw out, challenging him. "C'mon, big man. Hit me."

Joey rolled to his knees and jumped on his wife, pinning her beneath his body while pummeling her breasts with punches. Monica absorbed the blows with muted grunts, then attacked Joey as his fury ran out. She brought her knee up hard, jabbing him in the balls. He gurgled in pain and brought his knees up to his chest, rolling around the bed. But no position offered relief.

Monica braced her back against the headboard, pulled her legs back, then kicked her husband onto the floor. He landed with a loud thump, cracking his head on the night table. She continued her verbal assault, leaning over the edge of the bed. "What's the matter, big man? I thought you wanted it. Well, come and get it!" She reached out and again smacked Joey in the face.

"I told you before to stay the hell away from me," she said.

"You're my wife," he whined. "I got my rights."

"Oh, now I'm your wife. When you're out screwing around, you don't give a damn that I'm your wife. Now that you finally come home I'm supposed to roll over on my back and spread my legs wide for you. Do you remember I'm your wife when you're screwing that *putana?*"

"What are you talking about?"

Monica screamed and threw a box of tissues at Joey. "You think I'm stupid? I can always tell when you come home after sleeping with her. I can smell her on you. The smell of that whore Connie."

"You keep her out of this. And she's not a whore."

"You could have fooled me. What else would you call a woman who steals your husband?"

"Maybe if you'd fuck me a little more we wouldn't have all this trouble."

"If you stopped fucking me all the time, Joey, maybe we could get back what we lost." Tears dribbled from her eyes, leaving black streaks from her mascara. Monica slumped back in bed and sobbed loudly, burying her face in her hands.

Joey stood there watching her, not knowing what to do. And not caring either. He sat down on the bed and gently stroked her leg, moving his hand higher and higher up her thigh.

She shook his hand off. "Get out of this room," she said.

"Hey, I gotta sleep."

"You'll sleep all right. But not here. Why don't you see if Connie's got room in her bed for you tonight? Or do you need a reservation?"

"Gimme a break, will you? It's three o'clock in the morning. Where am I going to go?"

"You can go to hell, you sonofabitch!" Monica vaulted out of bed and slapped Joey's face. He backed up to avoid the blows but she kept up her relentless assault. The fury of her attack stunned him. The slaps stung his cheeks and he felt his face burning from the shame of having a woman beat him.

"*Basta!*" he shrieked. "I'll get out. I'll sleep on the couch. Just stay away from me, you fucking nut!"

Monica slammed the door so hard that the walls of the bedroom shook. Her fury sated, she leaned back against the door. A sobbing fit overcame her. She wept for her lost youth and lost dreams.

As the door slammed in his face, Joey felt a momentary sadness. He felt alone and unwanted. An invisible hand twisted his stomach into a knot, and he pressed his hands to his belly to ease the pain. *Bitch,* he thought. *It's a good thing I don't hit women or you'd be in for it. It's respect I have. I give to everyone but no one gives it to me.*

He walked to the bar and opened a bottle of Scotch. Not wanting to wash a dirty glass, he swigged a gulp straight from the bottle. The liquor seared a path down his throat and landed with a splash in his stomach. *Tastes so damn good. Even better than snatch!* When he remembered how Connie tasted after using that strawberry-flavored douche, he grinned and grew erect again.

Another swig of Scotch calmed him. He sat on the couch, throwing his leg over the arm. His left nut itched and he scratched it disinterestedly like a tired mongrel who's just too lazy to exert himself. *It was such a sweet deal. And I set it up all by myself. No help from Uncle Frankie. My fuckin' brother. He'd never help me out. He's too damn busy sucking up to Uncle Angelo. I did good. Unloaded all that shit on that dumb-ass nigger.* He laughed.

Jivin' me. Rappin' his shit. But I got the better deal. Ten grand for weak shit. I thought Uncle Angelo would be so proud of me. Finally doin' good on my own. No help

51

from no one. But do I get thanks? Or, "Great job, Joey"? No! That fat bastard burns my money. So they can't trace it to the family, he says. He's got no balls. He's soft. He should step down. Let younger men rule the business.

The Scotch fueled his fantasies of greatness and for a brief moment he saw himself as the head of a large family, with Uncle Angelo, Frankie, and Billy coming to him for permission to fart. The image made him laugh loudly. But it was silenced by the ice-cold eyes and skeletal face of Rocco Mazzi. He shuddered. *That creep would kill me if Uncle Angelo gave him the word. Fuck him. Fuck Uncle Angelo. Nobody tells Joey Castelli what to do. Fuck you, Billy. I ain't layin' low. And fuck you, nigger. You still owe me five big ones. You better get your black ass hot or it will get goddamn cold real quick.*

He staggered to the phone and dialed Larry's number. It rang fifteen times. *C'mon you bastard, answer the phone.*

"It better be good or I'll get your ass," said Larry.

"That you, cool?"

"My main man! Shit. You know what time it is?"

"I know what time it is. It's time you got off your ass and came up with the five grand you owe me."

"Man, what's your hurry? Don't you trust me?"

"No, I don't. I don't like getting stiffed in a deal."

"Man, I ain't jiving you. It's like this. That was some great shit. How can I get some more?"

This dumb ass don't even know he's been fucked, thought Joey. *I can unload all that shit on him.* "How much you need?"

This guy's so greedy, he don't know he's being set up, thought Larry. *These guineas ain't shit. The brothers are fools to let them control their business.* "How about twenty? Maybe forty cases of beer?"

"What kind?"

"Miller High Life." Larry chuckled at his joke.

"Look, cool breeze, before we deal you gotta pay for what you got already."

"I'm good for it, man. Didn't I come with ten dollars the last time you needed it?"

Sure you did. And it's ashes now. "Look, you make me an order and we deal. But I want the money for my last shipment up front. You dig? Otherwise it's off."

Oh, shit, I pushed too hard. I'm losin' him. "Hey, dude, lighten up. You'll get paid."

"Just make sure I get it before I'm dead, okay?" *If Uncle Angelo finds out about this, I'm fish food. But if I pull it off, I'll be a real big man.* "I'll call you tomorrow. No bread, no deal. You dig?"

"Be cool, my man," said Larry. "You can trust me."

CHAPTER 6

ED FLEMING grinned in triumph when Larry called in. "A meet, huh? Make it tonight. Tell him you want half a kilo."

"Half a kilo, man?"

"Yeah. Tell Joey-baby he'll get full payment on delivery. Plus whatever you owe him."

"You think he can get his hands on that much, so fast?"

Fleming's grin got bigger. "He'll handle it, if he wants his money. You just tell him it has to be tonight. If he can't come up with the goods, you'll have to go elsewhere. He'll show."

54

"Then you nail him. I hope I get a few tastes of what he's toting," Larry said.

"Don't push your luck, asshole." Fleming slammed his phone down. He headed down the hall, to the supervisors' offices. Outside Dick Powers's office, he slowed for a second, then continued down the hall, to knock on George Kohler's door.

As he outlined the setup, Fleming thought Kohler was going to have a stroke. His sallow face went doughy, and his lank brown hair almost stood on end.

"Castelli," George whispered, almost afraid to believe it.

Fleming could understand the reaction. Kohler hadn't had a big case in six months, since he arrived in the office. *What could you expect from a guy from Idaho? They expect a bunch of out-of-towners to clean up New York. What they need is New Yorkers—like me—like Dick Powers. Kohler may have been the Terror of the Midwest. But here, he's out of his league.*

"Um, Ed, can you do me a favor? I need to make a phone call." Kohler was dialing even before Fleming left. Fleming made a silent bet with himself. It had to be Washington.

A couple of minutes later, Kohler called him back in. "Washington is real pleased with this." George leaned back in his chair, a big "See what I did for you" look on his face. "They want him bad. The sky's the limit on this case."

How did this guy make supervisor? Fleming wondered. "Great. We have to reel him in tonight. The sooner the better."

"Shouldn't we plan—"

"This can't drag on past tonight." Fleming cut him off.

"We're in a race now. We've got to nail Joey Castle before somebody tips him off. That's why I set the meet as soon as possible. When Joey shows up with the goods, Larry will give us a signal, and we catch Joey's ass."

Kohler looked unconvinced. "We need to catch him red-handed, Fleming—nothing manufactured about this case. I know your reputation . . ."

"We'll catch him with the stuff in his hand," Fleming assured Kohler. *We'll have to. God,* he thought, *so much can go wrong.*

But Kohler seemed determined to *make* something go wrong. "I'm assigning four cars to look for Castelli," he said. "I'd be easier in my mind to have an eye on him before the delivery. Maybe we'll even see where he gets the stuff."

Fleming kept his face carefully neutral. Kohler was the boss. He'd just given him the case. If he wanted to fuck it up, it was up to him. Instinctively, he knew the best they could hope for was nailing Joey. No way could they hope to make the location of his plant.

As the afternoon wore on, Fleming got no word of success on the search for Joey Castelli. He found himself perversely relieved. If they hadn't found him, that meant Joey had no tail to discover.

Fleming checked with Larry. "Joey hasn't called yet, but he's going to," Larry assured him. "I'm packing my bags. After this, I'm out of here."

"Just moving out?" Fleming asked.

"Man, everything I want I can fit into two small suitcases. If you can't eat it, drink it, or screw it, it ain't worth having. Only thing better is cash money. How we doing on that?"

"Uncle's being generous," Fleming said. "You'll have thirty grand for a flash roll."

Joey Castle sat in the bar where he had first met Larry, nursing a Pinch and water. He glanced at his watch. He was supposed to call Larry soon.

I'm fucked, Joey thought. *No way am I gonna get that five thousand without another delivery. But Uncle Angelo told me never to deal with the* mulignan *again. If he knew I was even talking to him on the phone, he'd bust my ass.*

Uncle Angelo had gotten angry with him many times, but only once had he beaten him. *The first night I got Monica—busted her cherry.*

Monica's mother had called the police about "the animal" who had "raped" her sixteen-year-old angel. And because Monica was only sixteen, Joey was arrested.

Angelo got him home. Then he had banged Joey's head against the wall until he cracked the plaster. "You're going to marry that girl," he said.

When Joey refused, Uncle Angelo smashed him into the wall again. "The de Fabrizios are men of importance—Sicilians. You don't marry their niece, they'll fix you so you're no good with a woman ever again. Maybe *I* should do it!"

When Joey saw his own uncle pulling out a penknife, he had changed his tune. He got married. *Tied down to Monica because I got a piece of her ass. Because she was afraid God would make her pregnant, and told her mother—who told Uncle Angelo.*

Joey took another sip of his drink. No one could tell Uncle Angelo this time. Nobody would know, except himself and Larry. He finished his drink in a gulp. *Sure, I'll do the delivery. One last one—a big score. Billy will find out there's stuff missing from the plant, but he won't tell Uncle Angelo. Besides,* he convinced himself, *it's good business, selling to the* mulignans. *They pay better than our Italian customers—and they'll take lower-quality goods.*

He walked to the pay phone and dialed. "Hey, Richards, it's me again." His words slurred a little. *Damn, I'm feeling that booze.*

"I've been waiting on you," Larry said. "Everything all right for tonight?"

That sobered Joey up. "I don't know about tonight," he said. "That's . . ."

"Got to be tonight, man," Larry cut him off. "Or I shop elsewhere this trip."

When Joey didn't answer, he said, "Tell you what. I'll double the order."

Joey stared at the phone. "But you already doubled the order."

"Double the double," Larry responded.

"Double . . . ?" Joey said.

"Trouble with you Eye-talians is, you talk so much horseshit to make your business secret, it's a wonder you sell anything at all," Larry finally said. "Look. Give me a whole kilo. Two halves wrapped in two separate packages. Okay?"

"I got it," Joey said. "And you get this. It will cost you sixty thousand. You gotta have all the money."

"Man, don't sweat it," Larry replied. "I got it in my pocket."

"Okay." Joey leaned back in the phone booth. Now he

was in charge. "Nine o'clock. We meet the same place I met you last time. Understand?"

"I be there, nine sharp."

"You just stay in your car. I'll come to you." Joey hung up the phone. *All set up.*

Larry hung up his phone, smiling. He looked at the two bags lying on his bed, and the bills he'd just stacked on top of them. His working capital, ten thousand bucks.

Put that with Fleming's thirty grand, then tell Joey I have to owe him twenty for the extra half-kilo. He'll take it, rather than bringing the goods back. Larry's smile got wider. *Then Fleming gets Joey and his shit, and I get a half-key for ten thousand. Fleming probably even give me my money back, if he don't get too pissed off.*

He picked up the phone and dialed Fleming's office number. "We got him," he said. "Nine tonight. Twenty-third and Tenth."

Joey drove down Twenty-third Street in his brother Billy's gray Eldorado. *Nearly nine o'clock,* he thought, with a glance at the paper bag on the seat beside him. He'd just driven in through the Lincoln Tunnel. He and Billy had a beautiful stash in Hoboken, watched by an old couple who didn't ask questions.

All the way in, he'd checked the rearview mirrors, looking to see if he had a tail. There was none. Now, as he neared the meet, he scanned the streets, looking for cops.

Fleming made Ross park half a block away from Larry's car. "Here he comes."

Ross grunted uncomfortably. He was wearing a blond wig. From a distance, it was supposed to make him look like Fleming's girlfriend. Close up, it made them look like the Odd Couple. Fleming grinned and put his arm around Ross as Joey drove by.

Ross tried to shake the arm away.

"Now, Jack," said Fleming. "You don't want to spook him."

"Get the fuck off me!" Ross exploded.

Their car radio crackled. "Get a load of that Caddy," Kohler's voice came over. "I'm going to look great behind the wheel of that."

"Fucking section chiefs," Ross grumbled. "We nail the pushers, and they take their cars."

"Well, all our guys are alerted, now," Fleming said. He watched as Joey's head swiveled around, taking everything in but seeing nothing. Grover Alston was walking along Twenty-third. He blended in perfectly.

Joey rounded the block, then came around again. Passing right between Fleming and Kohler, he pulled into a space behind Larry. "Parking beside a fire hydrant," said Fleming. "Doesn't he know he's breaking the law?"

As Joey walked to Larry's car, Fleming's radio crackled again. "It's going down," Kohler said unnecessarily. "What's the signal, Ed? You call it."

"Let him leave Larry's car. When Larry blinks his lights, it means he's got the stuff. You take Joey, I'll get Larry." *Better to miss the bust than let Larry start playing with the goods,* he thought.

Joey jerked Larry's car door open and got inside. "Here's your kilo," he said, opening his bag. "Where's the money?"

"What's the rush, man?" Larry said. He could see Joey visibly jittering. "Hey! I told you I wanted it in two bags. Two separate packages."

"Fuck what you want!" Larry shouted. "You can break it up any way you like later. I want to see my money."

Larry opened the glove compartment, taking out two plastic bags. "We'll have to break it up first."

Joey grabbed his arm. "Look, you fuckin' nigger, don't dick around with me. You ain't touching shit until I get my money."

Larry passed him an envelope and reached for the paper bag. Joey kept it tightly under his arm as he riffled through the bills. "What the fuck is this?" he screamed. "You're short!"

"Hey, man, I'll make it good. It's just . . ."

Joey didn't stay to listen. He jumped out of the car. Larry stared after him, stunned.

When he saw the car door open, Fleming broadcast, "Get ready."

"He's still holding that bag!" Kohler's voice blared over the speaker.

Fleming stared for a second. "Maybe he's carrying the money in it. Wait for Larry's signal."

But Larry's lights didn't blink. Joey's car started. He peeled out.

Kohler's voice came out in a shriek. "What? What's going on!"

Fleming sat transfixed, in a daze. *What had gone wrong?* He grabbed the radio. "Follow him. Don't bust him. Let me check with Larry." He ran over to Larry as the other cars peeled out. Hauling the door open, he pulled Larry into the street. "What did you do? You fucked it up!"

"Man, that guy acting crazy!" Larry said. "He must have been snorting some bad shit or something. Ran out . . ."

"Don't hand me any bullshit!" Fleming smashed him

into the car. "You started screwing with him, didn't you? A little business of your own?"

Larry fumbled for words. The look in Fleming's eyes told him that the wrong thing said now would get him killed. "Look, he's still holding. I saw. A full kilo."

Fleming's car pulled up beside him. Ross was at the wheel. He'd pulled off his wig. "Guy's driving like a bat out of hell. Kohler wants to know what the fuck he's supposed to do."

Fleming threw himself into the car, grabbing the radio. "Bust him! Bust him! He's holding!" Even as he was talking, Ross had the tires screaming.

Half a mile south of them, Joey Castle careened down Ninth Avenue, his gas pedal to the floor. He didn't see the other traffic. He didn't see the DEA cars falling behind. He was driving blind. *Gotta get away from that fuckin'* mulignan. *Get someplace safe.*

He screeched along Mulberry and turned onto Hester. Without even thinking of it, he was heading for safety— home to Mamma.

Kohler's hysterical voice crackled over the radio. "We've lost him! We've lost him! He's down those fucking little streets in Little Italy! Has anybody got him?"

Fleming thought he was about to get sick on the floor. *That black sonofabitch . . . I'll kill him!*

One of the other agents got on the horn. "I've found his car, parked on Hester between Mott and . . . DeWitt. It's empty."

"Hey," said Ross. "Doesn't his mother live down there?"

Fleming's head snapped up. He was out of his funk. Dredging the address from his memory, he put it out on the radio. "We're on Mulberry, and we'll be there in two minutes. Don't wait. It's apartment 4A."

They pulled up on Hester, to find it blocked by the other six cars. Fleming rushed into the building. Running up the stairs, he found Kohler beside the door with three other guys. One was Agent Roberts, the resident door genius. He had his gun out, aimed at the lock.

"What the fuck are you waiting for?" Fleming yelled.

Roberts fired. Part of the wooden door split away from the lock. But it held as Roberts kicked at it. Fleming finally pushed him aside and bulled into the door with all his weight.

The door panel splintered and fell away, to reveal Mamma Castelli with Joey at her side. They held onto each other. *Who's holding up who?* Fleming thought.

Joey stepped forward as Fleming shouldered through the wrecked door. "What the hell do you guys think you're doing?" It would have sounded a lot better if Joey's voice hadn't cracked.

Fleming's answer was a backhand to the face that sounded like a pistol shot. Joey tottered back toward his mother, blinking his eyes to clear the tears.

"Not another word out of you," Fleming said, poking a finger into Joey's chest. "Unless you want to tell me where the goods are hidden."

Joey was opening his mouth to ask about a search warrant. But he looked at those big, beefy hands again and shut up.

"We're going to search this place," Fleming said.

Joey turned to his mother as she made a choking noise. Her eyes rolled up as she moaned. He grabbed her arm as she started slumping to the floor. Kohler was in the apartment now and grabbed her other arm. Together, he and Joey brought Mamma Castelli to a nearby stuffed chair. She crumpled into it.

The other agents froze in the doorway, looking at the woman's obvious distress.

"She's got a bad heart!" Joey screamed. "You gotta get those guys out of here!"

Fleming's face hardened. "Tell me where the goods are."

"There's nothing here. You're wasting your time. And you're gonna kill my mother."

Fleming's face didn't change.

"At least let me call a doctor," Joey said.

"Sure," Fleming said. "After we search."

Kohler looked apprehensively from the gasping woman to Fleming.

"Stay with Joey," Fleming suggested. "Let him take care of his mother."

The agents split up to search the apartment. Fleming hit the bathroom, checking the commode, rapping the walls for loose tiles. Roberts came in, tore open the medicine cabinet, sweeping the contents to the floor. He stepped on the bottles, breaking them, as he spilled the clothes from the hamper onto the mess. He stepped into the bedroom and came back with men's suits—Joey's and Billy's, Fleming guessed. Tearing open the seams, he threw the jackets onto the pile. Then, opening his fly, he pissed on the whole collection.

Fleming stepped out of the room, disgusted. *Fucking farm boys, showing they're tough. They'll never find anything.* Searches were the worst. You could look and look, and the goods could be under your nose. Once Fleming had searched a girl's entire apartment and found nothing. Later, the suspect had told Larry about her luck. Nobody had searched *her.* She'd shoved the stash in her panties. When Fleming had heard about that, he entered Agency folklore, going back to the apartment, kicking the door down, and bringing the suspect to the office dressed only in her drawers.

He came back to the living room to see Joey pleading with Kohler. "You guys gotta get out of here. We need a doctor. She's going to die. Please." He looked up at Kohler. "You're in charge here. I tell you, there's no stuff here. I swear to God. On my mother's head."

He followed up when he saw the irresolute look on Kohler's face. "I wouldn't bring anything here. To my mother's house!"

Kohler glanced around nervously. "Maybe we should call the hospital."

"She won't go," Joey said. "It will kill her. Call a doctor and get those guys out of here. They're getting her all upset."

Roberts reported in. "Nothing."

Kohler's shoulders sank. "We're going to get this woman a doctor, then we get the hell out of here." Fleming could see him already trying to figure out how to report this fiasco.

"Forget it, forget it," Joey said. "Just leave us alone."

"Wait a minute, wait a minute," Fleming said, stepping forward.

Joey flinched away from the big, crazy cop.

But Fleming was advancing on Mamma Castelli. "Let me help you up," he said solicitously.

The closer he came, the worse Mamma Castelli panted and moaned.

"Are you crazy?" Kohler yelled as Fleming grabbed the old woman by the arm.

"It's the one place we haven't searched," Fleming said, yanking Mamma Castelli from the chair.

65

Suddenly, her panting stopped. "Lousy cop bastards!" she screamed, grabbing for the arms of the chair. It tilted, and a brown paper bag spilled out from under the seat cushion.

CHAPTER 7

FLEMING sat at his desk, writing a report on the arrest. Outwardly, he looked calm, but inside, he was fuming. *So, Big George is annoyed at me for making him look like a fool. Didn't take that much work.* He threw his pen down. *Where does Kohler come off giving me lectures? I'm the one who saved the fucking bust!*

"Ed?" Jack Ross stood beside him. "We got a problem. He won't sign his fingerprint cards."

Fleming stared for a second. "What?"

Ross looked sheepish. "He says it's a new court ruling,

or something. He can't be forced to give evidence against himself, so he's not obliged to sign."

"Not obliged to sign, huh?" Fleming jammed his chair back. "I'll oblige him!"

He stalked into the lockup, pushing past two lower-ranking agents, to find Joey just washing the ink from his hands. "You sign those fucking fingerprint cards!" Fleming shouted.

Joey shrank back. He was afraid of this big maniac, especially when he learned he was the main agent on the case. "I—I don't have to." It came out as a squeak. Joey looked at the floor.

He didn't even see Fleming's fist come flying at him. It caught him right in the mouth, knocking him flat. The impact cut lips and gums. Joey put his hand to his mouth. It came away bloody.

"Sign!" Fleming stepped forward, his fist cocked for another shot.

Joey sprang to his feet and grabbed a pen. With shaking hands, he signed. Ross had to hold his handkerchief to Joey's mouth, to keep blood from dropping on the cards.

Joey used the handkerchief to stanch the flow of blood. Ross reached to take it back, but Fleming waved him away. "Get out of here," he said. "All of you."

Joey's eyes darted around as Ross and the guards left the room. He was certain he was going to get another beating from Fleming—a bad one, which Fleming didn't want witnesses to see.

Who is *this Fleming guy?* Joey wondered. *He acts instantly, no hesitation, nailing people, not giving a fuck about the law. Doesn't he know who I am? Who Uncle Angelo is? He's treating me like a nobody.* Joey stared dazedly around the lockup. It seemed as alien as if he'd just beamed in from another planet.

"Sorry about the punch," Fleming suddenly spoke up. "You had it coming, you know, with this jailhouse lawyer bullshit."

Joey's eyes were riveted on his face as Fleming began to pace back and forth in the small cell.

"I hear you wouldn't sign your personal property envelope," Fleming went on. "You said your watch and your money were missing." He shook his head. "You should know better than to complain. You were in the joint once."

He watched Joey stew for a second. Usually, Fleming didn't approach his prisoners so soon. He let a night in jail soften them up. But Joey was the perfect defendant. He'd been inside already. He knew what he was in for. Fleming smiled.

"Well, I'm going to make sure you get your watch and money back."

Joey made a small "Who cares?" gesture.

Fleming pushed his face into Joey's. "Oh, no," he said. "It's too late for graciousness. Besides, I'd have gotten that stuff anyway. See, you're mine now, and I don't steal. I lie and I cheat, but I don't steal."

Joey stared at the big red face looming before him. *Maybe this is my chance,* he thought. *Maybe he'll ask for money.*

Instead, Fleming stepped away, playing Joey like a fish. He lit two cigarettes, and handed one to Joey. Even though Joey didn't smoke, he took it. "I guess you know by now that Larry is a snitch." Fleming took a puff. "He's made fifty cases for me in three years, testified two dozen times in court. What a witness."

He looked at Joey, all business. "I'm telling you this so you'll understand the situation," he went on. "I know Larry scored a quarter of a kilo from you on Christmas Day . . ." He watched as Joey stiffened. "Larry did that under my direction. But we're not going to use that stuff. No, we're going to use the stuff from tonight. A whole kilo. And Larry was paying for it with government money."

Joey's cigarette just hung from his lips. It had gone out. Fleming reached over and relit it.

"Now, of course, we were going to pop you on Twenty-third Street, but you got cute there. So we wound up taking you at your mom's." He shook his head. "A shame. You standing there, swearing on your mother's head. It's a shame for us, too. I'd much rather have nailed you at the buy—if we had 'buys' on you, you'd be absolutely dead. But instead we've got a seizure case, and that gets into probable cause."

He looked into Joey's eyes. "If you talked to a smart lawyer, he'd say he might be able to beat this case. And he might, if the truth was told." Fleming moved closer again. His voice was a hoarse whisper. "But it's not gonna be told, Joey. I'm going to lie. Larry's going to lie. All the fine, upright agents in this office are going to lie. I give you my personal promise that you will get convicted on this rap. You'll get ten years, probably fifteen."

Joey was almost hypnotized as he stared up at that big face. "C-Can't we . . ." He hesitated, trying to find a safe way to phrase a bribe offer. "Can't we work something out?"

Fleming gave him a big grin. "You want me to sell out, Joey?"

Joey looked away, afraid to say it.

"C'mon, Joey, it's just us boys here. Don't be afraid to

say it. I don't want you for bribery. If I did, I'd just make it up, part of my report in black and white."

Fleming grabbed Joey's chin. "You haven't been paying attention to what I've been saying," he said. "It doesn't matter what you say. What matters is what I *say* you say. And I'll say this. There is no way you're going to buy out of this case. You might make some cops happy, but you're missing the whole thing. You've got to make *me* happy. I'm the only one who can help you. But I won't do it for money." Fleming's smile didn't reach his eyes. "Only one thing will make me break this case."

Joey didn't want to hear about it. He didn't want to think about it. But he still asked, "What?"

"I want me an importer, Joey. Just one little importer. One of our friends from down Colombia way, making a delivery."

Joey jumped back, bumping into the wall. "You gotta be shitting me," he said. "I'd rather do the time. Me, rat on a guy? I'd die first!"

Fleming stared at him, face frozen. *Sure, Joey-boy,* he thought. *You're a regular hero. That's why you're telling me so loud. To convince yourself.*

He simply shrugged. "Just think about it, Joey. No Italians. Nobody from your family. Nobody from your organization. Just a Colombian. But if you think protecting some spic is worth ten years . . ."

Fleming walked to the door of the lockup. He'd get no further tonight. It was now a matter of time—of how many sleepless nights Joey would spend.

Stopping in the doorway, he turned back. "I won't be seeing you until the trial. But if you're interested, just call me, or leave a message. Say, 'Montgomery wants to see you.' I'll know, and only I will know."

71

Fleming stepped through the door. "Do you know that German joint, Unter den Linden, in Pelham Bay?"

"Yeah," Joey said.

"When you call . . ." Fleming smiled. "*If* you call, just say, 'Montgomery, under the trees.' I'll know, and I'll be there that same night at nine o'clock—alone."

He slammed the cell door shut and walked out.

"Eddie, me boy!"

Fleming turned in the hallway to see Dick Powers coming toward him. He braced himself.

But Powers was all smiles. "Nice collar. You've got Peretti pissed as hell. He's going to expect a case a week like this one from Larry."

"Well, he can have him. The greedy bastard nearly screwed everything up," Fleming retorted.

Powers shook his head. "I tell you, Ed . . ." He mashed the toe of his shoe onto the floor, as if he'd just nailed a cockroach. "You've got to step on them." He grinned at Fleming. "How about a celebration drink?"

They walked into McAnn's on Park Row, and Fleming scowled at the imitation-wood paneling. "I hate this place," he muttered. "It's a shame they closed down Suerken's. That was a real bar."

Of course, all the help in the place knew Powers. In spite of the hour, they got a table up on the balcony. "The best for my friend here," Powers said, handing the waitress a hundred-dollar bill. "Glenlivet and water. Just keep them coming." He smiled. "Ah, whiskey," he said. "Mother's milk to a true Irishman."

As their drinks arrived, Fleming saw a familiar face down at the far end of the bar.

Kohler. The section chief was leaning forward, talking to somebody, jerking his hands nervously. He moved, and Fleming could see the person George was talking to. Roberts. And even at this distance, Fleming could see the flashy new watch on his wrist.

Powers followed Fleming's gaze. "Roberts and Kohler processed Castelli while you took the junk in for evidence."

"Yeah, well, I told Kohler the watch and the money had better be found." He shook his head. "I wouldn't be surprised if Kohler was in for a part of it. Half of a hundred and fifty bucks is probably his idea of a big score."

"Let's get out of here," Powers said. He gulped down the rest of his drink and stood up. "Keep the change, darling girl," he said to the waitress.

They headed uptown, to Weston's, and really started hitting the sauce. Everybody in the joint was coming over to their table, saying hello to Powers. Half of the guys looked like pimps, the rest looked like hoods. The place was also crawling with hookers, giving both of them exaggerated smiles. Eventually, Fleming knew, Powers would go off with one, and he could go home. Even now, he was making eyes at a blonde with the biggest tits Fleming had ever seen. Powers would be resting his head on them before the night was through.

It had been that way since the days when they were partners. Powers had a wife, but he loved his whores. As for Fleming, they made his skin crawl.

Powers took a big sip of his (fourth? fifth?) drink and shook his head at Fleming. "The farm boys turn everything into amateur night," he said, picking up the conversation they'd dropped nearly an hour earlier. "You should have kept this in the family, boyo."

I would have, if I thought I could trust you, you professional Irish prick, Fleming thought. He shrugged. "Kohler needed the case. That gave me a little leverage."

Silence fell between them.

"This case," Powers finally said. "You're sure it will hold water? You didn't bust him at a buy. You got him for holding. That means probable cause . . ."

Fleming looked at him. "This is the first time I ever heard you worrying about having enough evidence," he said.

"Well, this isn't any little shitass pusher," Powers responded. "We're talking about a member of the Tartagliano family here—Joey can afford the best defense lawyers. Can he beat it?"

"You want the truth, the whole truth, and nothing but the truth?" Fleming said. "Yeah, he could beat it. But he won't. I'm writing this case up myself. And it's going to be a work of art. After all," he grinned, "us Feds are all loyal, true, courageous, and holy. And we're talking about a convicted dope dealer, whose record shows he violated a little girl. This guy is going away for a long time."

"Even so," Powers began.

"No even so," Fleming cut in. "You taught me well. There's no defense against perjury."

CHAPTER 8

FELICIA knelt at her brother's feet and clutched the hem of his trousers in her hands, wringing it like a washcloth. "He's my son, Angelo. My baby. Don't hurt him."

"I won't tolerate disobedience—from anyone. He must be punished."

"Angelo, he's family. How can you do this to family?"

"Did Joey think of family when he went with that *mulignan* again—after I told him not to? He puts us all in danger. I must make an example of him."

Felicia clutched her chest, then tore at her hair. "Please. He's not strong like Billy. He makes mistakes but he means no harm. Have mercy on him. For Vincent, my dead husband, who died for you. Do you forget his sacrifice? For me, your sister! Please."

"Felicia, because you're my sister, I'm listening to you now. Not because of that son of yours. When Joey owed the gamblers, I paid his debts. When he went to prison, I protected him. I asked for nothing in return—just the respect to which I am entitled. And this is how he repays me."

Felicia sank back on her heels with a wail. Angelo helped her to her feet and spoke, his voice almost a whisper. "He's not a spoiled child anymore. He's a man. And he must pay for his actions." His tone was gentle, filled with love for his sister. But the harsh lines of his face showed his determination. "No more discussion. I have spoken."

Felicia wiped the tears from her eyes. "Do what you must, brother. But let him come back to me."

Angelo watched her go without comment. When the door to her bedroom closed he turned to Billy, who sat at the kitchen table. He sat opposite his nephew.

"My sister just doesn't understand." Angelo shook his head.

"Can you blame her?" Billy asked. "He's her son."

"He's worthless. A weasel. Look at him, arrested like a common criminal. Making his mother shield him like a child. He just can't be trusted."

"He's also my brother." A slight sheen of sweat appeared on Billy's forehead. "I know he's weak. He has no discipline. He thinks with his balls, not his brains. But . . ." He wet his lips. "Do you have to kill him?"

Angelo stood up, a shocked expression on his face. "Who said anything about killing him?"

Billy felt a surge of hope. "You know how he is. Impulsive. Always wanting attention. He just got carried away.

I can straighten him out. Let me talk to him . . ."

"No!" The cutting edge of Angelo's voice silenced his nephew. "The time for talk is done. He disobeyed my orders. I *should* kill him. He brings the government men sniffing around me."

Billy took a deep breath as he looked at his uncle's angry face. "The Feds are always around. They examine your bank account and they spy on your affairs. It's nothing new."

"There is a difference. Before they didn't know what to look for. Now it has a name. Cocaine." The veins on Angelo's temples stood out like angry red worms. "And that idiot brother of yours has led them to me. He will be punished—something he will remember. This is his last chance. Any more disobedience, and I wash my hands of him—forever."

Billy shivered, fearing for his brother. "What will you do?" he asked.

Angelo peered at Billy through hooded eyes. The flicker of a smile teased his lips. "*You* tell *me*. Or do you defy me as well?"

Billy didn't hesitate. He walked to the door and opened it. "Rocco. Achille. *Veni ca!*"

The two men shuffled into the room. They were a mismatched pair. Rocco wore a gray suit that was too big for him. His black shoes were scuffed and needed polish but his black eyes flashed in anticipation. Achille had better style sense and his well-cut blue suit fit him admirably. With his carefully styled hair, he looked more like a stockbroker than a button man. The two of them were opposites in everything except their devotion to their jobs.

They were coolly efficient and worked well as a team. Achille was the muscle and used his bulk to intimidate his victims. He rarely fired his pistol and preferred to use it to club his prey into submission. Rocco loved brutality and delighted in any session where he could inflict maximum pain. His favorite weapon was a razor-edged stiletto that he kept in a sheath on his right calf.

"My brother has not been behaving himself and needs to be taught a lesson," said Billy, addressing the two men in Italian.

Rocco's bullet eyes actually twinkled. "When?"

"Tonight. The lesson must be prompt if it's going to be remembered."

Angelo interrupted. "Stop talking in riddles. Speak your mind. What do you want them to do?"

Billy hesitated for a moment, then sighed. "Break his legs. Quick and neat. Give him this message. 'Orders are made to be obeyed. Disobey again and you will die.' Understand?"

"Sure thing, Mr. Tartagliano. We'll give him your message," said Achille. He and Rocco left the room.

Billy was sweating, and his hands shook as he poured a shot of whiskey. He downed it in one gulp, coughing as it went down. He made a second drink and sat down.

Angelo had been watching him. *A brother's love. A good thing. But wasted on Joey. Billy's a good boy. Respectful. He'll do fine.*

"So what did you learn of the investigation, Billy?" he asked.

"We didn't talk on the phone. We just set up a meeting."

"Can this one be trusted? There's a lot of pressure these days about uncovering corruption. Is he really what he appears to be? Or is he a spy?"

"He's ours, uncle. Have no fear."

"Me? I don't worry. But a prudent man checks out the dangers behind any business venture."

"He fears exposure. We have enough on him to put him in jail for life. He'll cooperate. But after this business is completed, we'll take our business elsewhere."

My nephew uses his head. A good quality. "Why look for others when this one is so reliable? A relationship must be developed slowly."

"There are ambitious men everywhere. And I have been examining replacements."

Angelo grinned. "So, his services will be terminated?"

"When we're through with him, uncle."

"You learn well, nephew."

Joey gunned his car at the red light. He wanted to get home and change in a hurry. Monica had gone to her mother's to spend the night. He thought of Connie's big tits and imagined his face between them. *Just a little longer, baby. I'll give you a tongue bath that'll make you scream.*

He leaned on his horn, but the light was deaf. It remained red. *What a fuckin' day. That damn narc. Does he think I'm crazy? Snitchin' on my own family. What does he think I am? He can go fuck himself. I'll go to jail. No way I'm gonna snitch for the Feds. C'mon, light. Change, dammit.*

His patience worn out, Joey sped across the intersection, narrowly missing a delivery van from a local Chinese restaurant. The driver jabbered at him in Cantonese while angrily waving his fist at him.

"Fuck you, asshole," Joey yelled. "You're in America now, you fucker. Speak English."

Joey drove into the garage of his building and pulled into his parking spot cursing the darkness. *Look at that damn light. Out again. Fuckin' super. When's he gonna put a damn bulb in?*

He locked up his car and strutted to the exit. Snapping his fingers to the beat of the song he hummed, Joey did not hear the scraping of feet from the shadows. But a primal survival sense caused him to hesitate and peer into the darkness. "Who's there?"

There's nothing there. Be cool. Think good thoughts and hot pussy. Connie, baby, you're really gonna get it tonight. I feel like an all-nighter.

"Hey, Joey. C'mere," said a voice in Italian.

Joey spun around and saw a hulking shape lurking behind him. "Who's that?"

"It's me, Joey. Achille."

"Hey, what's happening? What do you want?"

"You, Joey."

"Me? Why?"

"Because you pissed off the old man, and ya gotta pay for it," said a voice to his right. Joey turned and saw Rocco emerge from the shadows carrying a baseball bat.

Holy fuckin' shit. Uncle Angelo's gone nuts. They're gonna kill me. That bat. I know what he does with that.

Joey reacted quickly and tried to sprint to safety but Achille was too quick for him. The big man swung his fist in a huge arc, clipping Joey on the right ear, knocking him to the cement floor of the garage. Joey skidded on his face for a few feet, screaming until he stopped. He stood up on wobbly legs and Achille wrapped him up in a bear hug.

"Take it easy, kid," Achille said. "This ain't gonna be that bad."

"Leave me alone. I got money. I'll pay you. I'll give you

anything you want. You want snatch? I got babes for you. *Anything.* Just don't hurt me."

"I told ya the kid was a pussy, Achille," Rocco said. "He's got no fuckin' balls." Rocco hefted the bat in his arms and aimed for Joey's knees.

Joey screamed and squirmed in the grip of Achille. He kicked his legs out, nearly catching Rocco in the groin, but striking his thigh instead.

"Sonofabitch," spat Rocco. "You little fuckin' worm. I'll get you for that. Keep him still, dammit!"

"I'm tryin'," said Achille. He eased his hold for just a second to get a better grip, but Joey bolted free.

Rocco stuck the bat between Joey's legs and knocked him off balance. Joey slammed into a parked car with his face, breaking his nose.

He sat on the ground and cupped his hands to his nose. He stared in fascination at the blood pooling in his palm. As Rocco and Achille moved closer, he shook off the pain and tried to stand.

Rocco rammed the bat hard into Joey's nuts. Joey gagged as his stomach turned over, sending a stream of vomit streaking out of his mouth which landed on Rocco's pants.

"Fuck," he yelled and swung wildly with the bat, catching Joey in the shoulder. Joey sighed, then crumpled to the floor.

Achille reached out and grabbed the bat as Rocco swung it again. "The boss said to make it quick."

"Did you see what the little prick did? All over my fuckin' pants. This is gonna take a long while. I owe him."

Achille placed a ham-fisted hand on his shoulder and squeezed, causing Rocco to grimace in pain. "Later. Not now. He said make it quick. And we gotta pass the message. You fuck him up too much, he ain't gonna know what we're sayin'."

"He's gonna know. 'Cause I'm gonna tell him. Let me go." Achille released him and Rocco flexed his shoulder, which had gone numb from the pressure. "Hey, kid, you awake?"

Joey whimpered, and tried to curl into a fetal ball. Rocco knelt beside him, grabbed a handful of hair, and forced Joey to stare into his eyes. "Stop crying, you shit. The boss is pissed that you disobeyed him. This is your first and last warning. Understand?"

"Don't kill me. I got money . . ."

"Piss on your money, kid. We ain't gonna kill ya today. But I'm gonna bust your fuckin' legs."

Joey screamed and Rocco muffled his cries with a dirty handkerchief that he jammed in his mouth.

"C'mon, dammit," said Achille. "This is takin' too fuckin' long. Do it before somebody comes."

Rocco punched Joey in the jaw, snapping his head back. He fell backward, cracking his head against the concrete. Rocco picked up the bat and smashed Joey's right femur.

A muffled shriek make its way through the handkerchief.

"Quiet, Joey." Rocco laughed. "We'll be through in a minute."

Joey sat frozen as Rocco raised the bat again. It came down, shattering his left tibia. The sound of cracking cartilage and bone echoed in the garage, along with a strangled yell. Then came silence, as Joey lapsed into unconsciousness.

CHAPTER 9

I HEAR your friend Joey had an accident." Jack Ross took a sip of beer and rested his hip against his bar stool. "Broke his legs."

"Yeah." Fleming didn't sip beer, he inhaled it. One pop, and his stein was empty. "Told the cops he fell down a flight of stairs. They must make stairs awful funny in his building. They make the same kind of marks a baseball bat would."

Fleming hadn't been happy to hear about the leg-breaking. It set him back in his campaign to turn Joey. He hadn't expected Angelo Tartagliano to spank his errant nephew. Especially with a baseball bat.

The whole job had been pretty much of a disaster for the past weeks. Since Peretti had Larry, Fleming hadn't had a decent snitch—or a case—since nailing Joey. *Thank God Ross has some snitches,* Fleming thought. *Even if the best they can come up with is a grass bust.*

They were on surveillance, waiting for a Cuban guy who was going to score a load of marijuana. He was supposed to make delivery to Jack's bar stool by three in the afternoon. But Fleming and Ross had come to the neighborhood at nine in the morning, to keep an eye on the suspect's car. He'd need the car to transport the bulky load of dope. And they intended to follow him to his stash—or, if they were lucky, to his connection.

It was a good plan, but there was one factor Fleming and Ross hadn't counted on—both of them were seriously hung over. And there they were, at an ungodly hour, sitting in front of this guy's house. By ten o'clock, Ross had suggested going to the bar on the corner for a quick beer "to clear the cobwebs."

"I don't know about you, Ross," Fleming said. "You're turning into a real booze-hound." But he felt so lousy himself, he finally agreed to moving the car in front of the bar. They could still surveil the suspect's place, and they could take turns going in to have a drink.

By noon, they each had ten beers down, and were sitting together in the bar.

The bartender came over. "Another round?" he asked.

Ross put up his hand. "All this beer is bad for me," he said. "I'll switch to martinis."

The bartender looked at Fleming. "For you, too?"

"Nah. I'll stick with the beer."

They continued to drink, with Ross matching Fleming glass for glass. Fleming continued tossing his beers down. Ross sipped his martinis, meeting his glass halfway, exhaling after each mouthful, as if he'd been holding his breath.

Jesus, Fleming thought as he watched his partner. *I hope I never get as bad as this guy.*

As he watched, Ross carefully reached into his pocket and pulled out a small cosmetic mirror.

"What the hell is this?" Fleming asked.

"My handy pocket surveillance device," Ross replied with great dignity. "Stand this up on the bar, and we don't have to keep twisting our necks to keep an eye on the spic's car."

So they kept their seats, staring in the mirror.

People coming in for lunch looked at them askance, congregating at the far end of the bar with the bartender. "What are those two fucking guys doing?" Fleming heard a voice floating down from the knot of people.

"I dunno. You want to ask the big guy?"

Nobody did.

Finally, at two o'clock, Fleming caught sight of the Cuban's face in the mirror. "Come on! It's him! He's going to the car!"

"Let's get the bastard!" Ross sprang from his bar stool—and promptly fell flat on his face.

"Jack! Get up!"

Ross tried, but he was too drunk to move. And Fleming was too drunk, and laughing too hard, to lift him.

The Cuban pulled away, and Ross managed to pull down a bar stool in his efforts to get up. Finally, Fleming hauled his partner to his feet.

"You two—out of here. You've had enough!" The bartender was reaching under the bar.

"Fuck you!" Before Fleming could do anything, Ross flicked out his .38, and stuck it right in the bartender's nose. The guy keeled over in a dead faint.

"Lousy Irish bastard. Take our money, and then cut us off! Get up!" Ross waved his gun.

"Come on. We're leaving." Fleming grabbed Ross's free arm. "And put that away."

"Fucking bastards!" Ross said. But he holstered his gun as Fleming steered him to the door. "Didja see them making fun of us at the end of the bar? Didja?"

Fleming got them to the car. Ross flopped over on the seat, reaching for the wheel. "I'll drive."

"Fuck, no!" Fleming said. "I want us to get out of here alive!" He pulled away as fast as he dared.

Glancing in the rearview, he didn't see anyone on the street. *I hope nobody got our license,* he thought. *This would take one hell of a story to explain.*

At the office, Kohler did not give them a warm welcome. "I ought to reassign both of you," he said. "But I can't risk Ross with any of the younger agents. He'd probably get them killed." He glared at Fleming. "And you fucked up another case. How long do you think you can keep milking the Joey Castle thing?"

How long has it been between guineas for you, fuckface? Fleming silently asked.

Kohler pointed from his office to Ross, who was bent over his desk, laboriously stirring a cup of coffee. "Look at the two of you—dead drunk!"

Fleming stiffened. *Sure, I'm drunk. But don't go lumping me in with Ross.*

He turned and left the office, stopping off by Ross's desk.

"God, my stomach is killing me," Ross complained.

Fleming heard a fizzling sound coming from the coffee cup. He looked inside to see the liquid bubbling madly— and it was a clear amber, not coffee.

My partner, Fleming thought. *He drops Alka-Seltzer in straight Scotch!*

Kohler spent the rest of the day showing his displeasure with Fleming and Ross. "We're using you as backup while we go to nail Guillermo Pacheco tomorrow," he told Fleming. "Try not to drink too much lunch."

The bust looked straightforward. They'd be hitting a tenement in the South Bronx. Roberts and McCarthy would be on the rear fire escape. Kohler and Fleming would go in the front door. They'd find the stash in the refrigerator freezer. At the last minute, Kohler decided to leave Ross in the car.

Fleming stared around at the ruined buildings. It looked as if someone had carpet-bombed the whole neighborhood. *You'd have to need a bust pretty damn bad to work a case around here,* Fleming thought. They synchronized watches, then took up their positions.

They walked up the stairs to the apartment. Kohler checked his watch. "Eight o'clock," he muttered. "Let's move!"

Fleming went to kick the door down. *None of this knock-and-announce horseshit,* he thought. His kick landed right by the lock, but the door held.

Screams erupted around them. They could hear a wild rattling of venetian blinds, then a shot.

That set Kohler off. He aimed a tremendous kick at the door. His leg went right through the panel as he crashed into the wood. "I—I'm stuck!" he yelled, trying to push himself away.

Fleming now realized that the screaming and shot had come from the apartment next door. He turned to it, gun out, as the door swung open. There stood a baffled-looking Agent McCarthy. Behind him, Fleming could see Roberts. He must have been the first one in, because he was completely tangled up in a set of venetian blinds. As he thrashed around on the floor, he yelled, "Don't move, motherfucker!"

The guy he was yelling at was a Puerto Rican in his underwear, sitting at the dinner table. Beer dribbled down his chin as he sat there in shock. His wife lay at his feet; she'd fainted at the first crash.

As Fleming came in, the guy pulled himself together and began screaming in Spanish.

"You're in the wrong apartment," Fleming said. "We're supposed to go in . . ."

The rest of his words were cut off by a wild scream from Kohler. "Somebody's got my leg!" he yelled. "Oh, my God! They pulled off my shoe and they're biting my foot!"

Fleming grabbed McCarthy. "Come on, help me get him loose!" He turned to Roberts. "And when you get loose, search this place."

One on each arm, Fleming and McCarthy pulled Kohler free. He hopped around. "My shoe! My shoe!"

"Be glad they took it off, or you'd still be stuck in there."

Together now, they broke down the door, to confront an old woman clutching Kohler's shoe.

Kohler stared around. "No Pacheco?" he faltered.

"I don't think *any* of us got the right apartment," Fleming said.

"I got the motherfucker! I got him!" Ross came down the hall, marching a guy at gunpoint. The guy had his hands to his cheek, which was bleeding.

88

"I heard all the noise upstairs, then I see this guy running out of the house. So, I clocked him."

Kohler went pale. "That's not Pacheco."

"Pacheco?" The Puerto Rican in his underwear spoke up in heavily accented English. "He move out last week. That's my cousin from downstairs. He's late for work."

Roberts appeared. "Nothing in the freezer there. Do I start here, now?"

"No. No." Kohler began to back up, confronted by the group of screaming, wounded tenants. "Let's just get out of here. He flashed his badge at them. "See? See?" he yelled. "Federal Bureau of Investigation. FBI." He headed out of the building, followed by his agents. "Let's hope they just believe that."

On the drive home, Fleming was torn between laughing and throwing up. This had to be the worst bust of his career. It wasn't even a bust. But the image of Kohler, stuck in that door . . . and later, pulling off his sock (he never did get his shoe back) to reveal angry-looking toothmarks . . .

Fleming began to laugh, but stopped abruptly. *We're getting too sloppy—especially me. How can we expect to nail the Tartaglianos with a Looney-Tunes operation like this?*

He shook his head. *I haven't even checked in with the base operator today. Sloppy, sloppy.*

Picking up his radio, he called base. Routinely, the operator checked for messages. "No, nothing. Oh, wait. You had a call. Somebody named Montgomery. They just said to tell you 'Under the trees.' "

"Shit!" Fleming whispered, looking at his watch. It was ten minutes to nine, and he was a good half-hour's drive from Pelham.

CHAPTER 10

THE BAR was empty. *Goddammit,* thought Fleming, *where the hell is he?* The bartender looked up from the half-moon-shaped bar. "What do you have on tap?" Fleming asked. He looked around.

The room was large and round tables dotted the floor. A vintage jukebox squatted in a dimly lit corner. Along the far wall, a string of red vinyl booths hid in the shadows. Fleming strained his eyes and saw movement in one of the booths. He picked up his beer and casually strode to the jukebox. Dropping in a quarter, he quickly punched in three songs—not caring what he played.

He glanced at the booth. *Why the hell didn't he tell me he'd be in the back? The shit.* A closer inspection revealed that the man in the booth was an old fossil who was fumbling with a napkin in his lap.

"What do you want?" the old man croaked.

"Sorry, old man," said Fleming.

"Fuck off."

Fleming chuckled at the crusty old-timer and scanned the remaining booths. *Nothing. That sonofabitch isn't here.* "Hey, bartender, where's the john?" he asked.

"In the back."

As Fleming entered the lavatory his nose was assailed by an eye-watering stench. "God, do they ever clean this place?" he muttered. A pair of feet straddled a bowl in one of the stalls. He pushed the door open. A startled young man dropped his newspaper. "Hey, what's going on?" he asked.

Fleming had to laugh. "Sorry. I thought you were a friend of mine." He stepped out of the stall with a smile on his face.

"Jesus! A guy can't even take a crap in peace," muttered the young man. "Close the door, you asshole."

Fleming kept the door open with his hand. With his other hand, he pulled out his lighter, setting fire to the newspaper.

The young man frantically slammed the paper against the side of the stall, trying to put the fire out.

"Maybe you should piss on it, kid," Fleming advised.

The young man jumped up, a look of fury on his face. "I ought to kick your ass!"

"Yeah? Well, first you better cover yours."

The young man looked down at the trousers coiled around his ankles.

Fleming laughed and walked out of the men's room. He sat at the bar, still chuckling to himself. If only he could take care of Castelli as easily as that punk.

He ordered a new beer, downed it quickly, and nibbled on the stale peanuts in the bowl in front of him.

Behind him, the kid came barreling out of the men's room. "You fucking bastard!" he shouted.

Fleming didn't even get up from his stool. He just flicked open his jacket, showing his pistol. The young man went pasty-faced. "H-h-hey," he said.

"You don't look good, kid," said Fleming. "Maybe you should go home and go to bed."

Without another word, the young man fled the bar. Fleming grinned at the quick retreat. He whistled the bartender over and ordered a boilermaker.

He had just finished his beer when the door opened. Joey limped into the bar, using both a cane and a leg brace. Each step was pure hell and Joey grimaced in pain. He didn't look at Fleming, taking a seat at the far end of the room. Joey ordered Scotch, drained it in one gulp, and ordered another.

Fleming grabbed his drink and walked over. "You're late," he said.

"Fuck you. I ain't walkin' so good, if you haven't been payin' attention. It's hard for me to get along."

"Don't tell me your fucking problems. You have something to say to me?"

"Yeah. I don't like you, Fleming. You're a prick. You think you can push people around. I ain't gonna be pushed."

"Stop all this bullshit, Joey. You want to deal. That's why you're here."

"Why are you fucking with me? They moved my trial

date up. You have anything to do with that?"

Fleming held out his hands and grinned. "It's an election year. You know how they get. If you help me, I'll see what I can do to slow it up a bit."

"Slow it up? Why don't you kill it?"

Fleming's grin widened. "I can't do *that.* That would be dishonest. And you wouldn't want to break the law, would you? Then I'd be just like you and go to jail for a long time."

Joey wiped his sweating lip with his cocktail napkin. "What do you want from me?" he hissed.

"I want names, dates, and places. That's all."

"That's enough," Joey said.

"You don't want to go back to prison, do you?"

"You got that shit right. I'll help you. But I ain't turning in anyone from my family. You leave them out of this or it's no deal."

I got the punk now, thought Fleming. *Now to squeeze him.* "I make the deals, Joey. Not you. *Capische?* I'll tell you what I want."

Joey's eyes widened and he choked down his drink, coughing on the Scotch. *Sonofabitch. Uncle Angelo will know. He'll fuckin' know. I'm a dead man for sure.* "I need assurances. No one's gonna know who I am, right?"

"You'll be anonymous. Don't worry."

"I am worrying, dammit. You Feds got a man on Uncle Angelo's payroll."

Now it was Fleming's turn to be surprised. "Who?"

"I don't know. But it's a Fed. So you gotta keep it quiet or it's no fuckin' deal."

"I can't give you any guarantees."

"Then what the fuck am I doing here with you? You feed me this shitass line and then you won't protect me? Well, fuck you, buddy. You ain't getting shit from me."

93

Joey struggled to get out of the booth. He stood up and tried to walk away but Fleming grabbed his wrist and twisted it.

"Sit down, Joey. Or I'll bust your fuckin' arm this time."

Joey hesitated, then grimaced as a jolt of pain surged through his left knee. He stumbled into Fleming's arms.

"I'll be there, Joey," said Fleming, "to help you. But you've got to trust me." He eased Joey back into the booth.

Joey rubbed his knees, trying to erase the pain. "You don't get it, man. They find out I'm just talking to a fuckin' cop and I'm a dead man. You want me to snitch on them, too? My body will never be found if they find out."

"No one's going to, Joey."

"Bullshit. They always find out."

"Not from me. Only two people will know about you. Me and my boss. Trust me."

Joey laughed. "Trust you? Shit! I don't fuckin' trust nobody. You just keep me out of prison. That's all."

"You give me what I want and we'll help you."

"I ain't goin' back to jail."

"You won't. We'll kill the charges."

"And I ain't snitchin' on my family."

"I can't promise . . ."

"If you can't promise, it's no deal."

Fleming pretended to consider Joey's proposal. *I'll promise him anything he wants. I just want to get my hands on Poblete.* "Okay, Joey. You got it. But you better deliver."

"What do you want?"

"Jorge Poblete."

Joey whistled. Beads of perspiration studded his upper lip and he brushed them away with the back of his hand. "H-he's our main supplier."

"I know."

"I'm not allowed near him. They don't trust me enough."

"I want the sonofabitch."

"We're setting up a big deal."

"When?"

"We haven't worked out all the details. But a hundred keys are coming in."

"In one shipment?"

"I don't know."

"Then you better get your ass in gear." Fleming sat back and stared at Joey, who eyed him and turned over his glass. "We don't meet here no more. I'll be in touch."

"You do that," said Fleming.

Joey limped away, a pathetic figure. An unexpected surge of compassion washed over Fleming. *If he fucks up, they'll eat him alive.*

Fleming walked to the bar and threw a twenty to the bartender, who sat reading the afternoon paper. He walked away.

"Hey, mac," yelled the bartender, "you got change coming."

"Keep it," said Fleming. He stood on the sidewalk and took a deep breath, then expelled it in a coughing fit as his lungs filled with the fumes from an idling car. The car pulled into the street and chugged away, backfiring as it went.

As Fleming stepped off the curb, his foot skidded on a squishy mass. Barely keeping his balance, he looked down. *Just like I said. You work in shit, and some sticks to you.*

He searched for something to wipe his shoe but could see nothing. Finally, he had to settle for scraping the offensive mess on the curb. He headed home, convinced that he had removed all of it, unaware that its odor followed him.

Billy Castelli squeezed the phone in his hand. *This fuckin'* mulignan *is jerking me around.* "Who the fuck do you think you're talking to? Let me tell you something. You wouldn't be shit if we didn't set you up. Don't you forget it. You've only got one thing to do. You find this Larry guy for us. And when you find him, you let me know. Got that? Good. Do it." He slammed down the phone.

Angelo chuckled. "Billy, don't get so excited. You'll give yourself an ulcer." He sat in an overstuffed easy chair with a bemused smile on his face.

"I want that bastard, uncle." Billy paced on the Oriental rug.

"So do I, Billy. We'll get him. And when we do, we'll teach him a little lesson."

"It will be a final lesson if I have anything to say about it."

Angelo's smile was very wide and his eyes gleamed like a cherub. "You give him the lesson, Billy. I'm sure you'll show him justice."

"Why are you bowing to me, uncle? Suddenly, it's me who is making the decisions. You're the head of the family. Not me."

Angelo reached for a gnarled, brown Italian cigar, licked it like a Popsicle, and stuck it between his front teeth. He struck a match and gently touched it to the tip while sucking gently on the cigar. Its smoke swirled in ever-increasing spirals to the ceiling of the room. He blew a cloud of smoke directly at Billy, who coughed.

"This is my family. I've been making decisions for

many years. Always alone. Explaining to no one. But I grow old and tired. Someone has to be there to take over when I step down."

Billy hid his delight with a thoughtful expression. "It's too early to talk about retiring from the business, uncle. You still have years ahead of you."

I was right, thought Angelo, hiding his frown behind a bland expression. *He's ambitious. Maybe too ambitious for his own good. I must watch him carefully.* He stood up and turned his back to Billy. "Come here," he said.

Billy came over, wondering what his uncle was up to. Angelo whirled around. His hand shot out for Billy's shoulder, squeezing powerfully. The fingers dug deeply into the muscle, causing Billy to wince in pain. A smile crept over Angelo's face. He enjoyed his games and liked to humble would-be rivals.

"Do you know why I give you certain responsibilities?"

"To test me," said Billy.

Angelo shook his head. "You disappoint me, Billy."

"Why, uncle?" Billy was confused now, anxious of what was going to happen next. *I should have kept my mouth shut.*

"A man with my responsibilities must have loyal lieutenants, eager to carry out his orders."

"I've never been disloyal . . ."

Angelo squeezed Billy's shoulder as hard as he could, causing his nephew to yelp in pain. He forced the younger man to his knees while increasing the crushing pressure. Shock waves of agony assaulted Billy's shoulder, but he refused to beg his uncle to stop. Gradually, the pressure decreased and Billy heard his uncle chuckle.

"Never interrupt me, Billy. Never." He released his grip. Billy knelt before him. "A lieutenant anticipates the wishes of his leader and takes all steps to meet his leader's every wish. But you, nephew, have to be told what to do. Not a very good position for a lieutenant."

Billy got slowly to his feet. His eyes were masked and Angelo could not read his thoughts. He did not look his uncle in the eye. "I'm sorry, uncle. I've failed you."

"Did I say that you had failed me? I only said that you must learn to anticipate my wishes. You're young. But you'll learn. Let's take a walk. We must plan our strategy for our negotiations with Poblete."

CHAPTER 11

I TELL YOU, Bumpy, man, this white bitch was crazy." Larry interrupted his story for a quick sip from his glass. Johnny Walker Black, only the best. "She get her nose full of blow, then she want to dance with me. Next thing, she running her hand all over my Johnson. I see what she wants, so I give it to her. You know what I mean?"

Ellsworth Morgan, known to friends and enemies alike as "Bumpy," nodded. The dim lights of the bar reflected on the knobs and crags of his shaven head, showing how he'd won his nickname.

"And what do you think I find? She *shaved* down there.

I only thought fuckin' whores did that. But her old man, he a big-ass stockbroker or bank president, or some such fucking thing, and he don't like pussy hair. It was like porking a little girl—with big, round tits." Larry gave him a lewd smile as he shook his head. "I tell you, those white folks, they crazy. But I like to sell them the blow. You meet a better class of people."

Bumpy smiled, as if he enjoyed the joke. But he heard what Larry was really saying. Bumpy Morgan had come up the old-fashioned way, pushing heroin in Harlem back in the sixties. Pushing horse to blacks, because he was too black and ugly to push anywhere else. Now he pushed coke, too, but he couldn't go where Larry Richards could go. Bumpy Morgan smiled at Larry's face, that good-looking football player's face the white folks liked to buy from. The Italians would be fixing that face. Damn soon.

You may know the better class of people, motherfucker, but I know Angelo Tartagliano, Bumpy thought. *And his guys are bad news for smart niggers like you.* He'd dealt with Angelo years ago, and now with the Castle boys. During the big conspiracy trial, he'd been the only black to get nailed with the big-shot Italians. That made him hot shit in Harlem, but Bumpy knew what Angelo would do to a smart nigger. So he disappeared. Jumped bail and spent two years hiding out in a shack with an outhouse down in Hickory, North Carolina.

Then, when the case finally came to trial, he walked into the courtroom and pleaded guilty. The Feds tried hard. They offered him freedom. They offered freedom and money—and more money. Then they started with threats. But the Feds couldn't scare him as much as Angelo's people. Besides, this was an investment. He could show he was a stand-up guy, make the Italians believe that

Bumpy Morgan was a man with honor. And it worked. When he came out of prison, the Italians made Bumpy their main connection uptown. "Bumpy the King of Harlem," the street niggers would say. "Those Eyetalians, they don't mess up here unless they get Bumpy's permission." Talk like that made Bumpy Morgan an important man on the street . . . as long as no Italians heard it.

So Bumpy Morgan had respect, and lots of good clothes, and a table at Brownie's, where the rich white folks came to see the niggers and their colorful mating rituals. Especially the women—and Bumpy had lots of them, too, in the backs of their limousines. Johnny Brown ran a real clean place—no drugs, no guns, no fights. "You can talk business in here," he once told Bumpy. "Just don't *do* no business in here."

But Bumpy was going to do Larry Richards. That's why he was having drinks with him here. Larry would think he was safe.

At first, Bumpy wanted nothing to do with Larry. That was before Billy Castle had talked with him. "Angelo is not happy," he'd said. "He holds you responsible for introducing this snitch to Joey." Bumpy realized he had no choice then. And after ten minutes of listening to Larry Richards, he didn't mind setting him up.

"Let's talk business," he said. "I guess you must be running short on goods, after what happened on your last buy. Joey ain't walking too good yet, and he ain't talking about what happened, except there were Feds all over . . ."

Before Bumpy could finish his sentence, Larry's story was coming out. "There were Feds all over our asses, like flies on shit. Two cars chased me like all hell. I ain't been home since that went down."

Bumpy nodded. "I figure you be needing goods to sell,

and I got a connection—Italian, real good. He wants to deal, and he'll talk to you on my say-so. But Larry . . ." His face was serious as he grabbed Larry's arm. "There better be no fuckin' around. 'Cause I be responsible then, and have to straighten things out. Then I straighten you out. Understand?"

"I understand," Larry said. In his mind, Larry was already selling the Italian to the city narcs. And Bumpy? Well, he could take the blame. Let him straighten that out. Him and the fucking United States Marines. "Don't worry, man. I pay my way."

"That's another thing," Bumpy said. "Since this guy is my connection, I think I should get a piece. A weekly charge, depending on business. I won't take nothing now, but we talk about it later, okay?"

"Seems right to me, Bumpy."

They stepped out of Brownie's and onto the street. "The guy's in a car on the corner of the park. I'll give you a knockdown, then it's up to you. Don't mention my name again. And never, never mention Joey. Got that?"

"Okay."

Larry pushed his hands into his jacket pockets as they walked the couple of blocks to the car. It was a bright night, lots of moonlight, just a little too warm for a coat . . . but as Larry was finding, chilly without one. At least no wind was blowing. A lot of dudes stood on the Harlem streets, hands in their pockets like Larry, bopping a little to keep warm. They stepped aside when they saw Bumpy.

Just before they reached the car, Bumpy stopped for a second. "I better tell you now. This guy, he real ugly. Got no nose."

"What the fuck?" said Larry. "How that happen?"

"I don't know. He ain't the kind of guy you ask. And I

wouldn't stare at it, you know what I mean?" He walked up to the car. "The guy in the back is his bodyguard. Okay, here we go. You on your own."

Bumpy leaned in the passenger seat window and spoke to the driver. "Yo, Rocco, here's the guy I told you about. This is Larry."

Larry peered through the window. *Jesus,* he thought uneasily, *this is one ugly motherfucker. Even uglier than Bumpy.*

Rocco motioned Larry inside. As soon as Larry had the door closed beside him, the car pulled out. Rocco Mazzi sat behind the wheel. Achille Aspermonte sat right behind Larry.

Bumpy headed back to the bar. *Glad I'm not that guy,* he thought. As he reached the entrance to Brownie's, he kept walking. The streets seemed much colder, all of a sudden. Bumpy decided he'd take himself home.

Soon the car was out of Harlem, speeding down the West Side Highway, then to the Verrazano Bridge. Rocco kept a tight eye on the mirror, looking for a tail that never showed.

Larry looked at the two guys in the car, feeling his nervousness rise. They hadn't smiled or said a word during the whole trip. Almost as if they were pretending he wasn't in the car. Well, Larry could keep as quiet as they were. He knew that Italians were funny about business, so he would play their game. *Probably just checking me out,* he thought. *Things will be okay once I start talking to them.*

Whenever he had trouble, Larry had always talked his way out of it. That was because he always kept to Larry's Law: tell them one story, and never change it. Even hard-ass guys will believe you then. It was like the time he got kidnapped by the gang who was ripping off pushers. They'd heard in the street that Larry was a big dealer, so they grabbed him—and told him to give them $100,000 if he wanted his ass free.

Larry told them that he was all bullshit, that he was looking for credit . . . but he knew an Italian dealer who'd be good for $200,000. "Let me go," he said, "and I'll set this guy up."

The kidnappers didn't believe Larry at first. They spent hours beating on him. But he stuck to his story, and finally they decided to take him up on his offer. Larry called Fleming, and when the kidnappers came to get the Italian pusher, they found an undercover agent—with lots of backup. The three kidnappers were shot dead in the street, and Larry wound up with four bullet holes in him, all from the narcs agents. But he was alive, and the kidnappers weren't, all thanks to his gift for bullshitting. His problem now was, how could he bullshit these two Italians if they didn't want to talk?

Larry finally spoke up after they crossed the Verrazano Bridge. "Hey, man, I ain't used to the country. Where we goin'?"

Rocco answered by pulling the car off the road. Behind him, Larry heard a pistol being cocked. Then the cold metal of the barrel was jammed against his neck. "C'mon, man," he said calmly. "This ain't necessary."

But the situation only got more serious. Rocco's crater face turned to Larry. He also had a gun in his hand. "Lean forward. Put your fuckin' face on that dashboard."

Larry's head immediately landed on the dashboard, right on top of his hands. He winced as Rocco whipped his gun into the side of his head. "I didn't tell you to put your fuckin' hands up there. Just your head. Hands behind your back."

Achille grabbed each wrist, forcing a pair of hand-cuffs on.

"Hey." Larry's voice was a little wobbly now. "You guys cops or something?"

Rocco grabbed Larry's hair, twisting his head so viciously that his neck snapped like a set of knuckles popping. "No, punk," he said. "We're from Joey Castle. We're gonna take you someplace quiet, and peel you like a grape." Little dribbles of spit came from the sides of Rocco's mouth. Larry just stared in silence. For the first time in his life, he had nothing to say.

They drove to the far end of Staten Island, nearly to Perth Amboy. Rocco kept Larry's head down for the whole of the trip. "You won't need to see how to get back here," Rocco said.

He pulled up in front of a little house by the water. Rocco had used the place before. He knew the owners well, and they knew him well enough to stay away for a week. The nearest neighbors were a quarter of a mile away, and even the loudest screams wouldn't carry from the basement.

Rocco and Achille hustled Larry into the house, through the kitchen, and down a set of wooden stairs into the cellar—a big, bare room with a vinyl-tile floor and concrete walls painted white. In one corner, the oil burner and water heater sent a series of pipes across the ceiling. There was no furniture except for a couple of hardwood chairs, and the only light came from a couple of naked forty-watt bulbs hanging from wires set in the open-beam ceiling.

"Hey, man, we got to talk." The words almost burst from Larry's lips. "I got to talk to Joey. He got to hear my side . . ."

"Shut him up," Rocco said.

Achille Aspermonte rammed his fist four inches into Larry's gut. While Larry was bent over, retching, Achille yanked the jacket and shirt from his body, tearing them over the handcuffs. Then he tore the pants, stripping Larry completely naked. "Please, man," Larry wheezed. "We got to have a trial, or something."

Rocco slapped his hand across Larry's face. "You know what you're gonna get, nigger? I'll show you." He twisted Larry's head until it faced the far wall of the basement. About six feet off the floor was a metal hook, mounted on a heavy steel bracket. Larry had seen that kind of hook when he was a kid, in a meat packer's where his dad worked. He remembered his father picking up half a cow and ramming it onto a hook like that, letting it hang there for the butchers to cut up.

"Yeah, we're gonna hang you on that meat hook, and see how long it takes you to die," Rocco said. "If you don't move around too much, you can last pretty long. I had a guy hang there for a month once. But if you jump around, or try to pull yourself off, you go quicker." He smiled. "I give you about a week. A real hard week."

Larry's eyes darted from Rocco's wrecked face to Achille's as he frantically tried to come up with something to say, something to stop this. But his gifts completely failed him. When Achille came over and picked him up, Larry began to cry. "Please, man . . . PLEASE!" He kicked, he squirmed, but Achille silently lifted his body up, up, over the hook. Achille had to peer around Larry's body, making sure he had the hook lined up with just the right part of Larry's back. Then with a jerk, he pushed Larry onto the point of the hook.

Larry screamed for Fleming, he called to God, he yelled "Mamma!" He could feel the point pierce him, the warm wetness of blood spreading down his back, and Achille was still holding most of his weight. Then Achille let go. Larry's body dropped three inches, and the hook set itself well in his back. Blood began gushing from the enlarged wound. Larry tensed, afraid to move, afraid the hook would come tearing up through his neck, out the top of his head. His throat choked, his breath came in shallow pants, his face twisted, eyes shut tight.

Rocco wrapped his arms around Larry's legs and pulled down hard. The hook ripped through the tensed muscles, under and around the shoulder bones, then the point tore its way out through the flesh right in front of Larry's collarbone. Fresh blood ran down his chest. The noise that came out of Larry now was more animal than human—a guttural howl that went on and on, rising in pitch.

They removed the handcuffs, which had cut gashes a quarter-inch deep in Larry's wrists as he thrashed. For a few minutes he held still, screaming his throat raw. Then he tried to push himself off the hook. His feet were a foot off the floor, so he braced his heels against the wall, slipping in his own blood as it ran down the rough concrete.

Rocco Mazzi enjoyed the show. As Larry wriggled, he looked like a worm on a fishhook—and had about as much chance of getting off. The more Larry tried to reach back and free himself, the greater his pain. After an hour's struggle, it became unbearable. Larry passed out.

Achille had gone upstairs, returning with a box. Rocco opened it to reveal a battery-operated cattle prod. He twisted the control to "Maximum Shock," then rammed the prod into Larry's balls. A convulsive shudder went through Larry's body, making him jerk around on the hook. His wounds tore wider, and his bowels and bladder went into a flux, sending a stinking spray to mix with the blood puddling on the floor. Larry's back arched and his legs drummed uncontrollably against the wall, slipping as they tried to find some purchase in the thick, coagulating blood and filth.

"I just wanted to catch your attention, Larry," Rocco Mazzi said as he took the prod away. "If you're asleep when I come down tomorrow, I'll use my little alarm clock here. Until then, good night."

Fear had Joey Castelli's silk shirt plastered to his body. Now the sweat was soaking its way through his suit jacket. He just thanked God that it was a dark suit, so the stain didn't show. Then he worried that Billy would smell it. That made him sweat some more.

He looked over at his brother, sitting behind the wheel of the car. Was this really just a ride to Staten Island? Or was he being set up? Would they find him in a garbage can somewhere with a bullet in his head? Maybe they'd found out about him and Fleming. He ran their last meeting over again in his head, trying to remember anyone who might have been in the background. But it still seemed all right. *Maybe I should talk things out with Billy. Maybe Billy could . . . No. Billy couldn't help. He could only get me in deeper trouble.*

"The bridge is coming up." Billy broke the silence. "We should be there soon."

"I still don't understand," Joey said. "Why can't Rocco take care of this?"

"It's for you, Joey, for you. Uncle Angelo felt you'd want a part of him."

Things were just moving too fast for Joey. That evening, Billy had turned up with great news. "Uncle Angelo says everything's okay. He's forgiven you." That was the good part. Since his arrest, Joey hadn't been allowed anywhere near where Uncle Angelo might be . . . and, of course, he wasn't allowed to do any business. Now that was all over.

Then came the bad news. "And there's more. Rocco got that punk Larry."

"Got him?" Joey almost babbled. "Got him when? How did Rocco kill him?"

Billy grabbed his arms and gave him a gentle shake. "They got him a couple of days ago. But they didn't kill him. They got him on ice in Staten Island . . . holding him for you. You can burn him if you want."

"But . . . why . . ."

Billy shook him again. "Because Uncle Angelo loves you. He wants to show that he cares."

Joey picked up his cane and pointed at his broken leg. "I wouldn't do this to someone I hated. Maybe it would be better if he didn't care so much."

Billy shook his head. "Joey, you broke the rules. And you got off easy."

Joey had to admit that his brother was right. A broken leg was better than bullets in the brain. But, just in case, he'd insisted that Billy come along, too. If anything else was up, he'd be able to see it—to spot it in the way Rocco Mazzi reacted to Billy's presence.

They were halfway across the bridge before Joey spoke again. "Billy, do I really have to be there?" he asked. "Can't they just kill him? I don't want to see him again."

Billy's eyes left the lanes ahead of them. "You have to go. *You* have to do it. You can't refuse."

Joey shook his head. It was the first time he'd been ordered to kill someone. Everybody he knew had killed someone. But could he do it?

Billy looked at his brother, wondering the same thing. His first killing hadn't been easy. And Joey had never been strong. Ever since Dad got himself killed, Billy had been the man of the family. And Joey had taken advantage of it. Billy had fought Joey's fights, made good his debts, and gone to bat for him with Uncle Angelo. Even when Joey had knocked over Feldman's Drugstore, it was Billy who took the blame and spent the year in the state reform school.

But this was all up to Joey. This hit was a peace offering from Uncle Angelo, and there was no way out of it. Angelo expected that Joey would *want* to kill Larry. If not, he wouldn't think Joey was worth forgiving. "Look, Joey, it won't be bad. Just shoot him right away in the head. And don't look in his eyes."

They turned onto an unpaved road, then onto a dirt driveway that ran for about five hundred feet, until they parked in front of a frame house. The area was covered with heavy brush, so they couldn't see the house until they were almost on top of it. Joey remembered having been there years before, but couldn't remember why. He was extremely anxious, and it showed. Billy was anxious, too. Was Joey going to fuck up, or worse, run?

Achille Aspermonte met them at the door, and behind him was Rocco Mazzi. Joey and Billy stared in surprise.

They'd never seen Rocco without a suit—even the night he'd broken Joey's leg. Now he was wearing only an undershirt—and a "guinea tuxedo" at that.

He's fuckin' skin and bones, Joey thought. *A nothing guy.* It made him furious to think that Rocco, who looked like a corpse himself, could have put him through so much pain. But his sense of survival made him search Rocco's eyes for any hints of anger or surprise at Billy's presence. He stared until the silence became uncomfortable.

Billy finally broke the ice. "Look, the past is done and should be forgotten."

Rocco merely shrugged and went on with business. "I've got the *mulignan* in the basement, but he's almost dead. We've had him for three days, you know."

He led the way through the kitchen, to the cellar stairs. As soon as the door opened, Joey caught a hint of foulness. At the bottom of the stairs, the stench was killing—a combination of dried blood, excrement, and rotting flesh. And then they saw Larry—or what was left of him.

They'd never have recognized him. Larry sagged forward a little, his arms hanging lifelessly at his sides. He seemed glued to the wall by congealed blood. His head drooped to the right, lying on top of his shoulder, and his gut was bloated, like the little kids starving in Africa. But those kids didn't have bluish burns on their bellies. And below . . .

Joey's breath caught in his throat as he focused on a vein throbbing madly in Larry's prick. Rocco must have spent hours with the cattle prod. Electric shocks had swollen Larry's balls to twice their normal size, turning them an agonized purple. Hoarsely, Joey asked, "How does he stay up . . ." And then he saw the point of the hook, all bloody, with a hunk of rotting flesh draped from its tip. A hint of bone showed through the wound torn in Larry's shoulder—bent from the weight of Larry's hanging body.

"Jesus, Mary, and Joseph," Billy muttered, blessing himself.

Joey stood numb. In spite of all the tales of killings, all the war stories, even the death of his own father, he'd never heard anything to match this sight.

Rocco casually picked up the cattle prod and gave Larry a poke. "Hey, nigger, you got guests. Wake up."

Larry's whole body vibrated, even the fingers clenching spasmodically. His head jerked erect, revealing further grotesque deformities. The left side of Larry's face was dead from nerve damage. His right eye was fused shut, his left eye bulged from its socket. Even his lips were twisted and paralyzed, revealing some teeth.

"I think he recognizes you, Joey," Rocco said. "See? He's smiling." He took away the prod, and Larry collapsed as if someone had hit his "Off" switch. Rocco pulled a knife from his pocket. "Take your time." Joey still stood frozen, hardly conscious as the knife was slipped into his hand. Rocco's smile grew scornful.

"Give us a minute or two alone," Billy said abruptly in Italian. Rocco shrugged his shoulders and followed Achille up the stairs.

Billy put a hand on his brother's shoulder. "Come on, Joey, you've got to do it. Look at this poor bastard. Nobody deserves this."

Joey dropped the knife and reached under his coat, pulling out a gun.

Billy stared. "What are you doing with that?"

"I've been carrying it . . . ever since that night in the

garage." Joey aimed the gun at Larry's head, with only a slight quiver, until Billy touched his arm.

"You can't use that. Not here. A shot will carry like a scream never would. The neighbors will hear."

Joey watched his brother pick up the knife. "Billy, I . . . I *can't.*" His eyes filled with tears.

Billy nodded. "I know." He reached up to Larry's unmoving body. With one quick flick of the knife, he slashed the throat open.

Larry had been unconscious since the last time Rocco hit him with the cattle prod. He never felt a thing.

CHAPTER 12

N THE DRIVE back from Staten Island, Joey sagged against the passenger door of Billy's car, nibbling on his thumb. He didn't have much to say and just stared out the window. Billy didn't have much to say either. Each was lost in his own thoughts.

Never seen so much fuckin' blood in my life, thought Joey. *That sonofabitch Rocco. He really likes that shit. He laughed when he came back down and saw blood all over the place. Puddles and puddles. It's all over my shoes. And the smell is up my nose.* He blew his nose into his handkerchief. *How the fuck did they ever find him? I thought we were safe, sure as shit. They got eyes everywhere. I'm a real fucking shithead. Making that deal with Fleming. Well, he can go fuck himself. No way am I rattin' on my family. I'll go back to the joint. Better than being dead.*

Billy eyed the road, trying to concentrate on his driving. But all he could see was the blood pumping from Larry's neck. The first spurt hit him in the chest and he cursed his stupidity for not standing behind Larry when he sliced him up.

He brushed his fingers on his jacket and they came away sticky, making him gag. This wasn't his kind of work.ButRoccosureenjoyedit.*A hard-on. He had a fuckin' hard-on!* Billy shivered.

A station wagon abruptly changed lanes and Billy leaned on his horn while swerving hard to the right. The car went into a mild skid but Billy steered easily into it, gaining control of the car quickly. He stepped on the accelerator and brought his car up level with the wagon. In the front seat of the car was a young redheaded woman with a car full of kids. She was talking a mile a minute with a blonde woman while four kids jumped up and down in the backseat.

He honked his horn and rolled down his window. "What the fuck are you doing, lady?" he yelled.

The blonde calmly looked at him and raised her fist with the middle finger up. In case there was any doubt what she meant, she said, "Fuck you." Her partner showed more sense and quickly accelerated the station wagon.

Billy suppressed the urge to run the station wagon off the road. He turned to Joey. "Should we kill her?" He stifled a wild giggle.

Joey shook his head. "Nah. I got too many stains on my suit already. Let's get Rocco."

They both roared with laughter all the way back to Manhattan.

But Joey got serious as they came close to his apartment. He grabbed Billy's arm. "Hey, I'm not going back there. Not tonight."

"What the hell are you talking about?" said Billy. "That's your home. Your wife is waiting."

"Fuck her. She's probably over at her mother's anyway. Take me to Connie's."

"You nuts? What if our aunts see you?"

"Who gives a flying fuck? Fifteen minutes ago you slit some guy's throat. His blood is all over you. And you worry about some relatives seeing me visiting Connie?"

"That was business, Joey. I always take care of business. You listen to me. You better start wising up. You couldn't leave it alone and you got that guy killed. The only reason you're still alive is because you're blood. We got a big deal coming up and Uncle Angelo don't want no heat on us. So keep your nose clean. Is it so important to get laid tonight?"

"You better believe it, man. That could have been me on that fuckin' meat hook. I had to grab my nuts to make sure they were still there after you offed that dude. I'm fuckin' alive. And I'm gonna stay that way. Let me out here if you don't want to take me. I'll walk."

"Take it easy. I'll drive you. But I'll leave you off a block from her house. Go in the back way."

Joey smiled at his brother. "Thanks, Billy."

"Forget it, kid." As he stopped the car he turned to Joey. "It would be a lot easier if you just moved her out of the neighborhood. Set her up in some other place. That way you could come and go and no one would be any the wiser."

"As soon as I get back on my feet, I'll do that." He slid

to the door but Billy grabbed his arm. He stared at his younger brother and the love was clear in his eyes. The strength of Billy's emotions embarrassed Joey and he dropped his eyes.

Billy reached over and kissed his brother on the cheek while hugging him close to him. "Take care of yourself, Joey. And wise up, huh? Enjoy yourself."

"I will, Billy. Thanks for everything." Joey watched the car drive away. When it turned the corner, he walked slowly to Connie's apartment.

It was dusk and he moved from shadow to shadow. When he looked across the street, he saw his aunt Nina, leaning out the window. She was Angelo's sister and lived with her younger sister Jenny in the apartment directly across the street from Connie's on Mulberry Street.

Fucking old broad. Always minding everybody's business but her own. Joey waited in the shadows for a few minutes hoping his aunt would go inside. When he saw her put a pillow on the window sill he knew she was in for a long night of people-watching. Joey's legs stiffened up and needles of pain stitched his knees.

"Hey, Aunt Nina, how ya doin'?" he yelled and waved to his aunt.

Nina squinted in the darkness and tried to identify the voice. "Who's that?"

"It's me, Joey."

"It's late, Joey. Where's Monica?"

"Who cares? Hey, aunt, listen. If you want me, I'll be at Connie Buttafari's. You know where she lives." Boldly, he walked up the steps of the apartment building and rang the bell.

Connie answered the door. "Who is it?"

"It's me, baby, let me in." She buzzed him in. Joey

opened the door, waved once to his aunt, and stepped inside.

Connie had the door to her apartment opened and Joey's mouth went dry when he saw her. She was tall and wore her dark hair long so that it draped over her shoulders like a shawl. Her velvety skin was the color of heavy cream. She leaned against the door frame wearing a cinnamon-colored teddy, slit so high that Joey could see the curve of her hip. Her legs were long and smooth and the nails on her nicely shaped feet were painted ruby red to match the lipstick she favored.

"Madonne mi," Joey gasped. "Someone will see you, for Chrissake."

"Let them," she purred. "I missed you. Come to mamma, baby." She traced a circle with her finger beneath her left breast and let it trail down her flat stomach.

Joey growled and limped forward, burying his head in her ample breasts. She smelled of soap and lilacs and it drove Joey crazy. He pushed her into the apartment, shedding clothes as he went. Connie giggled throatily and let herself be mauled by Joey's eager hands. "Aren't you going to shut the door, Joey?" she asked. "Or do we cause a neighborhood scandal?"

Joey stopped just long enough to hit the door with his cane, slamming it shut. He dropped his brace and fumbled at his trousers.

Connie brushed his hands away and fell to her knees in front of him. Her fingers fluttered over his thighs and Joey's breath came in ragged gasps. She unzipped him and took his hardness into her soft hands. Joey moaned. She stroked him gently, delighting in the warmth which pulsated from his straining member.

She grabbed him in both hands. He wasn't as large as

her dead husband but he made up for his smallness by the vitality of his thrusts. She licked his quivering penis and Joey shivered with the delight of it all.

He closed his eyes, eager for the comforting warmth of her mouth, and was disappointed when she pulled away. "What are you stoppin' for?" he asked.

Connie stroked him with her hand. "Why are you in such a hurry tonight?" She teased him with her tongue, licking his entire length, then pulling away when he thrust forward.

Joey liked the game but he was too excited to wait. He twisted his fingers in Connie's hair and pulled her face into his groin. She was too aroused to resist and she took him, eagerly, into her mouth. It didn't take long. He climaxed in five strokes and Connie had to tilt her head to keep from choking. She pulled away as jets of sperm hit her in the chin and dribbled onto her breasts. She spit his semen into her palm and wiped it on his thighs. Joey was too excited to notice as he crumbled to the carpeted floor.

The two lay there together, totally spent. Connie had her head on Joey's stomach and ran her fingers along his thighs. His penis lay limply between his legs. She stroked it gently, and it stirred but did not get hard. Connie smiled as she remembered the first time they met.

It was at the Feast of St. Anthony and Connie was selling sausages from her uncle Tony's stand. The day had been long and she was exhausted. Her skin was sticky from the grease made by the grilled sausages and her eyes were reddened from the smoke. There were stains on her blouse and the backs of her hands had slight burns. Her feet hurt and all she wanted to do was take a bath and go to bed.

Halfway home, she stumbled on a soggy roll in the

street and turned her ankle. She landed in a puddle and sat there with tears streaming down her face. She couldn't stand and the pain made her cry. Suddenly, gentle hands slid under her armpits and helped her get slowly to her feet. She expected a grab at her breasts and readied her elbow for a quick jab. When it didn't come, she turned to examine her rescuer.

She was surprised it was Joey Castelli. He usually propositioned her in the street and she took delight in taunting him with her body, safe with the knowledge that he would never get into her pants. She considered him a pig and since he was married she avoided him. Not that she minded sleeping with married men—she had her share—but she just found him repulsive.

When he found that she couldn't walk, he carried her to her apartment. Once inside he laid her gently on the couch and put some ice around her swollen ankle. His gentleness and concern both disconcerted and aroused her. In less than five minutes, she seduced him and they had riotous sex on the floor of her living room.

They saw each other regularly after that. The sex was spontaneous and satisfying for the two of them. She felt sorry for Joey. He bragged and strutted like a peacock in public but was insecure and vulnerable when they were alone. Curiously, she found herself falling in love with him. It thrilled her that he needed her and even though she knew he would never leave Monica, she knew that he would always be hers.

In Connie, Joey found the companionship that he lacked in his marriage to Monica. After his legs were broken, he had been spending more time with Connie than with his wife. She gave him comfort and made him feel like a man. But what he loved about Connie the most was the way she satisfied him with her mouth. Monica would never do that.

"That was terrific, Connie," said Joey as she stroked her hair.

"I'm glad you came, Joey," she purred as she blew her breath along Joey's thighs.

"Me, too. Come here, baby." He scooted around on his buttocks until his head was near Connie's hip. His tongue glided wetly down her thighs while his hand gently pinched her nipples.

Connie moaned and spread her legs wide. Joey gently tugged on her pubic hairs with his teeth, then softly blew on her vagina. She grabbed his hair and pulled him down until his tongue slipped inside her while she slid under him and licked his testicles. In seconds, both were panting and thrashing on the carpet.

She felt the climax rising in her like a flood about to burst a dam and she did not want the pleasure to end. She rolled him over to his back and straddled him, her back to his face. Holding him steady, she lowered herself onto his penis, enjoying the way it felt as it filled her. Slowly she raised herself up, then down, until she found the proper rhythm.

Joey was in heaven. He stroked her silken back and watched her long hair bounce up and down on her shoulders. His heart pounded as the blood rushed to his head. A roaring sound filled his ears. He was getting the fucking of his life. He closed his eyes and imagined biting Connie's tits.

The brown nipples begged to be bitten and he nibbled the air as she screwed herself on his prick. He was almost there. Any second. As she looked over her shoulder he could see her tongue peeking from her ruby red lips. Then it turned into the bloody tip of a meat hook. Larry's tortured face disappeared in a splash of blood.

Joey's erection vanished as though it was never there. Frantically, Connie thrust harder and harder. She sobbed with the realization that her pleasure would be denied. Joey squirmed out from under her and sat up, hugging his right knee. He grimaced as a shock of pain zipped up his body and landed behind his left ear.

"What's the matter, Joey?" Connie moaned.

"Nothing, Connie. I just got a lot of things on my mind. I'm sorry."

His tone was sad and frightened and Connie stroked his cheek. "That's okay, baby, there are other times."

He hugged her until the breath whooshed out of her but he wouldn't let go. It was the first time he had ever hugged her like that and Connie decided that she liked the feeling. It gave her a new impression of Joey as strong and assertive. She snuggled against him.

Joey hoped that by squeezing Connie he could blot out the image of Larry, dancing on the end of that hook. But the image would not leave him. The harder he hugged her, the sharper the image became. That would never be him, he promised himself. He wasn't snitching for anyone. *Especially* Fleming.

CHAPTER 13

FLEMING crumpled the copy of the *Post* in his hands. Red headlines screamed "THE BODY UNDER THE BRIDGE." The front-page picture was fuzzy, but even with the grotesque deformities, Fleming had recognized Larry.

He forced himself to spread out the paper again and read all the gory details.

Kohler stopped by his desk. "Reading the paper on company time, Ed?" he asked. Then he saw the picture of Larry. "Hoo! That's a gross one!"

Fleming looked up at him. "Don't you recognize him? It's Larry."

Kohler's face changed. He leaned forward, studying the picture more carefully. "Hmmmmmm. So, he finally got caught up with." Kohler shook his head. "Well, he knew the game he was playing. And we all know the fate of informers."

Fleming's hands balled into fists as they held down the newspaper. He wanted to smash that pompous face. But, of course, he couldn't do that. He'd have to do it with words. "This isn't going to help us," he said. "Larry's information was a lot of our probable cause."

That shook Kohler up a little. He retreated to his office.

Word about Larry percolated among the guys. Ross and several others came up to say "Sorry." Powers passed, just raised his eyebrows, and shook his head. Fleming could read his meaning. *He got stepped on, Ed.*

Fleming was actually home early that evening. While Joan worked on dinner, he paced around the living room. *This is crazy,* he thought. *I keep feeling I should do something. But what?*

He picked up the phone and dialed Peretti at home. All he got was an answering machine—a funny tape with music. But even when Peretti was kidding around, his voice sounded all business. Fleming hung up at the tone.

"What's the matter?" Joan finally asked at the dinner table. She tried to lighten the tone. "It's got to be pretty bad, if *you* won't eat."

Fleming looked down at his plate. Most of his food was still there, just mixed around into a confusing mess. The peas were in the mashed potatoes, which covered part of the steak. He'd been trying to hide it, making it look like more had been eaten. Fleming shook his head. He hadn't done that since he was a kid.

"Come on, Ed." Joan's beautiful hazel eyes were giving him a direct look now. "What is it?"

He took a deep breath, then it all came out. "Larry's dead."

"Your snitch? Larry?"

"Yeah. Killed. It's spread all over the front of the *Post.* I recognized him from the pictures." His face sank into his hands as Joan went to get the paper.

She shuddered as she read. "This—this is terrible." She threw the paper down. "Tortured to death."

"Yeah," he muttered. "Terrible."

She stood behind him at the table, her hands gently rubbing his shoulders. "Do you want to talk about it?"

Fleming leaned back, feeling the warmth of her breasts against his head. He looked up into those eyes . . . How could he tell her what he was feeling? Would Larry still be alive if he hadn't started this case? He really hated this shitty job.

Finally, he shook his head. "I don't think so."

They had planned all week to catch a movie that evening. But, somehow, neither of them brought it up. They spent the evening hanging around the apartment, watching television, not speaking much. Finally, Joan announced she was going to bed.

Sometime later, Fleming stepped quietly into the darkened bedroom. He'd undressed in the bathroom, not wanting to disturb Joan.

But she was awake. "Ed," she said. "This has really upset you."

He sat heavily on the end of the bed, his back to her in the darkness. "It's stupid. He was just an informer. A guy I busted and turned into a tool. I didn't even *like* the guy."

He looked over his shoulder at Joan, but only saw her as an indistinct shape under the covers. "So why do I feel so angry?"

Fleming shook his head. "The way I figure it, they must have nailed Larry the same night I talked with Joey. The same fucking night! I didn't think that slimy little worm would have the guts to kill a guy. Especially this way." He slapped his hand against the mattress. "Poor Larry."

"I've been lying here, saying prayers for him."

Fleming blinked at the incongruity of it. Joan, lying in the dark, saying prayers for a pusher. He hadn't said a prayer since he was ten years old.

"Come to bed."

He slipped under the covers. Fleming didn't believe in dressing for bed. The coolness of the sheets against his skin made him sigh.

Then Joan rolled over to lean against his side, her breath tickling his ear.

"Didn't you . . . uh . . . forget to put something on?" he asked. The full weight of a breast lay on his arm, the warmth of her belly snuggled into him, her thatch of hair tickling at his hip.

"I thought maybe tonight I'd dispense with the PJs." Joan's fingers caressed his chest, walking their way through the heavy mat of hair, then working downward.

One of the things she always loved about Ed was how cuddly he was. Sometimes in bed, it was like hugging a giant teddy bear. He was big, strong, a government agent, and when he wrapped her in his arms, she never felt safer. Those big, capable hands had probably punched in more heads than she could count. But when they explored her body, they were gentle, almost tentative—and very exciting.

Tonight, though, she felt unyielding muscle as she cuddled into him. "Come on. *Relax,*" she whispered coaxingly. Her fingers trailed farther down, but he didn't respond.

Joan made a fist and rapped on his chest. "Hey. Anybody in there? You awake?"

She lay half over him, brushing her lips across his. "I don't do this for everybody, you know. The least you could do is appreciate it."

He laughed into her lips and kissed her—playfully at first, avoiding her lips. They were both laughing now. Then the kisses became more demanding, their tongues darting against each other.

Joan brought one leg up, rubbing against his thighs. She yelped as he slipped one arm beneath her, the other under her knee, and neatly flipped her on her back. He rolled over, onto her.

Both of them let out a deep sigh as the full lengths of their bodies caressed each other. Joan's nipples stiffened as they rubbed against Fleming's chest, her thighs opening as he lay between them.

Bracing himself on his elbows, he slipped one hand beneath Joan, caressing her neck, cradling her head, and lifting her face up to him. Their lips met again, tongues clashing. He kissed her cheeks, her eyes, her chin, the soft sides of her neck. Her head fell back, as if her neck could no longer support its weight.

"Mmmmmmmmmmmm," she murmured, wriggling against the friction as he slid lower on her body. He kissed along the soft, creamy skin of her neck, to the hollow below, onto the collarbones, and then down to her breasts.

She gasped as he planted feathery kisses around her erect nipples, pushing up to him. But he drew away.

Joan's eyes opened in surprise, to find Ed staring softly

down at her. "You know," he whispered, "I don't know how I'd survive without you. I don't mean just this . . ." He ran the tips of his fingers against the softness of her skin. "It's you—being with you."

His lips followed his fingers now. "I'll make this the best for you . . . the best," he promised, kissing the valley between her breasts, the undersides of them.

Then he left a trail of kisses along her ribs, moving onto the flesh of her belly. The muscles tightened beneath his lips as he tongued his way into her navel. He went lower still, under the covers, savoring the perfumed flesh, the warmth of her body. The tendons in her thighs tightened as he nuzzled through the soft tangle of hair at her loins.

Far away, he could hear soft sighs. "Oooooh—what're you . . ."

But he was lost in the darkness, in the feel of soft lips, and the warm musky taste he found there.

Joan's legs thrashed, kicking off the blankets. Her heels thudded into the mattress. Then they dug in, and her back arched as she pushed up her pelvis, offering herself to him. His hands cupped her frantically working buttocks as she pumped herself on his dipping tongue.

It seemed that he feasted forever, kneeling between her thighs. Joan's breath grew harsh, and her movements became erratic. Ed held her to him as she came in a series of tiny moans.

He leaned back on his heels, still between her wide-stretched thighs, feeling the tingling tightness in his own groin—like two pounds of sausage in a one-pound skin.

When he moved to lie on her, she rolled aside, coming up in a wobbly crouch on her hands and knees. "C'm'ere," she whispered. He came forward on his knees, and she rose up to lock him in an embrace. He gasped as his erection was trapped between their bellies.

Joan gave him a long, open-mouthed kiss. "Mmmmmm," she hummed, resting her face on his shoulder. Then she nipped him with her teeth.

He pulled back in surprise. While he was off-balance, Joan threw all her weight into him. He fell to the mattress, flat on his back, with Joan crouched over him. "Gotcha now," she said in a thick voice. Her thighs straddled his belly, and her hands rested firmly on his chest. "Stay down."

Ed lay very still as she scooted herself back along his lower abdomen, one hand still on his chest, the other one reaching behind her to grasp his erection. The light fluttering of her fingers along him made him close his eyes, as the muscles in his groin tightened.

Then she was rearing up, guiding him into her, sinking slowly onto him. She contracted herself around him, gripping him in a warm, damp vise of muscle. His fingers clenched the sheet. "God, you are fantastic," he said huskily.

She began working herself up and down, establishing her rhythm. Long, slow strokes at first, then gathering momentum. He began thrusting himself up to meet her on the downbeat, their flesh smacking together. Joan made little choking noises at each full penetration.

He opened his eyes to find they'd accustomed themselves to the dimness. Above him Joan rocked madly, as if moving to some orgiastic music only she could hear. Her breasts danced before him, and her eyes were half-lidded. She threw her head back, shaking, and her hair made a golden halo around her face. But no saint ever had that expression of ecstasy.

"It's—it's almost . . ." She crumpled forward as they both shuddered together.

Joan reeled back at the height of their climax with a loud gasp. Then she tumbled off him, bouncing bonelessly to the mattress.

She landed beside him with a long sigh, her face soft, her eyes closed, her hair tousled. Ed rose up on one elbow to regard her. Joan lay back in utter comfort, utter abandon, her thighs wide.

Gently, he reached down to retrieve the cast-off covers. "You'll freeze your tits off, lying around like that all night." She had no response. Asleep already?

He tucked the covers around her. With a little groan, eyes still shut tight, Joan snuggled into his body. Fleming lay back himself, eyes still open. He stayed that way half the night.

The next Monday afternoon, Fleming sat nursing a beer in Unter den Linden. Joey Castelli stepped up to his booth and sat down. He still used a cane, but his limp was noticeably better. "So, Joey, you're looking pretty good."

Joey was slimmer and in better shape than he'd been at his arrest.

"I—uh, I been exercising. Since my accident." Joey's eyes darted around. He quickly walked to the bar.

The place looked different in daylight, Fleming realized. Without knowing it, he'd become a night person, preferring the veil of darkness and dim lights to hide the imperfections of the world.

Joey came back with a fresh beer for Fleming. He had an extremely nervous look on his face. Fleming realized it was about Larry. *Well, I'm damned if I'm going to mention him to this weasel.* "We've got things to discuss," he said.

Joey flinched. But Fleming never brought up the subject of Larry. Neither of them would—ever.

"I've killed your trial date," Fleming said. "It won't come up until you're ready." He shrugged, as if it were nothing. Actually, it was nothing. He hadn't even bothered to have it done yet—preferring to test Joey's longevity as an informant.

"What did you tell the lawyers on your side?" Joey asked. "Didn't they wonder why?"

"I told them I'm not ready to reveal all the . . . details in the trial yet. They do what I tell them." He made a dismissing gesture. "But that's not what I wanted to talk about. I want to get into our deal. Get some specifics."

Joey shrank into himself, wrapping both hands around his drink. "Look, I can't do it. We've gotta cancel our agreement." He looked at Fleming's face to see how he was reacting.

But Fleming's face didn't change. He knew there'd be a couple of false starts before Joey would make the leap. He'd seen them all. And with him, turning a guy was an art. All he needed was the handle—gratitude, patriotism, fear. He still needed the handle on Joey, although he suspected he already knew what it was. He let the silence stretch, then finally asked, "What changed your mind?"

"No particular reason," Joey said. "I just can't do it. Look, I'm a stand-up guy. I don't rat on people. We're talking friends, family here. No way can I bring trouble to them." The more Joey talked, the more he convinced himself. He was almost proud of himself by the time he ended.

Fleming nodded. Yeah, he was right. Fear was the key. This guy was frightened to death of working with the Feds. It terrified him even more than going to jail—right now. But if it was one thing Ed Fleming knew, it was how to instill fear into people.

"Okay, Joey," he said, leaning back in his chair. "No hard feelings. I understand. It's your decision, and I can't argue with it." He even gave Joey a half-smile.

Joey puffed up. *I pulled it off!* he thought. "Hey, what can I say? I'm sorry if I caused you trouble with the trial delay."

Fleming shrugged. "No problem. A guy can change his mind. And don't worry about the calendar. I can have you in court, say . . . two weeks."

Joey choked on his drink. "Two weeks? What the fu— I mean, that's a lot sooner than it was before. Do you hafta do that? Can't you leave it alone for a while? It can't mean anything to you."

Fleming's face hardened like rock. "Look, scumbag. Let's get this straight. I owe you nothing. You owe me nothing. We had a deal, and now we don't. That's okay. I can't complain. While we had something going, I tried to help you. Now all I want to do is get this finished up, and on to the next case. As for you, you can take it up the ass. Understand?"

Joey sat where he was, shocked. "But—but, hey, man. Do you have to be so hard? Can't you give a guy a break?" A whining note came into his voice.

Fleming kept up the pressure. He stabbed his finger into Joey's chest. "Look, I don't dick around. I got a lot of work to do. So I want to be shut of your case as soon as possible. Just get used to it, Joey. You're gonna be spending the July Fourth weekend in the joint."

He got up. "I'm leaving now. And after I leave this bar, the whole deal thing is dead. I ain't holding up the trial after I start it again. Nobody makes me look like an ass-hole."

Fleming leaned over the table. "You won't get less than fifteen years. You'll be as old as your mother when you get out . . . And no broads in there." He gave Joey an unpleasant smile and walked for the door.

"Hey, Fleming!"

Fleming stood in the doorway, letting go a deep breath. It had been a big risk, but it had worked.

He walked back to the booth, where Joey sat jittering. Fear of prison had left him completely unstrung. He moistened his lips. "W—we got a deal, again."

Fleming sat down, talking in a low, reassuring voice. "Okay, the trial stays off. I don't want you to get involved, and I don't want to start off with a Colombian. We've got plenty of time for that. But you're going to have to show me some good faith. You've got to do something for me."

Joey stared down into his drink, his face slack and dejected. "What?" he said, looking up again. "What is it you want?"

"You gotta give me someone, Joey."

Joey's hands clenched around the drink. His eyes flared with panic. "I can't . . ."

Fleming leaned forward. "Look, I'll make it easy for you. I don't want any family, I don't want a *paisan*. Just give me a customer. How about Bumpy Morgan?"

Joey shook his head. "I don't do much business with Bumpy. He's Billy's customer. And you can't touch a guy like him. He went through the wars with the family. Everyone will be looking for the guy who did him."

But Fleming could see that Joey was thinking now. "I

need a customer, Joey. Can't you think of one? Even a nobody . . . that will do."

Joey looked up from his drink and nodded. "There is this one guy . . . Mike Davis. He's down in Philadelphia. Temple—a rich college punk. He deals for his hotshit friends. Well, this will burn his ass."

Fleming nodded as he wrote down the information. "Congratulations, Joey. You're not a virgin anymore."

"Hey, I ain't been a virgin since I was twelve."

"Yeah. But you just got fucked for real right now." Fleming leaned forward. "You just gave me one of Angelo's people. And you know what he does to snitches."

Joey stared at him, open-mouthed.

"From now on, I'm your only hope, you sorry sonofabitch."

CHAPTER 14

FLEMING AND ROSS sat in Kohler's office—part of their new Tuesday morning ritual. "Okay," Fleming said, "our man spilled wide open. We've got the outlines of the operation. Their couriers are diplomats, moving the shit under their immunity. I think he even gave away a little more than he intended. The guy who holds the stuff, who sits on the plant and brings the ten or twenty kilos at a time for Frankie Tartagliano to deliver to customers. The guy nobody sees."

"I know what a plant man is," Kohler said, annoyed. "You think you know who he is?"

"He wouldn't tell me—but he made a slip. He referred to a kid named Cantalope. And he said it when we were talking about the plant man. I don't think he even realized."

Fleming shrugged. "Anyway, I checked the files on the old conspiracy case. There in the pedigree sheets, there's a sister of Angelo's—Jenny Cantalope, widow of Guido Cantalope, mother of Guido, Jr., who now lives with his grandparents on Randall Avenue in the Bronx."

"And you think it's him?" Kohler said.

"There's no proof, but I've got a strong feeling. Jack thinks so, too."

Ross nodded. "The kid's about twenty-five, lives alone with his grandparents. The grandfather is bedridden, and the grandmother takes care of him. They never leave the house, so there's no chance of burglary—a big consideration. The kid's never been busted—clean as a whistle, but he's family. It all adds up."

Kohler nodded. Fleming could tell by the look on his face that he was trying to organize a report on this to Washington. "Okay," he said. "So when is the deal set for?"

"About six weeks," Fleming said. "They generally get a two-month supply. This one is going to be big—a hundred kilos."

"I've got to tell Washington." Kohler looked at Fleming as if he expected an argument. "There's no way around it."

"I'm not suggesting anything different, George," Fleming answered. "But I would like a couple of minutes with you."

Ross got up. "I can take a hint." He left the office and closed the door.

"You know, he's getting a little pissed at being kept in

the dark," Kohler said. "You haven't even told him about Joey . . ."

"*Nobody* knows about Joey—except me and you. Just like nobody knows about this case except the three of us, so far. This way, I can almost guarantee a hundred keys and Angelo Tartagliano. Once you tell Washington, God only knows what will happen and who will hear. Good-bye, guarantee."

"Jesus," said Kohler. "You make it sound like everyone's on that take."

Fleming shook his head. "I'm not even implying that. But it's a fact that people have a way of not keeping secrets. Word travels."

Kohler sighed. "So what do you suggest?"

"You go down to Washington. Tell the director and his assistant what we're into. I think they'll let us keep it quiet, and let us develop the case with one more agent up here—say, McCarthy. Tell them we can deliver a conspiracy case around the shit, and pull in Angelo, Vito Panella, Poblete, and the whole crew. With Joey testifying on the stand, we can pull the whole thing together."

Kohler agreed. So did Washington.

Assistant U.S. Attorney Andy Cavallera riffled through the files of reports. "These look pretty good," he said. "You guys must have had a busy two weeks."

Fleming nodded. He, Kohler, McCarthy, and Ross sat in a living-room-sized office in the Federal Courthouse. All of them looked pale and hollow-eyed—they'd been working fifteen-hour shifts, seven days a week.

Cavallera was just back from a Caribbean vacation,

looking bronzed and sleek. Fleming had been amused to discover he was taking the prosecution. "Wops versus wops," he'd said.

Cavallera looked at Kohler. "So far, the case is pretty solid—at least on some of these guys."

Fleming spoke up to answer. "We think so. With the shit, we figure we've got the Castellis, Bumpy Morgan, Frank Tartagliano, and Guido Cantalope pretty well wrapped up."

"Provided your informant testifies," Cavallera said.

Fleming had been carefully bringing Joey along. From a guy who'd never rat, he'd gone to an informant who just didn't want anybody to know. He still thought that he'd be off the hook after the bust. But it was only a matter of time before Fleming brought up the idea of testifying.

"Our guy will do it. He'll shit first, maybe have heart failure, but he'll do it. I'm going to fix it so he doesn't have a choice."

Cavallera nodded. "Good. That's critical if we're going to prosecute anyone other than those we catch with the 'smoking gun.' " He grinned at the phrase. "Now, problem two. Where do you plan on grabbing the stuff?"

Kohler spoke up. "We have several options. Since we'll know when it's coming, and who's coming, we can do it at Customs. We can take it at the diplomat's hotel room. We can take it at the exchange with the Gui—um, the Tartaglianos. Or, we can get it at Cantalope's pad. Now, which is the best time legally?"

Cavallera was silent for a moment. "I've talked this over with the State Department . . ." Seeing the agents shift nervously in their seats, he said, "Don't get excited. No names or specifics, although we'll have to tell them sometime. After all, we do work for the same government. And we do have a tight-lipped contact. He'll have to hear the full story before the arrest. He won't talk to the government involved. And anyway, we can't arrest or even detain this diplomat, whoever he is. He's got full immunity in America. In fact, we can't even stop and search him. We can't even question him."

"This guy can move shit into our country, and we can't even touch him?" Fleming burst out. "That is some bullshit!"

"Actually, it's called international law. And we have no choice." Cavallera shrugged. "Through State, we'll solicit the cooperation of the involved government, to get Merida to hand over the money and maybe testify."

Fleming couldn't help himself. "You mean, he even gets to hold on to the three million dollars?"

Cavallera nodded. "Once the Tartaglianos hand it to him, it's protected by diplomatic immunity. Why do you think Poblete uses diplomats?" He looked around at the agents. "That brings us to our final problem. It seems a shame to go through all this, seize the shit, and then let the real heavyweights get away. There's nothing in these reports that incriminates Angelo Tartagliano, Jorge Poblete, and most important of all, Vito Panella, the Don.

"Their names keep popping up throughout the case, but there isn't one surveillance report on them. Even if your informant testifies, there's no corroboration. You should really concentrate your efforts on Angelo and surveil him, hopefully with Panella. Know what I mean?"

Fleming looked at those raised eyebrows. Most government attorneys suspected that their agents lied on their reports—or at least engaged in overzealous exaggeration.

But Cavallera was the only one to come even close to mentioning it. "You mean, you want us to see them meet and talk about the cocaine deal."

"Well, surveillance with incriminating conversations would do the trick."

"I see," said Fleming. "We anticipated covering Poblete and Angelo when they meet on the delivery date, but right now Angelo is difficult to locate. I guess we could increase our efforts and single Angelo out."

"Good idea," said Cavallera. "After all, we want the main perps."

But the problem was, Angelo was nowhere to be found. And Joey wasn't close enough to find out.

All right, Fleming thought. *If we can't find Angelo, I guess we'll have to go after Vito Panella.*

The agents split into two shifts, each car following Panella twelve hours a day, seven days a week. Fleming only got home to sleep, which didn't help things with Joan.

Vito Panella was a readily available man, but he acted innocuously. Lots of people met with him, even known hoods, but they saw nobody connected with the case. Fleming began to wonder if he'd have to invent from scratch.

He was sitting in the car on a Sunday morning with McCarthy, watching Panella's girlfriend's apartment on Seventy-second Street. Ross and Kohler had followed him there the night before, as they had many nights before that. She was a superb blonde, and all four agents were jealous of the old man. Just looking at her made Fleming think about the last time he'd been with Joan.

Meanwhile, McCarthy lectured him about insects. "Now cockroaches, you don't have to worry if you've got them in the house. They look ugly, but they're really clean.

Flies are what you have to worry about. A fly shits every twelve seconds."

Fleming sat up in his seat. "What? Where the hell did you hear that crap?"

McCarthy said, "I'm not kidding. I read a book about it. A fly shits every time it lands, even on your food. This guy who wrote the book estimates that the average man eats about four pounds of fly shit in his lifetime."

Fleming couldn't help it. He threw his head back and laughed—a laugh that was abruptly cut off by the appearance of Vita Panella in the doorway. It was only nine o'clock, and within a moment Panella's car, with his bodyguard driving, picked him up and headed west.

McCarthy pulled out, forgetting about the open coffee containers on the dashboard. Both of them were soaked. Luckily, it was cold coffee.

They followed Panella's car discreetly, south to Sixty-third Street, west to Fifth Avenue, down to Sixty-second, where Panella got out of the car and walked into Central Park.

Fleming left McCarthy in the car and followed Panella along the lanes of the park, toward the zoo. Panella strolled along, never checking for a tail. His pace was so casual, so purposeless, that Fleming worried that the man was out for a stroll.

No way, he thought. *Panella is a real night person. Something big must have gotten him out of bed.*

Panella came up to a park bench and stopped, sitting down beside another man. They made no display of greeting or affection. But as Fleming neared them, his pulse began to pound. He only knew the man from photos, but he was sure. That was Angelo Tartagliano!

He passed them, confirming the ID. It was all he could

do to keep from staring at them. After all this time, here were his perps, passing the time of day in Central Park. Fleming walked a little farther along, then leaned against a statue where he could observe them without being observed.

They sat together for a few minutes, then rose and left together, parting company at the entrance to the park. Fleming didn't attempt to follow, letting each go his separate way. They'd met. He could write his report.

SUBJECT: General File, Angelo Tartagliano, *et al.*
    DATE: June 2, 1986
        BY: Edward W. Fleming, Narcotics Agent

Reference is made to all past memoranda relative to the General File investigation of Angelo Tartagliano, *et al.* On February 15, 1986, reliable informant "Montgomery" called me and reported that Angelo Tartagliano was going to meet Vito Panella the next day for the purpose of discussing a pending shipment of cocaine that was to be smuggled into the country, reportedly from Colombia. Both Tartagliano and Panella are identified in Federal Conspiracy case NYS: 9697. On February 16, 1986, Agent McCarthy and I were surveilling the premises of 463 East Seventy-second Street, the building where Panella resides with his paramour, one Rose Abbate, who occupies Apartment 14D. Also surveilling were Agents Ross and Kohler in a separate official Government Vehicle. At approximately 9:00 A.M., I observed Panella exit the above premises, enter a 1986 black Cadillac, driven by one Nick Penosi, believed to be his bodyguard/driver. The vehicle registration number is NY State 514 DIG, registered to the Avis Leasing Corp. They drove circuitously around Manhattan, ultimately arriving at Sixty-second Street on Fifth Avenue. The driver operated the vehicle quite suspiciously during the entire trip from the residence to the above site, and was obviously attempting to lose any surveillance which perchance might be on hand. Panella exited the vehicle and, acting quite furtively, entered Central Park.

Agents McCarthy, Kohler, Ross, and I followed the car, and Agent Kohler and I entered Central Park and observed Panella meet Angelo Tartagliano near a statue of Lafayette on a horse. The men sat on a nearby park bench and Agent Kohler and I could readily hear the conversation and most of the details. At one point Tartagliano was heard to tell Panella, "I expect to hear from Jorge any time now and he assures me that there will be a full one hundred kilos in the shipment." Panella nodded and said, "Very good. That makes me happy." At that point Panella handed Tartagliano an attaché case which he had been carrying. When Tartagliano opened it, Agent Kohler and I could see it was filled with hundred-dollar bills. The two men departed and Agents Kohler, McCarthy, Ross, and I terminated surveillance.

Edward W. Fleming
Narcotics Agent

Fleming leaned back at his desk. *This one should get me a fucking prize—best fiction of the year.*

CHAPTER 15

JOEY wanted to think, and he found that the winding, cluttered streets of Chinatown were very soothing to him. As he limped along, he felt his legs getting stronger with each step. He had a lot on his mind.

He was afraid that his arrangement with Fleming would leak out to his family and that he would die slowly and horribly at the hands of Rocco and Achille. *Hanging like a slab of meat in a slaughterhouse. They kept him there for days. Why didn't they just kill him? Why a fucking meat hook?*

The images of Larry's last seconds were imprinted on

144

his subconscious and he thought of that mutilated body at the strangest times. Twenty minutes ago he was screwing the ass off Connie. She was on all fours and waved her round buttocks at his face.

"Stick it in," she pleaded. "Hurry!"

He positioned himself behind her and eased himself into her. She tightened around him and he rammed home a final thrust. Connie grunted and drew her breath in through gritted teeth. The whooshing sound triggered the image of Larry writhing on the meat hook as his life leaked out of him through his slit throat. Joey lost his erection again.

Connie sighed. This was the fifth time in less than two weeks that he had been impotent. Such a poor performance from anyone else would have rated scorn from her, but her love for Joey made her search for the cause of Joey's distress. *It must be the trial,* she thought. *I'll make him feel better.*

She massaged his neck, working out the knotted muscles. His shoulders sagged. "That's great, Connie. Keep it up."

"What's the matter, Joey?"

Joey wanted to tell her everything. He had to talk to someone. But his sense of caution and his fear that she would not agree with him kept him silent.

"What do you say we get the hell out of New York? We can change our names and just get away."

"Why, Joey? You can beat that drug rap."

"It's not just the drugs. I'm in over my head," he said. "I don't know which way to turn."

"I can't help you, Joey. I don't know anyone. What about your uncle Angelo?"

"He won't help me."

"You're family, Joey. He won't let you go to prison."

Sure he won't. He'll just call those two sons of bitches to cut off my balls and stuff them down my throat. "Come on, Connie. Let's fuck this city. It's been nothing but trouble. I got no future. And I want to forget my past. Let's start new. Let's get married."

"You're still married to Monica. Don't you think you should get divorced first?" Connie reached out and stroked Joey's arm. He jerked it away from her.

"Why are you such a smartass? I'm fucking serious and you go bringing up Monica. We got nothing. She'll let me go. Even if she don't, we can skip off to Vegas and I can ditch her there."

"I don't know, Joey."

"Don't know what? I thought you loved me."

"I do. It's just that I never thought we would get married." Connie stood up and put on a flimsy silk robe. She lit a cigarette and puffed at it furiously while staring at Joey.

"What's that supposed to mean? I thought you loved me. Why do you think I'm sleeping with you anyway?"

Connie winked. "Don't you like what you see?" She opened her robe and flashed her naked body at him.

"Stop acting like a *putana,* Connie. I got a problem here."

"Yeah, you got a problem, all right." She pointed to his groin and smirked. "And it's right there dangling between your legs."

"Hey, fuck you. If I want to take shit like this, I'll go home to Monica. I don't gotta take it here. I'm leavin'." Joey threw on his clothes.

"Come on, Joey, I was only kidding. Don't leave."

"I gotta think, Connie. I'm taking a walk. I'll be back in

a little while." He had walked for three hours and found himself in Chinatown.

The exotic aromas of the many restaurants and the raw smells of car exhaust, fresh fish, and rotting garbage filled his nose. He stopped by a fruit stand and hefted a ripe orange in his hands. He held it up to the shopkeeper, who watched him warily.

"How much?"

"Fifty cents."

Joey flipped him two quarters. He held the orange up to his nose and inhaled the aroma from the navel end. Digging his fingernails into the skin, he pulled down a strip. In seconds he peeled the orange and tossed the rind into the street.

In front of him, a beer can leaned against the curb. Joey nudged it into the street and stomped on it hard, causing his knee to throb. Ignoring the pain which crested over him, he ground the can beneath his foot. He kicked the can and watched it scoot down the street, where it bounced into a parked blue sedan making a pinging metallic sound and leaving a slight dent in the rear panel.

Alerted by the sound, the driver got out and looked curiously at the damage to his car. As Joey tried to walk away, the man stepped forward to stop him. The man was large and pouchy with a bulbous, veiny nose from too much beer. He outweighed Joey by nearly a hundred pounds.

"Hey, where the hell do you think you're going?" he said as he grabbed Joey's arm.

Joey shook free of the grip and pulled out his pistol, ramming it into the shocked man's stomach. The man's eyes widened in fear. "Get the fuck away from me or I'll blow a fucking hole in your stomach."

"Don't shoot," pleaded the man. "I got a wife and kids."

"Where is she?" Joey hissed.

"She's getting some food . . ."

"I don't really give a shit." Joey put the pistol in his jacket pocket and kept up the pressure. "I ought to fuckin' kill you, motherfucker." He felt powerful with the pistol in his hands and delighted in watching the man's fear turn him into a quivering weakling.

"Please," whispered the man as tears bubbled from his eyes.

"Get back in your car and don't even look at me. Understand?" He jabbed the man once again.

The man clambered into his car, slammed the door, and sat hunched over the steering wheel while he anxiously eyed the Kam Hey Rice Shop. A chunky woman with dyed blond hair emerged carrying two large bags of food. She got into the blue car and it sped away before she got fully seated.

Joey chuckled. *Big fuckin' man. Was gonna whip my ass. But I showed him who was boss.* He patted the pistol in his pocket. *Got my little equalizer here. If I just see Rocco lookin' crooked at me, I'll blow him the fuck away.*

Stopping at a pay phone, he fumbled for a quarter and dialed Fleming's number. *Come on, you fuck. Answer, dammit!*

Ed Fleming slammed his fist into the kitchen table. "What is it with you?" he shouted. "I'm not in this door five minutes and you're on my damn case."

"Don't you dare use that tone of voice with me. I'm not one of your damn snitches."

"At least they know their place," he snapped.

Joan rocked back on her heels as though physically assaulted. "What the hell is that supposed to mean?"

"You can take it any way you want. I work a long day and take a lot of shit from the punks and my own bosses. I don't want to take it from you, too."

Joan grew white with anger. "You and your damn job. You've changed, Ed. You never have time for me anymore."

"I was with the Agency when we met. You knew what you were getting into. You didn't mind in the beginning. Why now?"

"You're acting crazy. Brooding all the time about that snitch who got killed. You stay out all damn night. Then you come home too tired—or too drunk—to do anything. What do you think this is? A hotel?"

"At least the room service is better." He smiled and gently stroked the line of her hip.

Grabbing a glass from the drainboard, she hurled it into Fleming's face, cutting his lip and cheek.

He stared at her in shock, dabbing away the blood with his handkerchief. "Jesus Christ," he finally said. "What the hell's the matter with you?"

"Haven't you been listening?" she said. "Don't you know what's going on? We can't fix this with a roll in the hay."

"You're really something. I'm in the middle of the biggest bust of my career. It can even mean a promotion and a desk job. Can't you wait until this thing is over?"

Joan's voice was quivering. "If we keep on like this, *we'll* be over before this case is."

Her outburst had a sobering effect on him. He reached out and hugged Joan, while stroking her hair. She was rigid in his arms. "I've got to do this thing. Please understand. You know, I'm under a lot of pressure."

"So am I, Ed. Not knowing where you go. I sit up late at night and wonder what you're doing. If you're safe . . ." She threw her arms around him, clutching tightly.

"I'm okay." Joan didn't relax her hold. "This isn't some little case, you know. This is really important. Just a little while longer. I can't quit now."

Joan looked up at him. "Can't you?"

"I can't quit my job," Fleming said flatly.

"Why not? With your experience you could become the head of security for some big outfit. Maybe even start your own business."

He pulled away from her. "Knock it off, Joan. This is getting us nowhere."

"That's because you never listen to what I have to say."

They were interrupted by the ringing of the phone. Fleming's hand went to the receiver but Joan grabbed it. "Let it ring, Ed. This is important. We've got to talk this out." Her eyes pleaded with him as he picked up the phone.

"Yes?" he said.

It was the office. Joey had called to speak to him. Fleming took the number down and dialed it.

Joey answered the phone.

"It's me. Joey. We gotta talk."

"When?"

"Today. I got information for you."

"Where?"

"You know the place Wing Lo's in Chinatown?"

"No."

"It's on Doyer Street. A basement place."

"When?"

"Thirty minutes."

"I'll be there." Fleming hung up the phone and turned to Joan. She was sitting at the kitchen table, her back to him.

"I've got to go. It's the job."

"It's always the job. When are we going to talk?"

"Tonight. I promise." As he bent down to kiss her, Joan pulled away. "Just go, Ed."

He shrugged. "Suit yourself."

As he left the apartment, Joan was tense and silent. Then she collapsed with a great wracking sob. She clutched at the table, her eyes blinded by tears. Pushing herself upright, she headed to the living room—to the liquor cabinet.

She threw open the door, reached for the Scotch—*his* whiskey. It took a moment to unscrew the cap. She put the bottle to her lips and threw back her head. The liquor burned a fiery path down her throat until she gagged. "Damn," she said, wiping the back of her hand across her lips. "Damn."

Wing Lo's was sandwiched between a fish market and a curio shop. Fleming walked past it twice before finding the grimy, soot-encrusted sign, which was the size of a license plate, hanging below a burned-out light bulb. He nearly stumbled going down the steep and cracked stairs.

A filthy glass door greeted him at the bottom of the stairs. He pushed it open and entered a dimly lit foyer. Fleming placed his hand on the butt of his pistol and took comfort from its presence on his hip. At the end of the foyer was a beaded curtain that he pushed aside.

He entered a noisy room, hazy with cigarette smoke

and cooking smells. There were twenty tables in the room, most of which were occupied by Chinese men and women, busily working their chopsticks over plates heaped high with food. In a corner, Fleming could see Joey fumbling with a pair of chopsticks and dropping rice all over himself and the table.

As he made his way to Joey's table, a smiling bald-headed Chinese man appeared by his side waving a grease-stained menu at him. Fleming grabbed the menu and sat at Joey's table.

The waiter hovered near. "You want drink?"

"Beer. What kind you got?" asked Fleming.

"Chinese beer."

"Is it cold?"

"Okay," was the reply. The man vanished behind a swinging door and returned seconds later with a dripping bottle of beer. He handed it to Fleming.

He took a sip. *Warm as piss.*

"Order now?"

"You better do it. This guy don't speak much English. If he goes away you won't see him again for an hour."

"Give me some wonton soup. Some spareribs and the chicken in black bean sauce." After each order the man would smile and blink his eyes as though photographing the words. He didn't write anything down. He repeated the order once to Fleming, then headed behind the swinging door.

Fleming turned to Joey. "He didn't write anything down."

"Don't worry about it. He never writes nothing down. And never makes a mistake on an order. I been watching him for the last thirty minutes."

"This looks like a real shit-hole, Joey."

"Don't be so fucking particular. Where do you want me to go? People know me around here."

Fleming wasn't in the mood for small talk. "What do you have for me?"

"My uncle told our customers to get their money ready. That means the shipment is coming in."

"How is it coming in?"

"Through Kennedy Airport. Carlos Merida is the courier. He's something in the U.N. From Venezuela."

"What about Poblete?"

"He's coming in on Thursday."

"That's two days from now. Will he have the junk?"

"Fuck no, Fleming. He don't go nowhere near it. He usually blows into town a day or two early. Then he and Uncle Angelo go out to eat."

"Where do they eat?"

"Nobody knows. That's decided by the two of them picking a name from a phone book."

"Why?"

Joey chuckled. "Uncle Angelo don't trust those spics. And Poblete feels the same way about us. So they pick out a spot at random. This way no one can set the other guy up."

"I've got to know where they meet."

"Forget it. Hey, why're you so worried about where they're going? You're gonna pick up Merida. Right?"

"Sure. Is he gonna have the stuff on him?"

"What do you think? That diplomatic pouch is sure getting a workout. You won't be able to touch him."

Fleming's soup came and he dug in. It was good. The wontons were well filled with meat and cooked to perfection. The broth was dark and tasted of scallions and ginger. "This food's okay," he said between sips. "So where does Merida go when he leaves the airport?"

"He goes to the Sheraton Centre. Uncle Frankie will meet him there."

"Where's your brother?"

"Probably with Uncle Angelo and Poblete."

"When will your uncle take possession of the cocaine?"

Joey stopped eating and stared at Fleming with a look of horror on his face. "What the fuck are you getting at? You told me that you only wanted Poblete and Merida. You said nothing about my family."

"I want that coke, Joey."

"Then nail that sonofabitch Merida at the airport. You can even pick up Rocco Mazzi and Achille Aspermonte. They'll be there."

"Who are they?"

"Just some button men my uncle uses. Both are bad asses. You'd do the taxpayers a big favor if you pulled them off the street for a while." Joey chuckled.

As Fleming finished his soup, the bowl was whisked away by the waiter and replaced by a heaping plate filled with spareribs. They were well cooked and were covered with a sweet, syrupy sauce. Fleming picked one up with his fingers and nibbled on the bone.

"Why don't Poblete and Angelo make the deal?"

"They don't trust each other. Besides, by meeting in a neutral place neither one has an advantage over the other. It's a safe way to exchange hostages without putting your life on the line. You know, Fleming, you're too damn interested in my family. You said they wouldn't get involved in this."

Fleming lashed out with a sparerib and smacked Joey

in the cheek. It wasn't a hard blow but the ribs left grease streaks on Joey's cheek and he sat back in his seat. "Cool your ass, punk. Who the fuck are you to call the shots on this? You're facing a prison rap. Don't forget that."

"You said you would get me off," whined Joey.

"I said I would try. You told me you'd be giving me some information on this operation. So far, you haven't told me a damn thing. All you do is dance around and feed me a bullshit story."

Joey's hand went to his jacket pocket. Fleming saw the move and knocked Joey from his chair with a punch to the jaw from his right fist. Joey tumbled from his chair, pulling his plate with him. Fleming calmly bent over and removed the pistol from Joey's jacket, carefully pocketing it. The clatter of breaking dishes silenced the noisy restaurant.

Fleming continued eating his spareribs while Joey righted his chair, rubbing his jaw. The restaurant returned to its normal noise levels.

"Give me back my gun," said Joey.

"In time," said Fleming. "Let's get one thing clear, Joey. You belong to me. You'll do just what you're fucking told to do. Or I'll yank your fucking chain and throw you back in jail again. I'm gonna get Angelo and Poblete and you're gonna help me do it."

"B-but you promised," said Joey as he fought back tears of fear.

"Promises don't mean shit, Joey. Not here. Not now."

"Please, Fleming. Not my family. They're all I got."

Fleming stared at Joey and his eyes turned to ice. He leaned back in his chair. "Lighten up, Joey. Don't you have the balls to do this?"

"Hey, there's no call for that. I got plenty of balls. It's

just . . . well, it's like this. I ain't never dealt with the heat before. I mean, like I always thought that snitching was so fucking low."

"Until you started doing it. Right, Joey?"

"What's with you, Fleming? You know, I ain't some jerk you can just push around. You fucking *need* me. Without my help, you got nothing. You got no case. Zip."

"Nice speech, Joey. But you don't want to go back to jail."

"Who the fuck does? But I'm thinking, if I gotta do this shit with no fucking guarantees of protection, then I might as well go back to the joint. I'd rather be fucked up on the inside then stone-assed dead."

"Oh, fuck this shit. I just had a fight—woman trouble. I guess I'm a little uptight," said Fleming.

"You should punch her out."

"I told you, Joey. I want Poblete and Merida. But to get them I have to know what they're doing at all times."

"I don't know what they're going to do. I told you, I don't go to the planning meetings. I hear things but I don't know much else."

"Listen, if I don't know more details, then your family could get picked up just like the rest. The more we know, the better we can prepare the bust so nothing goes wrong."

Joey wanted to believe Fleming. "I could find out more details, Fleming. We got time."

"You better get hot, Joey. There's only a couple of days left. Eat your food." He palmed the pistol and dropped it in Joey's lap. "See, Joey, I trust you. Why don't you trust me?"

Fleming's stomach twisted in a knot as he saw the gratitude flash on Joey's face. *The poor asshole doesn't know he's being set up. He actually trusts me. Just like Larry did.* The chicken and black bean sauce smelled delicious. But Fleming had lost his appetite.

CHAPTER 16

AT FLEMING'S SUGGESTION, Kohler waited until the afternoon before the bust to brief his agents. He gathered all the men from both his and Dick Powers's sections. Powers actually made this job easy by going out to lunch and not coming back. Assembling the twenty men, Kohler told them there was a major cocaine shipment coming in by way of a Venezuelan courier. He showed the men pictures of Carlos Merida. He didn't mention Angelo Tartagliano.

Each man was assigned a station and told to report early the next morning. There would be no surveillance to tip off the Italians—the operation would start with the diplomat at the airport. Men were assigned to watch for Jorge Poblete if he showed at the airport, and follow him to his meeting with Angelo Tartagliano. They'd wait for the exchange of cocaine and money between the Tartaglianos and Merida, then nail the Italians any way they could.

Fleming and Ross opted for a special assignment—recovering the money.

Kohler himself was to stay with the cocaine. He had no idea how or where the delivery would be made. But he knew how to cover it. His orders to the other agents were simple. "Arrest any sonofabitch who either speaks with a foreign accent or looks Italian and wrong. We'll sort them out later."

The next day, Dick Powers arrived at the office late, hung over and guilty. He knew his secretary was covering for him—every morning she cluttered his desk with mussed papers, a half-cup of coffee, and a dirty ashtray with a burning cigarette. He was halfway to his office before he realized things were too quiet. When he found out about the bust, he spent the day making frantic phone calls. But he never got any of the people he wanted to talk to.

The International Arrivals Building at JFK is a huge, cavernous place, with a large wall running the entire length of the structure. On one side, planes arrive from all over the world. On the other, friends and loved ones await the passengers. In between stand the people from Customs and Immigration.

A glassed-in balcony overlooks the Customs area, where people can watch their friends clear Customs. Once upon a time, the whole Customs floor had been visible, but people rapped madly on the glass partitions, trying to get the attention of various passengers. Now a screen cut the view to the passengers actually at the Customs tables. Even so, people rapped on the glass.

The agents never used the balcony. Why advertise their presence? In the same way, they never advised the Bureau of Customs about the case. If Customs could, it would seize the coke at the airport and be the hero.

It was a heavy morning. Six planeloads of people were being processed through Customs. And for every passenger, there seemed at least five people waiting to meet one. Fleming was glad for the crowd—it hid the agents in wait.

His interest now was to spot Jorge Poblete, to get a tail on him for the lunch with Angelo. Fleming knew Poblete had come in ahead of the courier, probably under an alias. But he was sure the Colombian would want to see his courier pass Customs.

Pan Am Flight 7 landed on schedule, and still there was no sign of Poblete. Merida waited until his bodyguard cleared Customs. Then he was greeted by a Customs official and his luggage was escorted through the checkpoint. *God, he has enough stuff,* Fleming thought.

As Merida said good-bye to the Customs official, Fleming looked at the litter of luggage. Garment bags, golf clubs—and six identical brown leather suitcases. They were brand-new and obviously had been purchased together. Fleming glanced over at Ross, who nodded and smiled. After all this surveillance and bullshit, here was the prize.

Merida started moving, and so did the agents. He entered a waiting limousine and drove off with an army of agents following.

He watched for Kohler to join the convoy, but instead the section chief headed for Fleming. He carried two suitcases to make him look like a traveler. As Fleming took one from him, Kohler whispered, "Don't look now, but Poblete is watching the whole damn thing from the observation balcony."

Fleming glanced up just in time to see Poblete leaving. "Get McCarthy on him," he said. "Then it's off to the Sheraton."

The radio traffic was fast and furious: McCarthy reporting that Poblete had arrived at La Cocotte for lunch. Other agents reporting that Merida had checked in at the Sheraton, with bellmen swarming all over his luggage. Just as Fleming and Kohler arrived at the hotel, the big one came over. "Little Daddy and the Melon are driving in."

Frankie Tartagliano and Guido Cantalope drove separate cars, just in case of accident or mechanical trouble. Now they pulled into the hotel's underground lot, parking next to each other and as close to the elevators as they could. They went up in the elevator as Fleming pulled in. The garage was good-sized and dark, with lots of room to hide four Agency cars—two near the ramp leading in, and two more near the elevator.

Fleming left Kohler in the car and disappeared into the next elevator.

Moments later, Kohler's radio erupted in static. Grover Alston, who was upstairs disguised as a maintenance man, was reporting in. "Two guys are on the way down in the elevator," his voice said, "carrying two suitcases each— heavy ones."

George Kohler sat in an agony of indecision. Tartagliano and Cantalope were on their way down. But Alston had said they were carrying only four suitcases.

"Where the hell are the other two?" he muttered. Would they go back to pick them up? Should he let them? Every second was bringing the elevator closer.

Finally, he hit the button on his radio. "They're coming down. Don't hit them while they load the stuff. Wait till I get the word."

He looked over the forces he'd deployed. A novice agent, Harold Denton, and Roberts were in one car, ready to pounce on Frankie Tartagliano with a carload of Powers's people. He and the remaining car would take Guido Cantalope.

Besides the four Agency cars in the garage, he had three more outside. The "Out" ramp led to Fifty-second Street, a one-way road, heading eastbound. He'd ordered the cars to park east of the ramp, ready to block the road. Not that they'd be needed. Kohler intended to nail these bastards before they reached the ramp.

Frankie and Guido stepped out of the elevator, staggering slightly under the weight of the suitcases. Guido had stowed his two in his trunk and was starting his car while Frankie was still wrestling his cases around.

Kohler broke into a cold sweat. What if Frankie stays to collect the rest, and Guido leaves? His men were almost quivering, ready to pounce on those guys. Any second, the guineas were going to make them. Then what?

Frankie got into his car.

Kohler snatched up his mike. "Take 'em! Take 'em!" He shouted the order so loudly, his men didn't even need the radio.

For Harold Denton, this was his first bust. He was even more nervous than Kohler. Especially since he was now busting guys in moving cars. At Kohler's order, he twisted the ignition. His target was Frankie Tartagliano. So when

Guido Cantalope moved first, he let him pass. Then he jerked into position, blocking Frankie Tartagliano from the exit ramp.

Unfortunately, he blocked everybody else off from the ramp.

One glance in the rearview mirror told Guido what was going on. He didn't hesitate. Reaching the top of the ramp, he turned right, against the traffic.

"Bust him! Bust that motherfucker!" Kohler screamed. But his cars weren't in position to intercept. Through honking horns and some screams, Guido made it to Seventh Avenue. He turned south, floored the gas, and headed for safety.

"Jesus Christ." Kohler moaned. "Where the fuck is Fleming?"

Ed Fleming shrugged into a bulletproof vest. He and Jack Ross stood by the emergency stairs on the sixth floor of the hotel when their radio finally crackled to life. "Two guys are on the way down in the elevator," Grover Alston's voice said, "carrying two suitcases each—heavy ones."

"I thought that spic brought in six suitcases," Ross said.

"They probably figure on coming back for them." Fleming smiled. "Doesn't matter. There's enough coke in the ones they've got to nail them a dozen times over." He stashed the radio in his pocket. "This is it," he said as they started down the stairs. "Let's just hope Kohler doesn't fuck up."

They reached the fifth-floor landing, opened the fire door, and drew their guns. Then they headed down the hall to Carlos Merida's suite.

Ross quietly worked the passkey in the lock, and gave

it a gentle push. The door opened three inches, then stopped—the chain was on. He glanced at Fleming. "We'll have to bust in."

For just a moment both men hesitated, the tension showing on their faces. Most busts caught the pusher on the agents' terms—alone, on the streets, or asleep in bed. But here, they were going in blind. Everything would depend on how many people were in there—and what they were doing. There was no choice, though. It was now or never.

"Here's how we'll do it," Ross whispered. "You go in low, I'll go in high, shouting the orders." He grinned. "I'm getting too old for this crouching shit." He shifted his shoulders. "Especially in these stupid vests." His face got serious. "We've been together on enough of these things, I don't have to tell you the obvious."

Fleming nodded, reciting the drill. "If in doubt, I shoot—and if I shoot, I shoot to kill."

They hit the door together, smashing it open and tearing the chain from the doorjamb. Merida looked up from the cases of money to see Ross stepping into the room with a gun in his hand. For a split second, his mouth hung open. Then he screamed, "Ramon!"

The bathroom door flew open and Merida's Colombian bodyguard burst out. One hand held up his pants. The other held a MAC-10 submachine gun. The rapid-fire roar of half the clip emptying drowned out whatever Ross was saying. If he was saying anything.

Fleming came in low, the blast of automatic fire above his head. Frantically, he squeezed his trigger—with that grease gun, this guy could get off three bullets to Fleming's one.

His first shot caught the Colombian in the shoulder,

throwing the machine gun off target. Fleming's arm was out straight, pumping shot after shot into the gunman's twitching body. He kept firing until his pistol was empty, and the Colombian was a bloody mess on the rug.

Fleming came out of his crouch, the gun still smoking in his hand. The stink of cordite burned in his nostrils, his ears rang from the gunfire in the confined space of the room.

"We got him, Jack!" His voice sounded loud, even to him.

Then Fleming saw that Jack was lying on the floor.

His head was back, and a little trickle of blood came from his cheek. Fleming started to kneel by his partner. On the way down, he noticed Ross's hair. It had flipped away from the back of his head.

Fleming reached out to adjust it, then stopped. That wasn't a wig. It was the top of Ross's head. A small reddish-gray stain had spread on the hotel rug.

A quick movement at the tail of his eye brought Fleming around. Merida scuttled from behind an overturned chair toward the doorway. Fleming shoved him away, slamming the door shut.

The diplomat backed up. "The money is right here. Please take it." Merida's eyes kept traveling between Fleming's gun and his stony face.

"Shut the fuck up." Fleming stood over Jack. Trying to find signs of life was a joke.

"Please, I'm with the United Nations," Merida began babbling as Fleming looked up from Ross's body. "I'm a diplomat. You're a policeman, aren't you? Call your State Department."

"I said SHUT UP!" Fleming rose to his feet, smashing Merida in the face with his now-empty revolver. He felt the crunch of nose cartilage breaking, and a crack from the cheekbone. Merida stumbled back, then collapsed on the carpet, a trickle of blood coming from his nostrils.

Fleming righted the overturned chair and dropped into it. Then, fishing into his jacket pocket, he found the hand radio. He looked at the carnage around him, then hit the "Transmit" button.

"Kohler, we've got ourselves a situation here. Some spic with a machine gun iced Jack before I could shoot. Then Merida went for the gun and had to be stopped—hard."

CHAPTER 17

JOAN FLEMING unlocked the door and stepped into the apartment. She'd stopped off for a drink after work this evening, but was sure she'd be home before Ed. When she saw a man slumped on the couch, she froze in surprise. It was Ed, and it was apparent that he'd been there for a long time. His jacket was off, his tie was tossed aside. A large green box sat on the coffee table, half-open. The Scotch bottle beside it lay on its side, empty. Then the red stains on his shirt registered.

"Blood! Oh, my God, are you all right?" She rushed to

the couch as Fleming opened his eyes and gazed blearily at her.

"It's nothing," he said as Joan's fingers touched the now-dried bloodstains. "The stuff on the cuff came from some asshole's nose. The rest . . ." He slammed the top of the footlocker. "The rest is Jack Ross."

Joan drew back. "Your partner? What happened? Is he . . .?"

"Dead." Fleming cut in. "Today was the big bust we've been working toward." In a colorless voice, he reported what had happened in the hotel room. The more Fleming talked, the farther away Joan moved down the couch. When his voice finally ran down, she was almost yelling.

"That could have been you. You could have been *killed*. I can't stand it anymore, Ed. First Larry, now Ross. When am I going to read about *you* on the front page of the *Post?*"

As she shouted at him, she watched Ed draw himself up on the couch. His face froze into what she thought of as his "work face"—a tight, icy mask. Sometimes when he came home, it took a little while for that mask to soften into the Ed she knew and loved. She quailed inside. He'd never looked at *her* that way before.

Fleming sat for a long moment, fists clenched, glaring at Joan as if she were an antagonist. His hand darted toward her, and she flinched. But he only grabbed her hand, smothering it in his. He stared at her with eyes like a lost child's.

"There are some things that are part of the job," he said. "We don't like to think about them, but they're always there. So we try to laugh them off, or have a couple of drinks too many to forget. There's no way to change them. You've got to understand that."

"That's what I'm just beginning to understand." Joan's voice hardened with anger. "Those cute stories you used to tell me about the job, they sounded like kids playing cops and robbers. But people bleed, and they die. It finally hit me when your snitch got killed—how upset you got. All this job makes you do is lie, and hurt, and take advantage of people. You've been kidding yourself, Ed. About this job . . . about this case . . . about how smart you are. You're not street-smart, you're just an opportunist!"

She jumped up from the couch and headed into the bedroom. Fleming silently trailed after her. "So what can I do? Give this up?"

"If you don't, you'll either get killed, or kill everything that's alive in you," Joan cut in. "Everything that makes me love you." She shrugged out of her blue linen jacket with short, angry movements. But all Fleming noticed was the swell of her breasts, moving freely under her blouse as she threw the jacket into the closet.

"I do love you," Fleming said, coming up behind Joan as she turned to unbutton her blouse. "Want me to prove it?" He slipped the blouse down over her arms, momentarily pinning them, and took her breasts in his hands.

Joan half-turned to find his lips on hers. She tried to push him away, but her arms were still caught in the blouse. She let it slide off, to float to the floor as Fleming ran his thumbs over her nipples.

She gasped into his mouth. "What do you think you're doing?"

"You called me an opportunist. I guess I'm grabbing an opportunity."

"Feels to me like you're grabbing my tits," Joan said, but Fleming covered her lips with another open-mouth kiss. "You're crazy. You're drunk."

169

"Yeah, but I'm also horny. One out of three isn't bad."

It was also true, he realized. Ever since the firefight in the hotel room, he'd known what he needed.

He crushed Joan in his arms. "Oh, shit," he muttered. "That sounds all wrong. I didn't just come home with a hard-on. I need *you*. After all the bullshit—lying, killing, and dying, I've gotta have someone to remind me that I'm still alive inside."

Sliding the strap of her camisole down her shoulder, he kissed along the open expanse of flesh, from her throat down to her chest. Under the lacy fabric her nipples were now erect. He went to kiss one, but she pushed him away with the ghost of her old laugh. "Hold it a second."

She tugged the camisole up until the lacy hem rose above her breasts.

"Much better." Fleming's hand slipped along the soft undercurve of flesh, savoring its fullness, his tongue grazing the blush-pink nipple. "Tastes better, too."

Joan drew the camisole completely off, shaking out her hair.

He ran his hands along the smooth skin of her sides, around to her back, pressing her to him. Then she was removing his tie, his shirt.

Fleming knelt, undoing the tab at Joan's waist, unzipping the light linen pants. He slid them down, running feathery kisses along the soft flesh of her belly. Now she stood before him only in a pair of white lace panties.

Joan's fingers slid under the elastic at her hips, rolling the panties down. Slowly, her dark blond pubic hair came into view. Ed kissed around it, then into it.

He stood up, opening his own trousers, pushing them off along with his shorts. Thick hair swirled over his chest, down his stomach, darkening at his loins . . .

Joan glanced at his erection, then turned away.

Fleming grinned. *She still hates to be caught looking,* he thought. He pursued her, nuzzling the nape of her neck. One hand cupped a breast, the other gently massaged its way between her thighs, his hardness rubbing into the crease between her buttocks. "Ed," she whispered, turning to him, the contours of her body merging into his.

They stumbled together to the bed. Joan lay on the coverlet, not even pulling it down. He lay beside her, kissing her hungrily, fingers breaching the soft dampness of her. She opened her thighs in welcome, murmuring into his shoulder, her fingers blindly searching downward to grasp him. Then she was guiding him into her. He hissed as he slid in to the hilt.

They moved together with a harsh rhythm, almost as if they were carrying on their earlier argument. His temples pounded with an urgency stirred by the sight and stink of blood.

As Fleming writhed in the embrace of Joan's thighs, a small part of his brain realized why she had worn slacks that day. The slight extra friction of her legs against his sides and back told him she hadn't shaved her legs. Somehow that prickly caress sent a shiver of passion rippling down his spine.

And then the argument reached its sweet conclusion. "Ogodgodgod." Joan's mutter was sharp, her hips working furiously, the sex flush bringing a delicate pink from her face to her breasts. A few more frenzied moments, and then they froze together.

They lay in the dimness of the room on their sides, silently facing each other. Fleming was running his hand along the sweet, lush curve of her hip, tracing the sweep up from the waist, then down to the knee. This recuperation time was both peaceful and filled with anticipation. Both of them knew that seconds was the best time, a long slow sharing after the hard edge of need had been blunted.

Joan crouched like a cat, pulling the bedspread around them. As she leaned over Fleming, her tousled hair and full breasts caressed him, her nipples teasingly tickling their way through his mat of chest hair.

"What do you think, soldier? Up to a rematch between the sheets?" Her hand stroked along his outer thigh, then moved inward. "Uh-oh. I think there are signs of life down here."

"Signs of lust is more like it."

Their lips were just meeting again when the phone rang. Seven rings later, Fleming finally picked up the receiver.

"This is Harold Denton," a hesitant voice said.

Fleming needed a moment to recall the kid at the bust.

"I was sent to cover Cantalope's place after the bust. When I got up here, I saw his car out front."

"Yeah?" Fleming didn't intend to give the kid any encouragement.

"I just went in to check our wiretap. And in the corner of the basement, I saw two brown suitcases. Like the ones from the airport." Denton's voice was rising in excitement. "I checked them out, and they had diplomatic seals."

"And?" Fleming couldn't keep the irritation out of his voice.

"I searched the basement. There was this big baby carriage, away in the back. And it was full of cocaine! I called Mr. Kohler, and he said to call you. He's already sending McCarthy over there."

Fleming swung his legs off the bed. "Who have you got there with you?" he asked.

"Roberts," came the answer.

"Well, you get back with him right away."

"D-do you think there'll be trouble?"

"No, I want you there to make sure that fucking thief doesn't steal any of it." Fleming started feeling around for his clothes.

"What's going on?" Joan's face was tight as she sat up in the bed.

"It's the bust. Still something to take care of."

"I thought you were finished."

"Just a little detail." Fleming gathered the clothes in his arms.

"You bastard!" Joan yelled at his retreating back as he headed for the living room. "You're really going to leave now? *Now*? You and your *fucking* job!"

The drive to the Bronx was short, but all the way, Fleming turned the angles over in his head. *Denton may have fucked up the bust, but he sure saved his ass, finding the rest of the cocaine. Now it's my turn. Maybe Cavallera and Kohler will get off my case if I tie Cantalope into this.*

He found a parking space on Randall Avenue and strolled casually into Guido Cantalope's apartment building. Moments later, he was in the basement. He stood in the gloom, looking around, until the stakeout agents recognized him. They emerged from the shadows. Both had their guns drawn.

"Glad you saw it was me," Fleming said. "We've had enough agents down on this case."

Denton holstered his pistol in embarrassment. "You begin to get a little jumpy in here after a while."

"Yeah," Roberts added. "We've been staking this place out since the bust went sour. And I don't know about you, but I'm starving."

173

"I see you didn't bring anything to eat or drink with you," Denton said. "We can wait while you get something."

Fleming shook his head. "I won't be needing anything. Just show me what we've got here."

Denton gave him the grand tour of the basement. He showed Fleming the old mattresses that hid the wiretap tape recorder. He pointed out the brown leather suitcases. Then he unveiled the pièce de résistance—the baby carriage full of cocaine.

Roberts's contribution was more practical. "There's a sink over here on the other side of the cellar." He pointed. "That's where we've been peeing."

They all froze as they heard footsteps cautiously descending the stairs. It was McCarthy.

Denton and Roberts left, wishing the two of them a happy stakeout. As soon as they were gone, Fleming turned to McCarthy. "We know he's up there. They heard him talking on the phone tap. But there's no way in hell this guy is ever coming down here. I stopped off to talk to my snitch on the way over. Angelo knows we've found the stuff. The word's out all over the street." He was about to tell McCarthy who the snitch was, but paranoia took over.

"Looks like somebody in our office is telling them what goes on. I don't know who, but it's definitely happening."

McCarthy just nodded his head, not shocked, merely acknowledging the information.

"There's nothing we can do about the leak. But there *is* something we can do here. As things stand, Kohler will keep up this stakeout for a week or two. Of course it will be dry, so he'll finally call it off. Then maybe there isn't enough evidence to nail Guido. He beats the rap."

McCarthy nodded again. "But we can do something about it?" He began to smile, anticipating the answer.

174

"If the mountain won't come to Mohammed, we can always bring Mohammed to the mountain."

The two of them headed upstairs.

When Guido Cantalope answered the knock on his door, he found two big strangers standing in front of him. "W-what do you want?" he said.

Fleming reached in, grabbing him by the hair, and pulled him through the doorway. Almost casually, he flung Cantalope down the first flight of stairs. Then he walked down to him. "Come on, punk. We're going down into the basement."

McCarthy and Fleming each took an arm, pulling Guido upright. They threw him over the railing, to tumble down the next flight. "No! No!" Guido began to shout. "I don't want to go down there!" He held onto the railing slats as the agents came to take him this time. They heaved together, tearing the slats loose.

Scrabbling frantically, Cantalope found a sturdy slat. It wouldn't pull loose. Sighing, McCarthy pulled out his gun. He smashed Guido's hands with the pistol butt until they let go.

Fleming glanced nervously up the stairway. Obviously, the other tenants could hear what was going on. But no one dared look out their doors, much less intervene.

By now, they had reached the door to the basement. Fleming kicked it open and sent Cantalope rolling down the steps, head over heels. At the bottom, Fleming picked up the weakly kicking punk, carried him to the baby carriage, and dropped him in. "Gotcha!"

The press conference was scheduled to catch the eleven o'clock news. Andy Cavallera had his hundred keys of

coke, which made a nice display on the table as he ex-
plained the arrest of Guido Cantalope. But it was referred
to strictly as "three hundred million dollars—street
value."

Fleming remembered the meeting between Cavallera
and Kohler over that point. "They won't understand the
significance of a hundred-kilo seizure," Cavallera had
said. "But put it to the public as money, and they'll understand that well enough."

Joey Castelli watched Cavallera on television. He knew
damn well that Guido Cantalope never went into that cellar on his own. *That Fleming,* he thought. *He's a fuckin'
animal!*

Fleming turned off the news before the conference was
half over. Rubbing his eyes, he lay back on the couch. He
had no reason to go down the hall to the bedroom. He'd
checked it out when he'd come home, hours before. It was
empty. Joan was gone.

CHAPTER 18

IT'S NOT *like the old days. Goddamn chinks taking over the old neighborhood. They're like rabbits. Pretty soon, we'll only have Mulberry Street. Can't even do business anymore. Now we got competition from the spics up in Harlem and every sonofabitch who gets off the damn boat from South America is dealing dope. I don't have enough damn trouble, the fucking Don chews me out like some lackey. Ow, this damn head!*

Angelo Tartagliano rubbed the sleep from his eyes in the back seat of his limousine. His temples throbbed and he rubbed them to release the pain. It was no use. The combination of a sleepless night and anger at the aborted deal had left him in a rage for hours that no amount of swearing could lessen.

I can't believe it, he thought. *All those months of planning shot to hell in a matter of minutes. But how did they find out? We were so careful. Everyone who knew the details was trustworthy. They were either family or close associates. It's just like the last time a buy went bad. Bumpy Morgan. That* mulignan *sonofabitch. He must have gone to the Feds. No. It can't be him. He didn't know where the meet was. But I'm going to find out today. Rocco will have a nice little job ahead of him. Whoever sold me out will—and slowly. Ah, this fucking headache just won't quit.*

He rapped on the glass partition and it slowly slid down. Rocco peered at his master from the shotgun seat. "What is it, boss?"

"I have a headache. Let's stop for some aspirin. And I want a cup of coffee."

"Sure thing, boss." He repeated the instructions in Italian and Achille drove the limousine to a neighborhood drugstore.

Rocco was out of the car before it had stopped and rushed into the pharmacy. Inside, an elderly woman with blue hair and glasses was carefully reading the instructions on a bottle of hair dye. Two teenage girls were giggling as they flirted with a young stock clerk. A tired-looking pharmacist sat on a stool behind the cash register. Rocco looked for the aspirin but couldn't find it.

"Hey, buddy, where's the aspirin?"

Before the pharmacist could reply, the old woman piped up. "I was before you, young man."

Rocco glanced at her and smirked. She was short and

wispy. Her skin seemed so thin that he could see the veins in her neck throb each time she spoke. "Give me a break, lady. Where's that aspirin?"

"I was before you. How dare you jump in front of me!" Her skin turned beet red and she started to shake, dropping the bottle of rinse to the floor. It shattered on impact, sending jets of the rinse out in all directions.

"Hey, watch it, lady," cried Rocco.

"It was your fault. You pushed me. If you weren't in such a hurry to jump to the head of the line, this would never have happened."

"What line? There's nobody here. Hey, bud. I asked you for the aspirin."

"It's on the bottom shelf," replied the pharmacist.

Rocco turned away from the woman and bent down to get the aspirin bottle. At that, the woman reached out and yanked on the sleeve of Rocco's jacket. He brushed her off by flicking his arm at her.

The unexpected move caught the woman unprepared. She lost her balance and tumbled into a display of pantyhose that came crashing down all around her. Rocco jumped back and reached for his pistol, unsure of what was going on. The stock clerk hurried to pick up the woman while the two girls erupted in peals of uncontrolled laughter. The pharmacist didn't move. He merely peered down at Rocco from his stool as though the situation didn't concern him.

Only his iron-hard control prevented Rocco from killing the woman and every one in the store. Dropping his hand to his side, he willed himself to be calm and tried to make light of an ever-worsening situation. He reached down to help the woman up, but she slapped his hands away.

"Get away from me, you brute." She stood up, shaking and wagging a long, gnarled finger at him. She pushed the stock clerk away. He shrugged his shoulders and went back to his work.

As the woman started yelling, the two teenagers rolled their eyes and waved to the clerk as they left the store. "Bummer," said one of them as she fluffed out her permed blond hair. She had squeezed herself into skintight white-striped blue jeans. And as she sauntered away, her buttocks twitched invitingly. The stock clerk enjoyed the view. "Really," agreed her partner, a hefty brunette wearing black stretch pants, a pink oversized sweatshirt, and white elf boots.

"You ought to be ashamed of yourself," yelled the blue-haired woman. She turned to the pharmacist who had come out from behind the counter. "Did you see what he did to me? I want you to call the police."

Rocco's fist clenched in frustration. It would be so easy to squeeze that chicken neck of hers. But he hesitated, fearful of the police and of Angelo, waiting outside.

"Lady, look, I'm really sorry. I really need those aspirins. They're for my mother. She's got this real bad arthritis and the pain makes her crazy."

"We've got arthritis pills right here," said the pharmacist, reaching for a different bottle of pills. "This is stronger than the aspirin and she should get some relief."

"What sort of medication is she on?"

Rocco giggled nervously. "She's not on any medication."

"Why not?" asked the old lady, her anger momentarily forgotten as she listened to someone else's problems.

"She's ninety. And never been sick a day in her life." Out of the corner of his eye he saw the old woman nod her head in sympathy. He decided to play his story to her. "She doesn't trust doctors. I been trying to get her to go to the doctor but she refuses. So she makes me get aspirins. Says it makes her feel better."

"I've never been sick either," answered the woman. "Lately, my back has been bothering me. Nothing I do seems to work." She rubbed the small of her back. "Ow. When you pushed me, I fell and hurt it again."

"Lady, I'm really sorry. I didn't mean anything. It's just that I'm so worried about my mother . . ."

"You're a good son. Worrying about your mother. Buying her medicine. My children never even come to visit me. Five children. Each rottener than the next."

Rocco patted the woman on the wrist as he steered her toward the cash register. "Kids are lousy. I'm an only child. If I don't look after my mother, who will?"

The woman nodded in agreement. "You're a good boy," she said. "But you shouldn't break into line."

"You're right, lady."

"You should have asked first." The woman fumbled in her purse and pulled out a crumpled tissue. She blew her nose and dabbed at her mouth.

"Could I go in front of you, ma'am?" asked Rocco, hating the thought of humbling himself to this old woman. Every instinct he had screamed at him to punch this tiny bag of skin and bones. As he stared into the Coke-bottle-thick glasses the woman wore, he wondered how she could see at all. *I'd cut my fucking throat if I ended up like you, old woman. You're one step in the grave. I'd even give you a push if I wasn't in such a hurry.*

The woman pretended to consider the request. "All right, young man. But next time, mind your manners."

Rocco paid for the aspirins and fled the store. He

opened the door of the limo and slid in. The car pulled away immediately.

"What the hell did you do?" asked Angelo. "Make them yourself?"

"Sorry, boss. There was this old broad . . ."

"I don't want to hear your excuses," roared Angelo. "I just want a fucking aspirin. Can't anybody do anything right?"

Rocco tucked his chin into his chest and stared intently ahead while Angelo filled the car with his curses. He spotted a diner ahead and told Achille to pull in.

"What the hell are we stopping for? This isn't where the meet is."

"You wanted some coffee, boss," said Rocco.

Before Angelo could reply, a jab of pain punched at his right eye. He rubbed his eyes, trying for relief. "Hurry it up this time, will you?"

Rocco bolted from the car and ran up the steps of the diner. Angelo sat back in his seat. *Poblete told me the buy was clean. No one on his side knew that the deal was on for yesterday. Who? It had to be that fucking Bumpy Morgan. Nobody sells me out to the Feds. But what if he isn't the one? I worked long and hard to establish a good organization in Harlem. Who'll run it if Morgan's not there? Fuck it. The family will run it. Just like always. There's plenty of nickel-and-dime punks who would wet themselves at the thought of being front men for this family.*

The door opened and Rocco handed Angelo a cup of steaming black coffee. Angelo popped two aspirins in his mouth and washed them down with the brew. He cupped his hands over the Styrofoam cup, enjoying the warmth. Holding the cup to his temples, he felt the heat ease the headache.

"Take it easy, boss. Rest your eyes. I'll wake you up when we get to the meet." Rocco took the cup from Angelo's hands and chucked it through the open window.

The car moved into traffic and Angelo tried to get some rest. But he couldn't erase last night's disaster from his mind. The bust was bad enough, but what infuriated Angelo was the way he was treated by Vito Panella.

Summoned to his home last night like an errand boy, not the head of my own family. And I stood there with my hat in my hand while he sat in his kitchen drinking espresso. He didn't even offer me a chair.

"I must not be implicated in this business. You must find the person responsible for this treachery and make him pay in a suitable way." Don Vito sipped from the delicate china cup. With his mane of thick silver hair and regal features, he was the picture of an old-fashioned gentleman enjoying his espresso. But his hooded eyes never left Angelo's face.

"He will be found," replied Angelo.

"Then you know who it is?"

"No. But I have my suspicions."

Don Vito made a face. "Suspicions are like spiderwebs. They ensnare everything that lands on them. We do not have the time to waste on this business. Our losses last night were not that great. But it has brought us to the attention of the government agents. They are like jackals who rip and pull at our skin and they will not rest until I am behind bars."

"The family is in jeopardy, Don Vito . . ."

"Idiot," screamed Vito. *"I* am the family. The Don. What happens to the rest of you does not concern me. You have pledged me your loyalty with your blood oath. Do you forget this?"

183

"No, Don Vito . . ."

"I'm glad that your memory has not failed you—like your people have."

Angelo's stomach writhed with anger at the insult. He concealed the pain and stood straight. "It is not known where the leak was. But I . . ."

"No excuses. Just find out who is responsible and eliminate him. Now leave me."

Don Vito finished his demitasse. As he lowered his cup to the saucer, his hand shook—just the faintest tremor—but enough to rattle the china.

Angelo stared for a long moment. *The Don is afraid.*

"Didn't I tell you to go?" Don Vito's eyes flashed a warning.

Angelo responded with a smile. "Of course, Don Vito. You must be protected at all times. It is your right as the head of the family. I will find the traitor."

"Leave me!" Vito's voice was almost a scream.

Rocco gently shook the napping Angelo. "We're here."

Angelo opened his eyes and was instantly awake. His headache had subsided. He left the limo and walked into the Bay Diner, leaving Rocco and Achille behind. Only he, Frankie, and Billy knew the identity of the man in the DEA on the family's payroll.

He stepped up to the cash register and spoke to the hostess. "I'm meeting Mr. Smith," he said.

"Sure thing," said the young woman brightly. "This way, please."

As she led him to the rear of the diner, Angelo looked around. The restaurant was nearly deserted. There were just two patrons and they both sat at the counter. One, a young black man with glasses, underlined passages in a thick textbook with a lime-colored highlighter. The other was a middle-aged man in work clothes and a three-day growth of beard reading a tabloid newspaper and sucking on a cigarette. Neither seemed much of a threat to Angelo.

The hostess stopped a few feet in front of him. She gestured to a solitary booth with high leather sides that hid the customer from sight. "Mr. Smith, your party is here."

Angelo slid into the booth across from Dick Powers. "How are you feeling, Mr. Smith?" he asked.

"Pretty good, Mr. Jones," said Powers. "Glad you could join me for breakfast."

CHAPTER 19

DICK POWERS wondered why Angelo Tartagliano had called this face-to-face meeting. Previously, he had dealt with either Frankie or Billy Castelli and always by telephone. *It must be pretty important for Angelo, himself, to meet me in a public place.*

"I'm glad we finally met," murmured Powers, eager to curry favor with the man who controlled his money. *The guy looks like a bus driver with that blue windbreaker, blue slacks, white shirt, and black shoes. All he needs is a pair of white socks to complete the picture. I can't picture him as the head of a crime family. He looks more like somebody's uncle.*

Angelo ignored the remark. "How is the food in this place?" *So this is the man who accepts my money for information. Even though he wears dungarees and a work shirt, he looks like a fashion model. Hair too neatly combed. This is one who is very vain about his appearance. Even the nails are manicured. He likes to be looked at, yet he never meets my eyes. Why not? Is he afraid of me? Or is he just pretending humility? Such vanity can be exciting in a woman. In a man, it is a vice. He is too concerned with appearances. So I must get below the surface. Who knows what I will find. I must watch this one carefully.*

"I don't know."

"Why not?"

"I've never been here before. Less chance of being recognized that way." *He must think I'm pretty damn stupid.* "You called this meet, not me. You worried that I'm setting you up? Search me for a wire." *That will shake his cage.*

Angelo and Powers locked eyes in a contest for the psychological control of this meeting. Powers felt confident that he could outlast the older man. Subtly, the color and shape of Angelo's eyes changed. They went from a murky brown to a bright amber. The effect was startling. Powers began to sweat and droplets formed on his forehead and upper lip. The deeper he peered into Angelo's eyes the more worried he became. *What the fuck am I doing? Those eyes. They laugh and change colors. And they're cold. Like the hand of death. I can feel them stealing my soul.*

He weakens quickly. For a moment I thought I detected defiance but I see only fear and confusion. He panics. Not a good quality for a Judas. He can read my eyes, so I will give him something to remember, thought Angelo.

I'm a fucking dead man. A corpse. This sonofabitch is going to kill me. He thinks I'm a threat to him. I can feel it, sure as shit. No way I'm going to blow this deal. The money's too good. Enough of this game. I don't want trouble with this man. Powers shivered and broke the eye contact.

Angelo smiled. *He understood. But he is still expendable. I'll keep him for his information. When I've learned all that there is to know, it will be his time to play with the fish. I don't want him to suspect that. Even the rabbit will fight when cornered.* "A silly game, trying to out-stare an opponent. I used to play it as a child, but I could never win. My eyes always blinked."

"You did pretty good on me. Don't get bent out of shape. I didn't mean anything by it. It was just a stupid game." *Don't make this man angry,* thought Powers.

"Why take offense? We've just met. You don't know me. And I do not know you. So we test each other to see our strengths." *He acknowledges my superiority. Good. But he's not to be trusted. He's a paid informer. Not much different from the scum I seek.*

Powers was eager to change the subject. This meeting was not turning out the way he expected. "Let's eat. After that long ride, you must be hungry. I'm starved."

"I'm an early riser and I breakfast when I awaken." Angelo looked at his watch—a battered Timex. "Ten-thirty. Not yet time for my next meal but early enough for a light snack."

They were interrupted by the waitress, who took their

orders. Powers ordered a hearty breakfast of steak and eggs. Angelo chose a chocolate donut and a large glass of milk.

While waiting for the food, the two men made small talk. Powers, now totally intimidated by Angelo, followed his lead wherever he took the conversation. Angelo delighted in leading him around by the nose.

"Looks like rain," said Powers.

"There will be no rain."

"But the papers said . . ."

"The papers print lies." Angelo thumped his knee with his fist. "My knee was broken many years ago. When it healed it gave me a dividend. It throbs whenever rain is due." He smacked it again. "Nothing. No pain. No rain."

Powers backed off. Searching for a neutral subject, he hefted the water glass in his hands. "This Long Island water is great. It makes good coffee."

Angelo sniffed the clear liquid and wrinkled his nose. "Too many chemicals in this water—they weaken the brew. Smell it."

"Water doesn't have any smell."

"This does. Smell it," Angelo ordered.

Powers held the glass to his nose. "I can't smell anything."

"That's because you smoke those disgusting cigarettes. It ruins your sense of smell. How can you enjoy your food? The aroma of a dish must be inhaled to be appreciated." Angelo chuckled. *He's so eager to please, he'll do whatever I want.*

The sonofabitch. He's jerking me around like a damn puppet. Nobody does that to me. Powers lit a cigarette from the one already in the ashtray. He inhaled deeply and held the puff in his lungs. *Don't like cigarettes, huh?*

Well, sniff this. He slowly exhaled the plume of smoke directly at Angelo.

The smoke stung Angelo's eyes, but he didn't rub them. Nor would he fan the smoke away with his hands. *I made him angry,* he thought. *He doesn't take long. Dangerous. Very dangerous. A liability that must be erased as soon as our business is done. Enough of these games.*

"I like smoking," said Powers. "It relaxes me. And I've been doing it too long to stop now. So I guess you'll just have to live with it for the time being, huh?"

Angelo heard the anger in his tone. "You're very feisty for a man with one foot in the grave," he said quietly.

The waitress brought their orders. After she left, Powers stared at Angelo, who nibbled delicately at his donut. "Are you threatening me, bucko?"

"Of course not," said Angelo. "Why should I do that? We're here to discuss business, not act like children daring each other to step over a line in the dirt. Read the label on your cigarette package. If you won't listen to me, maybe you'll listen to your own Surgeon General."

What the fuck am I doing? thought Powers. *This isn't going well at all. I'm gonna blow this deal.* He massaged his temples with his fingertips. "Look, I have a lot of things on my mind. I'm in a rotten mood. I'm sorry."

"Accepted." Angelo took a sip of milk. "Did you find out what happened?"

"It's not much."

"It is something."

"One of our agents has an inside man in your organization."

"What is his name?"

"I don't know. It's being kept under wraps. Only the agent and his superior know all the details."

"What are they after?"

"You."

Angelo again sipped his milk, then wiped his lips with his napkin. "What have they learned so far?"

"That Poblete is your supplier. They had the two of you under surveillance on the day of the bust."

"Then they saw nothing. We had a simple lunch. The courier—how was he identified?"

"By the informant."

Angelo rubbed his head. His headache had returned. "This agent. What is his name?"

"Ed Fleming."

"I must know who his informant is. What kind of a man is this Fleming?"

"He's good."

"That's not what I'm asking. Tell me about the man himself."

"We were partners once. I taught him everything he knows. He knows the street and he's not afraid to break the rules."

"Explain."

"This low-level French diplomat was smuggling coke in his diplomatic pouch. We couldn't touch him. The guy laughed at us. Fleming wanted him bad. We followed him everywhere for a month and came up with nothing. So Fleming hired these two porno actors and had one made up to look like the Frenchman. We shot ten rolls of film. The best shot was this one guy taking it up the ass. We superimposed the Frenchman's face on the guy being fucked. Fleming had copies of the photos made and sent one to the guy's wife. The other was sent to the Sûreté. He was recalled in less than a week. We never heard of him again."

"So. He's a man who's not afraid to go after what he wants."

"He's a real smart sonofabitch."

"Tell me about the other arrests. Surely you must have some idea of what his plans are next."

Powers squirmed in his seat. "I haven't seen the actual reports. Fleming keeps them locked up, you know. But from what I've been able to learn from other agents, there's going to be a piss-load of arrests coming up soon."

"Speak plain. Who are the targets?"

"Your nephews, the Castelli boys, are on the hit list. So is Poblete. Even Vito Panella is a marked man."

So, the Don is in danger. Good. Let him know how it feels to fear prison looming over his head. "How was he implicated? Tell me about it."

"Both you and Panella . . ."

"Don't speak his name in public. Have respect for the man. Call him 'The Don' as befits his rank."

"I didn't mean any disrespect."

"Go on. How were we connected?"

"You were under surveillance. I haven't seen the report, but I've heard . . ."

"There's a lot you haven't seen. How is it you hear so much, but have so little proof?"

Powers flushed. "Each agent keeps his own files. Unless you have a need to know, the files aren't opened up. This way, an operation won't be compromised by too many people knowing all the details. As a supervisor, I can examine any files. But if I go poking my nose into everything, it'll make people suspicious."

"Why didn't you have this information ready when we met today?"

"I didn't think you'd ask me these questions."

"Why do you think that I called this meeting? Because I wanted to meet you?" Angelo's voice sliced through Powers. "You're paid very well to keep me informed of any threats to my organization. Yet I never hear about this Fleming business—until it's too late to do anything about it."

The waitress sauntered over but was brushed away by Powers. "Leave us alone, honey." He handed her a fifty-dollar bill. The girl's eyes widened in surprise. "This is for the bill. Keep the change and don't disturb us."

"Okay, sir. Thanks a lot." The smiling woman quickly left them alone.

Angelo gritted his teeth. "And now you bring attention to us with your stupidity. This meeting is over. Your money will brand your face in that one's mind. Generosity for no service is always remembered. You make too many mistakes. I don't know if I want someone so careless working for me."

"Look, Tartagliano. Who the hell do you think you're talking to? You don't own me. I call my own shots. And don't you forget it. I don't have to give you shit. How about that?"

Angelo kicked Powers under the table. The unexpected assault disconcerted and shocked Dick. As he reached for his knee, Angelo captured his right hand and bent his pinkie straight up. He stared into Dick's eyes, which were filled with pain. "I could break it, just like that. I *do* own you. Body and soul. You're mine. Just a flick of my wrist and I break your pinkie. That's how I hold your life in my hands. And that of your family."

"Leave them out of this," said Dick through clenched teeth.

"But they're very much in this. My money has bought them so many things. A new television set, a VCR, stereo equipment. You're smart. You don't make big purchases. Just enough not to draw suspicion on yourself for extravagance. But it can end tomorrow if you ever cross me again. Am I understood?" He bent the finger as far back as it could go without breaking.

"Yeah, I got it. I'm not stupid."

"Good." Angelo released him. "I need two things from you. I need the name of the informant. He must be found and eliminated. He puts all of us in danger. And I need Fleming. His investigation is bad for business and must be stopped. As my enemy, he's dangerous. Maybe he can work for me."

"You're wasting your time. He can't be bought," said Dick, rubbing his finger.

"Everyone can be bought, if the price is right. So let him name his price. He won't even have to count it. He can weigh it. And it will be all for him."

"What about me? When I approach him he'll know I'm on the pad. I'll be useless to you."

Angelo smiled. "Two birds sing better than one. Each of you will be well rewarded for your services." He reached into his pocket and handed Powers a folded bill.

Powers unfolded it and blinked. It was a thousand-dollar bill. He quickly crumpled the bill and stuffed it in his shirt pocket.

"There will be fifty of these if you succeed," said Angelo. "But if you fail . . ." He let the thought trail off.

Dick Powers sat stiffly in the booth for a moment after Angelo had left the diner. How was he going to get Fleming to turn? Puzzling over the question, he stood up to leave. The waitress came over.

"Thank you, sir," she said, smiling broadly at him. "Have a nice day."

That fuck was right. This one will remember. Why the fuck did I do such a stupid goddamn thing? He brushed by the waitress, not responding.

In the parking lot, he saw a large black limousine pulling out into the traffic. He grinned. *He's hot shit, that Tartagliano. Reams my ass out for giving that broad a big tip because it draws too much attention to us, yet he drives to this meet in a limo. Guinea bastard. He'll get his one day. I just hope I'm there to see it.*

The drive back to New Jersey was long and infuriating. One lane of the Belt Parkway was closed for repairs and the traffic crawled along. Powers tried listening to the radio but found the monotony of AM rock-and-roll boring. He switched to the FM band but liked the album-oriented stations no better. Opening his glove compartment, he put a Clancy Brothers tape into the cassette deck and sang Irish songs for the rest of his trip.

His house was empty. Anne had gone into Manhattan for the day and the kids were all in school. Dick went up to the bedroom, took off his clothes, and hopped under a hot shower. The drumming of the water on his back relaxed him. As he toweled himself dry, he spotted the scale. *So Angelo is going to pay Fleming by the pound.* He grinned. *Wonder what he'll ask?*

He picked up his revolver that he had tossed on the bed. He flicked open the weapon and pulled out a .38-caliber bullet. He squeezed the round in his palm, then flung it against the far wall of the bedroom. Then he wondered how many twenty-dollar bills there were in a pound.

* * *

195

Angelo's headache was worse than ever. As he sat in the limousine, he tried to relax. But the thought of the traitor incessantly gnawed at him. He would find this worm, and death would be slow in coming. This would be an example to all who would break their oaths of silence and loyalty.

He opened the glass partition. "Rocco."

"Yes, boss."

"Tell Achille to be very careful. Take the long way home. And make sure that we haven't been followed." He closed the partition.

He picked up the modular phone and dialed a number.

"Hello," said Billy Castelli.

"You and your brother are coming to my house for dinner tonight. Call Frankie and let him know."

"Who else?"

" 'Sally Boy' Pantusco. Carlo Meruzzi and Vinnie Capella. We're having veal."

"Sounds good, uncle. Want me to bring the wine?"

"If you like. We eat at eight."

He hung up the phone and leaned back. Rubbing his temples, he massaged away the headache. *It was so simple in the old days. Just the whores and the gambling. The police would look the other way because everyone had vices. Then we discovered the white powder. The devil's snow. Covering us all with its deadly blanket. Destroyer of children. Corrupter of the innocent. Maker of money and power. More than I ever dreamed possible. The family has never been so well off. Or so much in mortal danger from our enemies. I must protect my blood. It is my responsibility. My duty.*

CHAPTER 20

JOEY CASTELLI ran as fast as he could, but the snarling German shepherds were right at his heels. One lunged forward, grabbing Joey's leg in his teeth. Its sharp teeth punctured Joey's calf and blood bubbled from the wounds. As he screamed in pain, he punched the dog as hard as he could behind its left ear. The animal yelped and relaxed its grip. That was all the time he needed. He jerked free and stumbled ahead, leaving a trail of blood behind him.

The scent aroused the second dog, who hurled itself at Joey and thumped him in the back, knocking him off his feet. He tried to scramble away, but the creature snagged Joey's ankle in its mouth. He bit down, crushing Joey's ankle. Joey howled in agony. Frantically he kicked the dog in the nose, but the animal would not release its grip.

Joey made a fist and pounded on the animal's head. It whined and whimpered as it backed away, staring at Joey, searching for any sign of fear or weakness. Warily it circled Joey, who dragged himself out of the animal's reach. Inching forward, it lunged for Joey's hand and trapped his pinkie in its mouth. Shaking its head violently, it snapped the finger off at the second joint and swallowed it.

As Joey bellowed in pain, the animal howled—a savage call that was answered by other dogs. Suddenly, Joey was surrounded. A panting Doberman slavered as it growled and crawled forward, nipping at Joey's exposed body parts. It darted out and ripped a hunk of skin from Joey's forearm. Shaking the bloody hunk of meat in its mouth, it ate the prize in three bites.

Joey tried to scream but his vocal cords made no sounds. The other animals attacked. One buried its teeth in Joey's stomach until his steaming intestines spilled to the ground. Another lunged for Joey's groin and tore at his penis and testicles. A German shepherd straddled his chest and bared its bloody teeth to Joey.

Its eyes were black and bottomless. Joey lost himself in them, terrified by the animal's presence. Joey shut his eyes tightly like a kid trying to hide from the bogeyman. When he opened them, he was lying in his bed, bathed in sweat.

Joey sat straight up. His heart thumped so hard that his chest hurt. He fumbled for the light and turned it on.

The bedroom was a mess. Clothes were draped over every piece of furniture. The bedcovers were stained and dirty. Monica had still not returned and Joey, a natural slob, left his clothes where he dropped them. He pulled at his hair until it hurt. *They fucking know. They know. And my own damn brother is gonna drive me there. To the same damn house where he iced Larry.*

He reached for the pistol that he kept under his pillow. *I ain't going down without a fight. I'll fucking blast anyone who makes a move for me.* The weight of the 9mm was comforting. He sighted down its barrel and blew an imaginary hole in Rocco Mazzi's chest. *You first, motherfucker.* The alarm went off. Billy would be there in fifteen minutes.

Joey sniffed his underarms. *Whew, no time for a shower.* He stripped off his underwear and rolled on some deodorant. Dressing quickly, he thrust the pistol in his jacket pocket. He was ready. Just in time, too. Billy arrived promptly at seven-fifteen.

The ride to Staten Island was long and the brothers had very little to say to each other. Each was lost in his own thoughts.

I had to be the big man. Always trying to make deals. And it fucking backfired on me. And I couldn't leave it alone. Uncle Angelo told me to knock it off. But I didn't listen. I had all the answers. That's why Larry's dead. I fucking killed the sonofabitch. Why? Somebody bad-rapped the dude. So that prick Mazzi worked him over. And they wanted me to kill him. Why me? I ain't never killed nobody. And this buy goes all to shit. That cocksucker Fleming. Leaving me all high and fucking dry. Joey's legs started shaking.

Billy concentrated on the road. He sensed Joey's discomfort and wondered why his brother was so nervous. *Look at him shaking like a kid. My own brother. A fucking waste. We could have had the power in this family. But*

Joey had to go it his own way. Never thinking. Just acting and reacting. Like some dog you stir up by ringing a bell. Thickheaded sonofabitch. Never should have killed that Larry. It was Joey's job. This whole fucking thing is all wrong. Bad timing.

The house was not brightly lit, and Billy nearly missed it in the dark. He pulled into the driveway. "Let's go, Joey, end of the line," he said.

But Joey was lost in his thoughts and didn't hear him. *I wonder how they're gonna do it to me?* He shivered, remembering how much Rocco delighted in using the baseball bat on him.

Billy was out of the car, and was waiting for his brother. "Hurry it up, Joey. Uncle Angelo isn't here yet. We still got time."

"T-time for what?" Joey cringed in fear.

"What the hell's the matter with you? Get the fuck inside. You'll really piss your uncle off if you're late this time." He grabbed Joey under the arm and steered him into the house.

They were the first ones there. Billy gave the house a quick once-over and, satisfied that it was clean, turned on the outside light. This was a sign to the others that it was safe to enter.

Carlo Meruzzi was the first to arrive. The bespectacled, white-haired, seventy-eight-year-old former university professor gave Billy a big hug. "Good evening, Billy. How's the wife and kids?" He ignored Joey as though he were a bug on the wall.

The snub by Meruzzi only heightened Joey's anxiety. *He didn't even talk to me. I'm dead already. Wonder who'll get the job of killing me?*

"Sally Boy" Pantusco and Vinnie Capella came into the house within minutes of each other. They had little to say and took their seats around the table. It was five minutes to eight.

At the stroke of eight, Angelo Tartagliano entered the room. He still wore the same clothes he wore for his meeting with Powers. Flanking him like two bookends were Rocco and Achille. The two positioned themselves at either end of the room and their eyes never left the table. Frankie appeared moments later and took the last empty chair.

Angelo took his seat. "I spoke with Poblete. He tells me that the trouble is on our side."

"You're damn right," said "Sally Boy." "The damn Feds knew just where to look when they took our goods away. It was as if they were briefed on exactly what to look for."

"But who would inform on the family?" asked Carlo.

"That's what we're here to find out," snapped Angelo. "Today, I had a meeting with our eyes and ears in the DEA." He hesitated and looked at each man seated around the table, enjoying the sense of anticipation that he read in their faces.

Here it comes. Sweet Jesus. He knows it's me. Joey's knees began shaking. He reached into his jacket and tightened his grip on the pistol. His motion was not lost on Achille, who positioned himself directly behind Joey.

Achille's eyes hardened, yet he did not pull Joey's arm from his pocket. He was Angelo's relative, after all. But Achille watched the younger Castelli very carefully.

Angelo continued. "My contact with the Feds says that an informer is responsible for all of our difficulties. He's fingered me and Frankie, my nephews, and Guido. With

Merida busted, Jorge's supply line is in a shambles. It must be rebuilt before any new deliveries can be made."

"Where does that leave us?" asked Meruzzi. "And what about our money?"

"So far the rest of you haven't been implicated. But your money is gone. All of our money is gone. There will be no refunds or credits. The Colombians say that they won't resume delivery unless we pay up front from now on."

"Impossible," roared Carlo.

"It has to be," said Angelo. "There is another condition. The informant must be eliminated."

Joey's legs shook so much that "Sally Boy" Pantusco looked questioningly at him. "Hey, kid, you gotta piss? Go do it. You keep on shakin' like that, you piss your pants."

"Oh, yeah," said Joey. "Thanks a lot." He stood up and left the room. In the bathroom, he pulled out his penis and tried to urinate. He was dry. *Dammit. I'm goin' fuckin' nuts here. Why the hell don't Uncle Angelo just fuckin' kill me? Why is he toying with me?*

He splashed water on his face. Patting the pistol in his jacket pocket, he felt safe. *Nobody better fuck with me tonight. I'm in no damn mood.* Joey laughed nervously. *What the hell am I going to do? How am I going to get out of this?*

Staring at himself in the bathroom mirror, Joey was shocked at how drawn he looked. Blood streaks crisscrossed his eyes that were underlined by heavy black bags. A host of pimples had erupted on his forehead. Dry skin flaked on his nose and chin like old paint on a plaster wall. *I look like shit,* he thought. He splashed his face with water and rejoined the meeting.

Smoke hung heavily in the dining room. Angelo had lit

a cigar and waved it for emphasis. He was still speaking. "The agent handling the case is named Fleming. My contact will try to reach him."

Joey's stomach twisted in a knot. *They buy Fleming and I'm dead. There's no reason for him to cover for me. But he's a Fed. He won't punk out on me.*

"What if he can't be reached?" asked Pantusco.

"He'll be reached. One way or the other."

I gotta get out of this place. I can't stand it. He's got to know. Look at him. Sucking on that damn cigar like it was his mother's tit. I'll die hard, uncle. Maybe I'll even take you with me, you old scumbag. What? He's talking to me.

"What did you say, uncle?"

"I said that this whole mess started when you made the deal with that *mulignan.* Where did you meet him?"

"At Zebra's in the Village. I told you that."

Angelo's eyes widened and he nodded imperceptibly at Achille, who moved quickly behind Joey and punched him in the jaw, sending him tumbling to the floor. Stunned, Joey lay on his back and stared at the ceiling. No one moved to his defense.

So this is how it all ends, thought Joey. *On my fucking back. Now what? A bullet? Or Rocco's stiletto?* He closed his eyes and waited for the end.

"Get him up," commanded Angelo.

Achille picked Joey up and deposited him once again in his chair. Joey's ears were ringing and his eyes wouldn't focus but he heard his uncle's next words distinctly. "Why are you sticking up for that *mulignan?*"

I've got an out. He doesn't think it's me. I can pull this off and save my ass if I can keep my head. It's Bumpy he wants. That ugly black bastard is gonna get it. I'm gonna live. The ringing in his ears became a loud whooshing sound and Joey swallowed, trying to equalize the pressure. "He's my friend."

"That kind can never be a friend. When the Feds arrested you where was your friend?"

He bought it. Now to play it out. "He was nowhere. And I took the rap." His ears cleared. Forcing a tear from his eye, he started to shiver.

"Stop this crying like a woman. Where is your pride?"

"I got pride," Joey yelled. He stuck out his jaw defiantly. "I been tryin' all my life to make you respect me. To say that I'm a man. Is it my fault I made a mistake?"

Billy was embarrassed by Joey's public humiliation and he was furious that Morgan was being implicated as the snitch. "Shut up, Joey," he said. "Why this thing about Morgan, uncle? He's been trustworthy for many years. Why are you suddenly pointing at him?"

"This Morgan knows too much about our operation. He knew how the drop was to be made. Merida was followed. Me and Poblete were watched. And Guido was arrested. They knew our every move. Now how can that be possible?"

"Someone had to tell them," answered Pantusco, delighted to contribute to the meeting.

Angelo frowned at the intrusion. "In this room are the only people I trust. We have been doing business for many years. Suddenly, the business goes wrong. I ask myself, what's different? Then I remember. Billy, when you and Joey got busted this *mulignan* vanished for two years."

"He did, the sonofabitch," said Joey.

"And then when they was cross-examining you on the stand, who comes strutting into court like a peacock?"

"Bumpy," whispered Billy. "But he went to prison, too."

"Sure he did. But he was paroled after eighteen months. When did you get your parole, Billy?"

"I served my full time."

"What about you, Joey?"

"I got out with Billy. That bastard cut a deal. He sold us out."

"I'm not convinced," said Billy. "Morgan's always been straight with us. He's the only one who puts his money up front. And he always makes the biggest buys."

Angelo waved his hands. "It means nothing. The more he buys the better his price. Who else outside of this room knew all the details of the deal? And why wasn't he implicated by our Federal contact?"

"But he doesn't know anything. Just that a shipment was coming in. He didn't know where or how."

Angelo stood and sneered. "How many people in this room knew even that much? Bumpy knows that Frankie makes the pickup. He also knows that Poblete is our main supplier. Tell me, you're a smart man, how much information do the Feds need to make a case?" He leaned over the table and stared deeply into Billy's eyes. "How much did you tell him, Billy?"

What the fuck is going on here? That bastard is blaming Billy. Nobody fucks with my brother. "You're full of shit, uncle." Joey kicked over his chair and thrust his hand in his pocket, reaching for his pistol.

Both Achille and Rocco reacted instantly. Two pistols were leveled at Joey.

I can make it, Joey thought. *I can kill them both, but the first bullet is for that fat fuck of an uncle.* He tightened his grip on the pistol.

"Stop!" roared Angelo.

Rocco looked disappointed as he holstered his weapon.

Achille didn't understand what was said and only acted when Rocco lowered his pistol.

"Take your hand out of your pocket, Joey," Angelo said quietly. When Joey was slow in responding, Angelo slammed his fist on the table. "Now!"

Joey jumped, but kept his hand locked around the pistol grip. Angelo moved quickly to his nephew's side. Clamping a hand over his shoulder he forced Joey to his knees.

"Take your hand out slowly, Joey," Angelo ordered.

Joey obeyed. As the pistol inched out of the pocket, Angelo grabbed it and pulled it from Joey's hand. In one motion, he dropped the pistol on the table while back-handing Joey in the face, sending him hurtling into the wall. The men sitting at the table were numbed by the rapid turn of events. None moved.

His face stinging, blood dripping from his nose, Joey wheeled around and glared at his uncle. "My brother did not betray you."

"I never said he did."

"Then why . . .?"

Angelo hefted the pistol in his hands. "You would have used this on me?" he whispered. "On your own blood?"

What's the fucking use? He knows. Why is he jerking me around? "Nobody calls my brother a snitch. I'll kill anyone who even thinks it."

"I believe you would, Joseph."

He's never called me Joseph before. What's going on here?

Angelo tossed Joey his pistol. "Put it away, Joseph." Joey sat down as Angelo began pacing with his hands behind his back. He faced the table once again. *Maybe I've misjudged my nephew. He shows the fire of his youth and risked getting killed to protect his brother's honor. Perhaps it's time I think of him as a man.*

Billy regained his composure. "Uncle, we have our contact. Why can't we wait until he tells us who the snitch is?"

"Because we have no time," said Angelo. "We need a delivery in the next two weeks or there will be serious consequences. Already they're mumbling on the streets. No, I won't sacrifice the position of this family because some *mulignan* sold out to the Feds."

"What if you're wrong?" asked Billy.

Angelo shrugged his shoulders. "With that kind, it makes no difference. Besides, it will serve as an example to anyone else who may have ideas." He stood. "I have finished. Leave. All of you except Joey and Billy. We have things to discuss."

Bumpy Morgan licked his fingers clean. He smacked his lips, tossed away the chicken bones, and looked at his watch. It was ten-thirty. Time for his meeting with the Castle brothers.

Brownie's Place was jumping. Bumpy had never seen it so crowded. Or filled with so many fine-looking women. He rubbed his balls as a stone fox with malt-colored skin and a low-cut cocktail dress that exposed three-quarters of her breasts slinked by him. She wore her hair in a natural and smiled broadly at Bumpy.

"Mmmmm. Hey, baby, you lookin' fine. How about making an old man feel young again? Let's play telephone operator." He ogled her huge tits and licked his lips.

She flashed him a big smile as she slid her fingers sensually between her cleavage. Her red tongue peeked from her teeth and fluttered over her lips. "Sugar," she said sweetly. "The call costs a dollar and you can call anytime you want. I'm in the book." She blew a kiss at him and sauntered off.

Bumpy eyed her hungrily, then regretfully looked at his watch again. Ten forty-five. He walked to the park.

The night creatures had taken over the park. Small-time dealers peddled drugs to anyone with some spare bucks. Working girls eased their tired feet by sitting on the benches, careful to keep most of their legs in view as they fished for clients. Underaged kids swigged beer and liquor from brown paper bags. Bumpy felt at home as he passed greetings to several of the denizens of the park.

He wasn't waiting long when a car stopped across the street. The front door opened and he slid in beside the driver. He heard a crinkling sound, and broke into a smile. Plastic. Even on their car seats. But when he saw Rocco Mazzi, the smile froze on his face.

"Hi, Bumpy," said a voice from the back seat.

He looked over his shoulder and saw both Billy and Joey Castelli sitting close together. Billy was smiling.

"What's he doing here?" asked Bumpy as he jerked his head at Rocco. "I thought we was meetin' alone."

"We got business after we leave you. Don't worry about him. He's just the driver," said Billy.

"He's the ugliest fucker I ever saw." Rocco didn't react at all. He kept his eyes on the road. Bumpy relaxed a little. *Let me get this over with. The dude's cold. Makes my skin crawl.* "What about the next delivery? How long before I get my shit? You're sitting on a lot of money of mine."

"Relax, Bumpy. We've had to change our plans. The shipment is due in two weeks."

"That ain't quick enough. My customers be gettin' jumpy. I gots to get me some shit real fast."

Joey stared at Bumpy. *For a* mulignan *he's awfully pushy.* "What's your hurry, man?"

"Don't you listen, chump?" said Bumpy. "I laid some heavy bread on you dudes. And now you jivin' me. I want my delivery."

The car slowed, then stopped abruptly for a light. Bumpy lost his balance and slid gently into the dashboard. His head bumped the windshield. "Ow," he said. He turned to chew out Rocco and got an ice pick jabbed in his left eye.

Rocco pushed the ice pick as far as it could go. Bumpy grunted once, then fell backward, hitting his head on the door. His mouth flopped open. Blood and vitreous humor mingled together and dribbled down his cheek. His body shivered then went still. Rocco grabbed him by the belt buckle and pulled him down. A honking horn reminded Rocco that the light changed color. He pushed down the accelerator.

"Where to, boss?" he asked.

"Stop at the next corner. Me and Joey will get out there. You get rid of Bumpy."

"Where?"

"Drop him at Ferry Point Park. And Rocco, make sure you leave a message telling everyone that this *mulignan* bastard was a snitch."

"I'll handle it."

After dropping off Joey and Billy, Rocco drove slowly with a corpse in the front seat. He glanced at Bumpy's body and laughed.

At Ferry Point Park, Rocco drove to a desolate section

of the parking lot and parked. He glanced furtively around and was convinced that there was no one around. Reaching down, he drew his stiletto from his calf sheath and tested the blade. *Razor sharp. Perfect.*

He pulled the body up to a sitting position so that it leaned against the door. Straddling Bumpy's body, he yanked his tongue from his mouth. With one quick slice, he severed the tongue and held it in his hand. Pulling the ice pick from Bumpy's eye, he used it to impale the tongue on the black man's forehead. It wasn't easy going. After a few minutes of pushing, the ice pick finally penetrated Bumpy's skull. Rocco was covered with sweat, his breath came in gulps, and his chest heaved from the exertion, but he was having the time of his life.

As he sat back and stared at the corpse, he realized that it just didn't look right. He smiled when it came to him. Taking Bumpy's right hand, he positioned the thumb in Bumpy's mouth, then closed his jaw around it. It gave the impression that he was sucking his thumb. *There,* he thought. *Just what was missing.*

He leaned over the body and opened the door. The body tumbled to the ground. Closing the door, he moved behind the steering wheel and drove slowly away.

CHAPTER 21

JOEY CASTELLI'S PALMS were damp. No matter how many times he wiped them, they were still wet. He paced the floor in his apartment, a look of panic fixed on his face. Stopping by the phone, he hesitated, then dialed the familiar number.

"Hello," said a bored voice on the other end of the receiver.

"Can I talk to Fleming?"

"Who is this?"

"Just tell him that Montgomery's calling."

"Sure. Wait one."

Come on. Come on. Hurry it up, dammit. Never should have trusted him. Shoulda taken the rap and did my time.

"What do you want?" asked Fleming.

"Is everything okay?"

"How many damn times are you going to call me? I told you that you have nothing to worry about. When are you going to start trusting me?"

"I don't trust nobody." Joey laughed. "Did you find him?"

"Sure we did. He was dead. You knew that."

"What about the other thing?" Joey clenched the receiver tight in his hands. *That guy had to reach Fleming by now. He told him all about me. I'm a dead man.*

"You were right. He approached me."

"What happened?"

"You're still alive, aren't you? Now stop bugging me. I told you I'd handle this. You got nothing to worry about. Don't lose your nerve. And, dammit, stop calling me." He slammed down the phone, causing the other agents in the room to look up from their desks. Fleming ignored their questioning glances.

He plopped down behind his desk and put his feet up. Placing his hands behind his head, he stared at the stained, cream-colored wall. *Who the hell picks out the colors for these damn offices? Cream, for Chrissake. What the hell is this supposed to be? A ladies' lounge or a government office? This is going all wrong. Powers on the pad. Trying to bribe me for Joey's name. Then making veiled threats if I didn't cooperate. Dick was never very subtle.*

He should have been suspicious at the way Powers pumped him for information, but he never suspected his friend was corrupt. They had stopped for drinks after work the day before, sitting at a far booth away from all the noise at the bar. "This whole bust has been one big fuckup," said Powers. "It's going nowhere. You got zero."

"I've got enough," said Fleming defensively.

"Bullshit. You got some low-level disposables. The big guys are still free and clear. You know, you can make a lot of enemies in a job like this."

"Tell me something I don't know already."

"It's all so much bullshit anyway. Look, boyo, you ever see any big shot get nabbed over any of this?"

Fleming was silent.

"Of course not," continued Powers. "Because they walk. Every swinging dick among them. And what do you get for it? Ulcers. A busted-up marriage. A booze-soaked liver."

"What are you trying to tell me, Dick?"

Powers sighed and patted Fleming on the shoulder. "Be smart. Drop this thing. There are some people who would be very pleased if you lost interest in this case."

Well, I'll be fucking damned, thought Fleming. *I knew you cut corners, but I never expected you to sell out.* He pretended to think about the proposal. "You want the number of my Swiss bank account?" He grinned.

"If that's where you want the money sent."

Fleming sat up. "What is this, Dick? Are you trying to bribe me?"

"You know, Ed, you got no damn brains. Guts, yes. But you left your brains someplace. Stop being a Pollyanna. You know what I'm talking about."

"I know what," replied Fleming. "I just don't know why."

"Don't you worry yourself about it, boyo. You just think about the offer."

"How much?"

Powers considered the question. "How about twenty grand?"

Fleming laughed. "You're one cheap sonofabitch. Make it two-fifty and we'll do some talking."

"You're crazy. They'll never go for that."

Fleming leaned across the table so that his nose almost touched Dick's. "That's my price. No negotiation." He sat back in his chair, laughing inside. *That should shut him up.*

Powers returned his stare and measured his friend. "You surprise me, Ed. I guess I had you pegged wrong. This isn't your first, is it?"

Fleming waved that aside, eager to end this discussion. "Never mind about that. What do you say?"

"You got it. Where do you want it sent?"

Fleming stared for a moment, then decided to go along with the joke. "I've got a post office box . . ."

"Not so fast, Ed. I gotta have something first."

Now it was Fleming's turn for a measuring glance. "What?"

"I want the guy who clued you in to the bust."

Fleming's reaction was immediate. "No fucking way. He's not gonna end up like Larry. Forget it. No deal." He stood up and tried to leave the table, but Powers grabbed his hand.

"Sit down, Ed." When Fleming hesitated, Powers flicked open his jacket so that his pistol could be seen. The message was not lost on Fleming. He sat down. "You're gonna play, Ed. Or you won't be around to get the final score."

"You're not getting his name."

"Why do you give a shit, Ed? Protecting that scum. Give

him up. They're gonna find out sooner or later. It might as well be from you. That way you can show them you're on their side."

"Let me think about it."

"Don't think too long, friend. You have twenty-four hours to make up your mind." As Fleming got up to leave, Powers held up his hand.

"Now what?" asked Fleming.

Powers reached into his shirt and pulled out a tiny receiver. "Don't fuck me up, Ed. I got it all down on tape. I want that name. And I want it fast."

Fleming glanced at his watch and noticed that it was nearly one-thirty. He peeked into Kohler's office, but it was empty. Glancing around the office, he saw an agent surrounded by huge stacks of reports. "Hey, Lamberti, where'd he go?"

Fred Lamberti looked up from the mound of paperwork that littered his desk. The dark-haired former Marine liked field work but dreaded the paperwork that followed. "He went to lunch with Dick Powers," he said.

"You know where?"

"What do I look like, his secretary?" snapped Lamberti.

"Nah. Your legs aren't good enough."

"Go to hell, Fleming."

Dammit, thought Fleming. *He's out pumping Kohler. That stupid sonofabitch will spill his guts.* He hurried from the office and headed for McAnn's, but they were not there. Nor were they in the rest of the spots where Kohler usually liked to go. Smothering the thoughts that raced around his brain, he calmed himself enough to wait in his car, hoping that one of them would call in on the radio.

The jumble of radio traffic droned on monotonously and Fleming scarcely paid attention. Experienced agents quickly learned to ignore any transmission that didn't immediately concern them. At five o'clock, Kohler called in.

His voice was slurred and Fleming turned up the volume to catch his every word. *What if Powers shot him?* he wondered. But the disjointed character of the transmission convinced Fleming that Kohler was drunk. He broke into Kohler's message.

"I want to talk to you," interrupted Fleming. "Back at the office. In ten minutes."

"Howya doin', buddy? No talkin' just now. Need sleep. W-wonderful s-sleep. No more talkin'. Bye-bye."

"Dammit, listen to me. Come in. Come in." *That bastard sounds like he's drunk out of his damn mind.* Fleming pounded angrily on his steering wheel. *That asshole. He probably told Powers all about Joey. And signed his fucking death warrant. I've got to find out what he said.*

Fleming's car stopped in front of Kohler's colonial in Holmdel, New Jersey. There were no lights on and no cars in the driveway. He waited patiently for Kohler to arrive.

A slate-blue sedan turned onto the street and had a difficult time keeping to the center of the road. It wobbled right and left, narrowly missing two parked cars. *This has to be Kohler,* thought Fleming.

The sedan turned into Kohler's driveway but drove instead up on the front lawn, where it stopped. The door opened. George Kohler stumbled from the car and fell, face first, on the grass. He curled his head into the crook of his arm and tried to sleep.

Fleming bolted from his car. He reached Kohler and pulled him to his feet. The odor of vomit and beer assailed his nostrils and the front of Kohler's jacket was wet.

"Jesus Christ, George. What the hell are you doing?"

"That you, Fleming?" Kohler peered at him from hooded eyes. He burped, sending a noxious blast of air into Fleming's face.

"You're fucking drunk," yelled Fleming.

"I couldn't fuck if you held it for me." He giggled. "Just let me sleep." He went limp in Fleming's arms.

Reaching into Kohler's pocket, Fleming pulled out his house keys. Then he slung him over his shoulder in a fireman's carry, lugged him into the house, and dropped him on the family room sofa. He opened up some cabinets and found a can of coffee, but couldn't find a coffeepot. On the sofa, Kohler snored peacefully.

Fleming shook him awake. "Where's the coffeepot?"

"Huh?"

"Listen to me, dammit. Where's the coffeepot?"

"Don't want no coffee. Just sleep. Let me sleep."

Fleming shook him, but Kohler was snoring loudly once again. He slung him over his shoulders like a sack of potatoes and carried him upstairs. Locating the master bedroom, he lugged him into the bathroom. He lay Kohler in the tub and turned on an ice-cold shower.

At first, the water had no effect and Kohler still slept. Suddenly, he shivered and his eyes snapped open. Not knowing where he was, he tried to stand and slipped in the tub. The water drenched his soiled suit and pelted him in the face. "What the fuck?" he shouted and tried to turn off the spigots.

Fleming slapped his hands away. "George. It's me, Ed. Do you hear me?"

"Yeah, I hear you. I'm not deaf. What the hell's going on here?"

"Did you have lunch with Powers?"

"What of it? Can't this wait till tomorrow? I'm beat." He tried to close his eyes but Fleming pried them open with his fingers.

Fleming was getting soaking wet but didn't care. He had to find out what Kohler told Powers. Slapping Kohler's face, he yelled at him. "Did you tell him about my snitch?"

Kohler opened his eyes. "You don't have no snatch, Ed. You got a prick. Shouldn't drink so much."

"Dammit. Did you tell him about Joey?"

"He knew all about him."

"What are you talking about? Only you and I knew his name."

Kohler slapped at Fleming with a limp-wristed motion. "I know that. He told me you wanted him to put him under pro-*tec*-tion. So I told him who he was."

"I never told him shit. What else did you tell him?" Fleming shook Kohler by the shoulders, trying to keep him awake.

"Told him about Davis."

Just fucking great. He's not only got Joey's name, but the proof that he's my snitch. Fleming reared back and punched Kohler in the stomach. Kohler burped, then vomited into the tub. As the bathroom filled with the vile smell of beer and decaying food, Fleming lost whatever control he had left.

Grabbing Kohler by the hair, he dragged him from the tub and held him over the toilet bowl. Kohler obliged him and sent another stream of vomit into the bowl. As he retched and gagged, Fleming kept slapping his face.

"You big-mouthed, stupid sonofabitch. Do you know what you just did?"

"Yep. I just peed in my pants."

Fleming dunked Kohler's head in the vomit-filled bowl.

He held him there for a couple of seconds then pulled him out.

Gasping for air, Kohler waved his arms. "Hey, Ed, flush the bowl, will ya?" he choked. "This stuff smells like shit."

Fleming lifted Kohler to his feet and punched him once in the jaw. Kohler's head snapped back and he lost consciousness. Fleming dropped him in the tub, under the running shower.

He raced to the bedroom and dialed Joey's number. *Be there. Answer it,* he pleaded silently. After twenty-five rings, he hung up. *Got to get back to the city.*

Kohler was unconscious in the tub. Fleming shut off the water and stared down at his supervisor. "You just killed a man, you shithead," he said aloud. "You killed him just as if you pulled the trigger yourself." Kohler hiccupped. More vomit dribbled from his mouth.

Fleming's stomach spasmed and he swallowed hard to keep from puking. He raced from the house, taking huge gulps of fresh air. When his stomach calmed, he drove back to Manhattan, hoping to find Joey in the city.

The ringing of the telephone jarred Frankie Tartagliano from a restless sleep. He sat up on the couch. For a moment, he didn't know where he was and it was only when he heard his brother's voice that he remembered being summoned to Angelo's house the night before. Angelo didn't say much and was clearly preoccupied, but he wanted Frankie by his side. So the two men waited all night until Frankie drifted off to sleep at four in the morning.

As Frankie rubbed the sleep from his eyes, he heard only snatches of the one-sided conversation. But he could see Angelo's face. It turned beet red, as though it would explode, then it sagged and Angelo looked like an old man. He hung up the phone.

"What is it, brother?" asked Frankie. "Bad news?"

"The worst," said Angelo. "We have discovered the traitor."

Frankie was instantly alert. "Who is the sonofabitch?"

"Your nephew Joey."

Frankie's mouth dropped in shock. "You're crazy. He's family."

"I have proof."

"It's bullshit. He's a fucked-up kid. But he's no traitor."

Angelo sagged in his chair. *"Basta,* Frankie. He's the one. There is no doubt."

"How did you find out?"

"My Federal informer got his name from Fleming's supervisor. But I didn't believe him at first."

"What convinced you?"

"He also got another name. Mike Davis."

"Who the hell is he?"

"The one from Philly. The college punk, who only buys to sell to his rich friends. Rocco and Achille had a little talk with him."

"That little *schifosa!"* Frankie stood up and paced the floor. "What's he got to do with all this anyway?"

"Sit down, Frankie," said Angelo. "And listen. Davis was picked up by the Feds the day before the buy went bad. He was Joey's man, and only Joey knew about him. A nickel-and-dime punk."

"But why would Joey do such a thing?"

"Because he's afraid of going back to prison. He's made a deal with the Feds."

"What deal?"

"I don't know. And I don't care."

"I just don't believe it," said Frankie.

"What's not to believe?" said Angelo. "That the blood of my blood could ever be an informer? He's weak. I've always known that. I made allowances for him. So did you. We always knew what he was like. But we chose to ignore it because he was family. No more. I have no nephew."

"Where is this Davis?"

"He's dead. Rocco disposed of him when he was finished."

"So what do we do now?"

Angelo's eyes went cold. "Joey is a threat to us. And he must be treated like any other traitor. Billy is going to be very busy . . ."

"No!" Frankie yelled. "Not Billy. You can't expect him to kill his own brother."

"He must demonstrate his loyalty . . ."

"I'll do it."

"You?"

"He'll never suspect me. We're friends. We grew up together. I'll make it fast and painless."

Angelo forced a smile. "This must happen soon—before we make any further plans."

"I'll take care of it, Angelo." He strode over to his brother and kissed him on the forehead. "The next time you hear about our nephew will be when he's dead." He left the room.

Angelo shuffled out of the study and walked to his bedroom where he lay on his back, staring at the ceiling. *Joseph, you're a disappointment to me. Your courage the other night came from the fear of exposure, not love of your brother. Your father was a man. Why couldn't you take after him?* In moments, he was asleep.

CHAPTER 22

FRANKIE TARTAGLIANO took careful aim at Joey's photograph on the wall and cocked the hammer of the pistol. He squeezed the trigger and the sound of the hammer striking the cylinder startled him each time. Holding the open revolver in his right hand, he spun the cylinder with his left hand. After carefully inserting five bullets, he closed the cylinder with a flick of the wrist. Next came the sound muffler. The bulky, long cylindrical extension was designed to lessen the report of the weapon. It also made the gun awkward and hard to hold steady. Frankie debated its practicality. Caution won out and he shoved the silenced pistol into the waistband of his gray trousers.

He put on a navy blue sport jacket and buttoned it. Checking his image in the mirror, he was pleased to see that the pistol did not show. Frankie rummaged through his dresser drawer and pulled out a picture.

It showed Billy, Frankie, and Joey pretending to be muscle men at Rockaway Beach. *Look at us,* he thought. *Skinny as hell and having the time of our lives. I buried Joey in the sand that day so that only his face was uncovered. He even made me cover him all the way. Just breathed through a straw that I stuck in his mouth. Looked like a sand dune. Someone almost stuck an umbrella in him.* Frankie chuckled as he remembered the shocked look on the woman's face when the sand dune got up and started walking away.

But that was another time and they were all different people then. Now Joey would be buried for real and he would be the executioner. Frankie's hands started shaking and he stared at them in wonder. He poured himself a shot of Scotch and gulped it down. His hands were rock-steady.

The street noises from the San Gennaro feast filtered into his apartment. Frankie stuck his head out of the window. Joey never missed the feast. He'd kill him there. Hoisting his pants up with both hands, Frankie took a deep breath. *Too bad, kid,* he thought. *You shoulda kept your mouth shut.* He shut the light in the kitchen and locked up his apartment, then walked out into the streets to find Joey.

The eleven-day orgy of food and games known as the San Gennaro Feast in New York's Little Italy usually begins on or about September 19. The feast commemorates the martyrdom of Gennaro, the bishop of Benevento in the third century A.D. He was sentenced to death by the Roman proconsul Timothy for giving comfort to imprisoned Christians.

After his arrest, he was subjected to torture but never renounced his faith. As punishment, he was hurled headfirst into a furnace. Miraculously, he escaped unharmed. But his tormentors did not give up and Gennaro was beheaded. A woman who cared for his body put some drops of his blood into a glass vial. The blood soon solidified.

As the legend goes, some forty years after Gennaro's death his relics were being moved to Naples when the powdered blood liquefied. Neapolitans made him their patron saint and pray to Gennaro for favors and protection from disasters. Begun in New York in the 1920s by local businessmen and religious leaders, the once small, local festival now stretched along most of Mulberry Street from Chinatown to Kenmare Street.

Brightly colored booths lined both sides of Mulberry Street, offering a dizzying variety of games of chance and a belly-bursting choice of food. The smells of cooking sausages, zeppolles, pizza, calzone, and other delights made Joey Castelli's mouth water. He hadn't gone very far when he stopped at a sausage stand that used a barbecue pit instead of a griddle.

"Hey, *paisan*," he said. "How are the sausages?"

A pimply-faced teenager grinned in return. "Best in town."

"Let me have a samich. One sweet and one hot. And gimme a lot of onions." He watched hungrily as the youngster filled the hero.

Joey flipped the kid his money and bit down into the hero. It was terrific. The sausages were burnt on the out-side and juicy on the inside. The onions were crisp, not soggy. Now all he needed was a bottle of beer to wash it all down. Finding a stand, he ordered a Beck's. It was ice-cold.

This is great, Joey thought. *A nice big hero and a cold beer. The sun is shining and I got laid twenty minutes ago. Things couldn't be better.* He finished the hero and drained the bottle of beer. A belch worked its way out of his stomach, causing a blonde midwestern tourist to wrin-kle her nose in distaste.

"Do you mind?" she asked primly as she stared disgust-edly at Joey.

"Not at all, lady," Joey replied. He burped again in her face. "I got that one from real deep so you can bring it back home with ya."

The woman backed away from Joey, who chuckled at her discomfort.

"What's the matter, lady? Ain't you got no smells where ya come from?" He was going to harass her further but the sight of two burly policemen made him cringe. He averted his eyes and walked right by them.

He searched the crowd for his mother but he didn't see her. The parade was going to begin soon and it was his family's custom to attach dollar bills to the statue of San Gennaro as it was carried past. His mother believed that by doing that, good fortune would shine on the Castelli family for the coming year.

Joey thought it was all so much shit but he didn't want to disappoint his mother. Besides, this year he needed all the luck he could get. Maybe San Gennaro would get him out of this mess. Just up ahead he could see his mother and

Billy standing on the corner of Grand and Mulberry streets. He waved to them in the crowd but they did not see him.

The crush of people got thick as the statue wended its way up the street. Joey was jostled and pushed until he found himself sandwiched between a heavy, moustached Italian woman and a short, baldheaded priest.

A hand reached out and tapped Joey on the shoulder. He brushed it off angrily. The tapping became a punch, and Joey spun around. "Hey, what's it with you?" he yelled.

"What are you doin' there, Joey? Why aren't you with your mother? She's been looking all over for you." It was Uncle Frankie.

"I got here late." He elbowed the woman behind him. "Keep off me, lady. Stop poking me. What do you think this is?"

The woman ignored him and continued to press forward. Joey couldn't believe it. He threw up his hands in frustration and squirmed his way to his uncle.

"Fuckin' nuts, these religious assholes. They'd climb right up my ass if they could get a better look at that damn statue."

"Watch it, Joey. That's a saint." Frankie blessed himself as the statue went by.

"Not you, too, Uncle Frankie? I thought you was different."

"What's the matter, Joey? Don't ya believe in the saint?"

"I don't believe in nothin' but warm pussy and hot food." He chuckled at his joke. "What are ya doin', Uncle Frankie? I don't usually see you here."

"I was lookin' for you. Come with me. I want to show you something."

"What is it?"

"Come on. You'll get a kick out of this."

Joey followed Frankie through the thick crowds. It was slow going and more than once Frankie had to wait for his nephew. But he was not about to let Joey out of his sight. At Hester Street, Frankie turned left. Joey stayed right behind him.

"What's this about?"

"Not now," said Frankie. "Come on."

"Where we going?"

"Mott Street. Now shut up and come on. There are too many ears here."

What the hell is this all about? wondered Joey. *What the hell is on Mott Street?*

The pedestrian traffic was thinner and Joey walked beside his uncle. Frankie stopped in front of a tall iron grating that blocked off an alley. He pushed the gate open and stepped into the shadows.

"Hurry it up, Joey," snapped Frankie.

He's awfully nervous, thought Joey. *I don't like this alley one damn bit. No way I'm going in there.* Joey hesitated at the entrance to the alley but Frankie reached out, grabbed him by the shirt front, and pulled him off his feet. He threw Joey into a garbage can.

As Joey tried to right himself, Frankie reached into his waistband and pulled out the silenced pistol. Joey's eyes grew wide and he got on his knees. "What are you doing, Uncle Frankie? For God's sake, I didn't do nothin'."

"Shut up, Joey. Don't make this any harder than it has to be." He aimed at Joey's head. "Just stand still. This will be real quick if you don't struggle. I don't want to hurt you."

"But why?"

"Angelo knows that you sold him out. You gotta pay."

"Holy Mother of God, don't shoot me." Joey buried his head in his hands and refused to look at his uncle.

Even in death, he'll act like a worm, Frankie thought. "Get up. Die like a man." He cocked the pistol and pointed it at Joey's head.

Joey raised his tear-stained face to his uncle. *Think of something. Quick! Or you're dead!* "Don't let me die like this. Not like this. Give me time to say a prayer."

Frankie took careful aim and started squeezing the trigger.

"Please, Uncle Frankie, just one prayer. How long can it take? Ten seconds? Fifteen seconds?"

"Make it quick." Frankie lowered the pistol and Joey saw the opportunity he was searching for. He butted Frankie in the stomach with his head.

Frankie's breath whooshed out of his lungs and he staggered backward. Joey scrambled to his feet and rammed his shoulder into Frankie's chest. His uncle flew off his feet and struck the wall of the alley. He slid down the wall, gasping for breath as Joey fled the alley.

Joey slipped on a tomato and fell into a pile of garbage-filled crates. As he tried to get up, he kept slipping on wet garbage. Scuttling forward on his hands and knees, he tried to get some distance between himself and Frankie.

It took a minute for Frankie to catch his breath. *Sonofabitch. The little shit got away.* He reached for his pistol. Grabbing it by the trigger, he jammed it into his trousers but the silencer snagged on his pant leg. As he pushed it down, the revolver went off, sending a bullet scorching down his thigh.

"Oh, fuck!" he cried. *"Madre mia!* I'm shot!" His leg was wet and sticky. Unbuckling his pants, he dropped his trousers and examined the wound. An angry red line traveled down the inside of his thigh. It burned like fire and hurt like hell but he could see it wasn't serious. *You'll pay for this, Joey. You'll pay.*

He picked up the pistol and unscrewed the silencer. "Piece of shit." He hurled it down the alley and ran out onto Mott Street. He looked carefully but saw no sign of Joey. Taking off his jacket, he draped it over his arm, making sure that it covered his pistol.

Blood was staining his slacks but he didn't care. He wanted Joey dead, and nothing was going to stop him.

When Joey reached Mulberry Street, he hoped to lose himself in the crowds. He saw Billy waving to him. *Billy, too?* he wondered but he didn't wait for an answer. Pushing his way down the crowded street, he got many angry looks that turned meek when they saw the terror on Joey's face. A path cleared for him in the crush of people.

At Hester Street, Joey hesitated, then ran straight for Connie's house. *She'll protect me,* he thought. *Got to get outta here. Need money. Got to hide.* He tripped on the steps of Connie's apartment building. Reaching her door, he pounded on it with his fists.

"Open up, Connie! Open up!" he yelled. "Hurry."

"Keep your shirt on," came the reply from behind the closed door. It opened just a crack as Connie peered out to see who it was. Joey hit the door with his shoulder. The safety chain snapped and Joey burst inside, knocking Connie off her feet. He slammed the door shut.

"Where's my gun?" he shrieked.

"What's going on?" Connie replied as she shook her head to clear the black dots that danced before her eyes.

Joey ran into the bedroom and started ripping the bed apart. He flung the pillows over his shoulder, then ripped the covers from the bed. Whimpering like a frightened child, he shook both hands by his sides. *Think. Think,* he commanded. *Where did I leave the fucking gun?*

Frankie limped to Mulberry Street. It was impossible to see where Joey had gone. *Dammit. Angelo's gonna be pissed. I let that shithead get away.* He bullied his way into the throng, grimacing each time he took a step. *I'll find that bastard.*

A quick movement to his right made him swivel his head and he saw Billy coming toward him.

"Hey, Uncle Frankie, what are you doing here?" he asked.

"Where's your brother?"

"I just saw him a couple of minutes ago. What do you want him for?"

"We got business. Where'd he go?"

"I saw him go up Hester. He's probably goin' to Connie's house."

Frankie brushed by him, a look of cold anger on his face, and Billy noticed the limp. When he looked at Frankie's leg he saw blood dripping from the trouser leg. "Frankie! What is it? You okay?" He reached for his uncle's arm but Frankie pushed him away with his left arm. Billy saw the pistol under the jacket.

He tried to grab Frankie. "What are you gonna do? What happened?"

Frankie came up to Billy and jammed the pistol into Billy's stomach. "You stay the fuck out of this, Billy. It's your brother I want." He shoved Billy into a jewelry vendor, knocking over the stand. As Billy struggled to right himself, Frankie hurried to Hester Street, his limp getting worse with each step.

Billy struggled to his feet and silenced the shouting vendor by giving him a hundred-dollar bill. The man smiled and pocketed the money as Billy raced off. He saw his mother talking with some friends. Pulling her aside, he whispered urgently to her. "Call Angelo. He's put a hit out on Joey. I'll try to stop Frankie. Hurry."

Felicia's face became a mask of horror and she blessed herself as Billy hurled himself into the crowd.

Joey found his pistol in Connie's underwear drawer, wrapped in a black teddy. He unwrapped the garment and fumbled at the magazine release. The magazine slipped into his hand and he checked the bullets. *All here. Now where's my money?*

"What the hell did you do to my room?" shouted Connie. "This place's a fucking mess."

"Frankie's trying to kill me," Joey said. "You gotta help me get out of here."

Connie stared at him, her face a mixture of fear and surprise. "What the hell did you do?"

"It's not important. You got to help me."

"No way, Joey. I may be dumb but even I know that Frankie don't do anything without Angelo's say-so. I'm not getting involved in this. Let me out of here." She backed out of the room.

"Stop! You gotta help me," Joey cried. He ran after her and tried to tackle her in the living room but missed. Connie reached the door and yanked it open.

Frankie whacked her in the cheek with his pistol and popped two quick shots off at Joey, who stood staring at him with his mouth wide open. Both shots went wide. One shattered a lamp. The other buried itself in the sofa.

As he stepped into the room, Connie swung her fist and hit Frankie in the ear. The unexpected attack stunned him and he took his eyes off Joey for just a second. Joey hurled himself at his uncle and hit him high in the chest, knocking him into the hallway where he landed on his back.

Joey stomped on Frankie's gun hand but his uncle would not let go of the weapon. He kneed Frankie in the nose, breaking it instantly. As blood ran down his face, Frankie fought to remain conscious. Joey grabbed him by the hair and pounded his head on the floor until Frankie's mouth lolled open. The pistol eased from his hands.

Grabbing his uncle by the feet, he dragged him into Connie's apartment. He picked up Frankie's pistol and thrust it into his back pocket. Joey's breath came in ragged gasps as he stared at his semi-conscious uncle. Connie sat sobbing in the corner, rubbing her swollen cheek already turning black and blue.

What the fuck am I gonna do? How am I gonna get out of this? he thought. He turned to Connie. "Oh, shut the fuck up, Connie. You ain't hurt that bad. Let me think."

"Joey, look out," Connie shrieked.

Frankie swung at Joey with a hassock, but missed. Joey ducked and punched his uncle in the stomach. Frankie grunted but kept on coming. He gripped Joey in a bear hug and started squeezing the life out of him.

Joey couldn't catch his breath. He was getting dizzy. "Connie, help me. Help me! He's killing me!" But Connie couldn't move. Fear rooted her in the corner, her eyes wide. Joey slumped over Frankie's shoulder and his vision blurred. In desperation, he set his teeth into the lobe of Frankie's ear. Frankie yelled, loosening his hold.

Joey didn't loosen his. Blood filled his mouth as he twisted his head, ripping the earlobe right off Frankie's head with a mighty jerk.

Now Frankie howled in pain and dropped Joey to the

floor. He cupped his hand to his ear to stem the flow of blood and bellowed when he realized that Joey had bitten part of it off. He growled and faced Joey, who had pulled his pistol and pointed it at his uncle.

Joey tried to speak but realized that he still held Frankie's earlobe in his teeth. He spat it to the floor. "Stay the fuck away, Frankie. I'll kill you. I swear it."

"You're a dead man, Joey. It's only a matter of time." He inched forward.

"Don't make me kill you," Joey pleaded as his finger tightened on the trigger.

Frankie's eyes narrowed and he stepped closer.

BANG! A tiny hole appeared below Frankie's right eye. He staggered. Joey fired again. This round caught Frankie in the chest. He stumbled, then fell to his knees. Frankie stared at his chest in shock for a split second before falling face first to the floor.

Joey giggled in hysteria, then walked over to his dead uncle and kicked him in the side. The body absorbed the blow but did not move. "I told you to leave me alone, Frankie," he said. "But you wouldn't listen." He turned to Connie. "You heard me, Connie. Didn't you?"

"You killed him. You *killed* him." Connie pulled her legs up and hugged them, burying her face in her knees. "Don't hurt me."

Joey ran to Connie and dropped down beside her. "I didn't want to do it. He made me." He tried to hug her, but she pushed him away.

"You've got to get out of here. You can't stay here. Get out." She got slowly to her feet. "Go on, get out of here."

A pounding on the door startled her. "Who's that?" she yelled.

"It's me, Billy. Where's my brother? I got to talk to him."

The door opened and Billy stepped inside. He was stunned by the sight that awaited him. Joey sat against the wall, blood smeared on his lips and chin, a pistol dangling from his hand. Connie was standing, the right side of her face swollen and misshapen, purple bruises getting darker. In the center of the living room lay Frankie Tartagliano, facedown on the rug, a dark stain beneath him.

"What the fuck happened?" Billy said. He knelt beside Frankie and put his fingers near the carotid artery on Frankie's neck. There was no pulse. "He's dead. What the hell did you do?"

"He tried to kill me, Billy," sobbed Joey.

"Why?"

"I don't know. He just went fucking nuts."

Billy walked over to his brother, took the pistol from his hands, then calmly slapped Joey across the face. "Don't give me that shit. Frankie didn't do nothing without orders from Uncle Angelo."

"Why would uncle want to kill me?"

Billy suddenly knew the truth. "You dumb bastard. *You're* the one. You sold us out."

"I . . ."

"You fucking sold us out. My own brother."

"Billy, you gotta help me. I had no choice. I don't want to go back to prison."

Billy aimed the pistol at Joey. "I ought to kill you myself. You sonofabitch. Do you know what you've done? You put us all in danger. First you pull that dumbass stunt and nearly get Mamma arrested, then you fink on us to the Feds."

"Billy, please let me live. You're my brother. Don't let this happen to me."

"Shut up. Let me think." Billy stood rooted to the floor,

tears misting his eyes as he stared down at Frankie's body. But after a couple of minutes, his voice was cold, all business. "You're damn lucky it's noisy out there. If they wasn't lightin' off firecrackers and shit the cops would be all over this place. Connie, cover up Frankie with a sheet or something." His control wavered for a second. "Have some respect for the dead. And you—" He faced Joey. "I'll try to get you out of this."

"Please," begged Joey.

"But this is the last fucking time. Get the fuck out of New York. Get out of the country."

"Where?"

"You can go to hell for all I care. Just keep away from me and Mamma. You're dead as far as we're concerned. I'll talk to Uncle Angelo. See if I can calm him down. You shouldn't have killed Frankie. He'll never forgive you for that."

"Don't tell him . . ."

"Shut up, Joey. You stay here. Don't fucking move. I'll be back in a little while. I'll figure something out." Billy left the apartment.

Joey and Connie tried straightening up the apartment to keep busy. But it was no use. Frankie's corpse reminded both of them that there was no turning back now. They had to stay together and the thought made both of them uncomfortable.

Both of them took turns drinking from a full bottle of Scotch. In less than an hour the bottle was nearly empty but neither was drunk. The phone rang, startling them. It rang ten times, but Connie made no move to pick it up.

"Answer it, dammit," Joey said.

"Do it yourself," replied Connie.

Joey snarled at her and grabbed the receiver. He held

235

it away from his ear. "Who is it?" he inquired timidly.

"It's me, Fleming."

"What do you want?"

"Angelo knows you're my snitch. You've got to lay low for a while until I can get you some protection."

"You're hot shit, Fleming. You're really hot shit. But you're too fucking late."

He slammed the receiver down on its cradle, then laughed until he cried.

CHAPTER 23

ANGELO gritted his teeth and kept clenching and unclenching his fists. His lips were pulled across his teeth in an evil grimace. But it was his eyes that stopped Billy from saying anything further. They were black dots burning with the fury of anger and glinting with the fire of revenge.

"Are you sure Frankie's dead?" he asked.

"He's dead. No pulse. Even the blood stopped spreading. I don't think Joey meant to kill him."

Angelo's eyes burned a hole through Billy's chest and pierced his heart. "Are you defending him?" he whispered, so softly that Billy had to strain to hear him.

Watch what you say, Billy. This is no time for mistakes. One wrong word and you'll be dead. "No," he replied with an even voice.

"You'd better not. Trouble. He's been nothing but trouble from the day he was born. I don't know how your father could have made a kid like him. It's as though he isn't even a member of the family. Always on his own. Never listening. And now a traitor. And a murderer. You took his gun. Why didn't you kill him yourself?"

"Connie was still there. I didn't want no witnesses."

"She's a *putana.* No one will miss her."

"She's got family, uncle. And they wouldn't take kindly to such a drastic action."

"Now I take orders from you? You tell me my business? *You,* who only just got off your mother's tit? She's nobody. You dispose of her like you would throw away the shell of a nut."

Now he's after Connie. That fucking brother of mine. He's put all of us in danger. Well, not me. And not Connie. She may be a whore but she don't deserve to die for his bullshit. "Uncle, this whole business with Joey is destroying our family. I take the responsibility. But who could figure that he would become an informer? I should have had Rocco kill him instead of breaking his legs."

I must see how loyal he really is. He says the right things, but I've got to be sure. "You would have killed your own brother? For disobedience?"

"Uncle, I won't lie to you. I love Joey. He's my brother. But the family comes first. It comes before Jean and my sons. Even my own mother, your sister, is second. I would die for you."

Angelo reached into his desk, pulled out a pistol, cocked

it, and aimed at Billy. He fired. The loud report echoed in the study, bringing both Rocco and Achille bursting into the room, their pistols at the ready. Angelo stopped them by raising his hand.

"Leave us. You're not needed."

Rocco hesitated and Achille kept his pistol trained at Billy, who hadn't moved a muscle.

"Are you deaf?" yelled Angelo. "Get the hell out of here."

As his bodyguards backed out of the room, Angelo again pointed his weapon at Billy. He came out from behind the desk and walked up to his nephew, placing the barrel of the pistol in Billy's ear.

The barrel was warm from its recent discharge, yet the feel of the metal on his ear made Billy shiver. *This is it. I'm fucking getting killed because of that sonofabitch brother of mine. At least I'm out of it. I'm tired of it all. The deceit. The fear. I got no life but the family. Now I'll be free of it at last.* He stared into his uncle's eyes. *I want one last look at you, motherfucker. You won't see me beg. I'm a better man than you'll ever be.*

"Good-bye, Billy," said Angelo. The hammer clicked on an empty chamber, but Billy still did not move. His calmness infuriated the older man. "What's the matter with you? Got icewater for blood?"

"If I gotta die, I'll die like a man. Not some shitassed coward."

Angelo slapped him on the shoulder. "That's what I want to hear." He flung the pistol to the sofa. "Blanks. It's not loaded. I just wanted to see how you would react. You had no fear. That's good. Very good. Now, when are you going to kill Joey?"

"I'm not," Billy replied. Angelo's face reddened in

anger. Before he could reply, Billy went smoothly on. "Joey's holed up in Connie's apartment. He's scared shit-less. He ain't goin' nowhere. But he did kill Frankie. And he's still got two pistols. If I tried to take him out, he'd probably kill me, too. And I'm not about to lose my life to that little prick."

"So what do you propose?"

"I need one hundred thousand dollars. I'll tell him that you never want to see him in New York again. And that if you do, you'll order him killed. He's stupid. He'll be-lieve it."

"Then what?"

"I'll give him a one-way plane ticket."

Angelo snorted. "My brother is dead and you give his killer money and a plane ticket. I don't like the sound of this."

Billy's eyes narrowed. "You'll like the rest . . ."

Frankie's body was draped in a sheet. Connie sat on the sofa, holding a bag of ice on her swollen cheek. She thumbed through a magazine with her free hand. Every time Joey moved closer to her, she would smack him with the magazine.

"C'mon, Connie, give me a break," Joey said.

"Keep your hands off me, Joey. I told you before I don't want nothing more to do with you."

"What is it with you? Just this morning you screwed my brains out. Now you treat me like I got the clap."

"This morning was different. You weren't a murderer then."

"Hey, watch it with that murderer shit. You saw what

he did. He tried to kill me. What was I supposed to do? Let him?"

Connie threw her magazine on the floor and stood up. Crossing her arms across her chest, she tapped her foot on the rug. Suddenly, she kicked out her foot, knocking over the coffee table. Joey grabbed for a glass candy jar and caught it before it hit the floor. But a cut-glass vase filled with artificial flowers shattered into three pieces.

"When the hell is your brother coming back? And what about that body? It just can't stay here like this."

"What do you want me to do, Connie? Sling him over my shoulder and throw him out with the trash? Billy told me to wait. And that's just what I'm going to do. Now you just sit down and keep your mouth shut."

His tone sliced through Connie like a knife. She started to reply, but this was a different Joey from the one she had slept with earlier in the day. Gone was the weasel. In his place was a skittish, dangerous man. The tension had hooded his eyes and left him physically drained. But each time he held one of the pistols, he seemed to grow in size. He was more confident now, and the weapons were his courage.

When there was a knock on the door, Connie nearly screamed. Joey silenced her by clamping his hand over her mouth. He held her in front of him as he aimed the 9mm automatic at the door.

"Who is it?"

"Open up. It's me, Billy."

Joey followed Connie to the door and stood with his back to the wall. When the door opened, he wanted a clear shot at whoever followed his brother into the apartment.

Connie waited for him to position himself before letting Billy in.

He entered rapidly, carrying a briefcase and a suitcase.

"How'd it go?" asked Joey.

Billy looked pained. "Not good. He really wants you dead. You never should have killed Frankie. If it wasn't for Mamma, he would have sent Rocco and Achille after you."

"Mamma knows?"

"What the hell do you think? Frankie was her brother, for God's sake. You hurt her deeply, Joey. But you're her son. She pleaded for your life and Uncle Angelo agreed to let you go."

"What? That's great." Joey smiled.

"No, it's not. You got to get out of the country. Fast. He's giving you twelve hours to do it. If you're not gone, you're dead."

"How the hell am I supposed to do that? I'm fucking broke."

Billy put the briefcase on the dining room table and opened it. Inside it was filled with stacks of hundred-dollar bills. Joey whistled. Even Connie's eyes grew wide at the sight of all that money.

"There's a hundred grand here. It's money to make a new start. Take it. I packed you some clothes in the suitcase. Now come on, let's get out of here."

"What about me?" asked Connie.

"Go visit your family. Everything will be okay."

"What about this body? It can't just stay here. I gotta live here."

Billy gently stroked her cheek. "He'll be gone when you return. But you gotta keep your mouth shut."

"Ain't the cops gonna find out?"

"The cops couldn't catch a cold. No one's gonna find

out. If they do, you won't live to see the night. Do I make myself clear?"

Connie nodded.

"Now get out of here. Anybody asks you about your cheek, you tell them that you walked into a stickball bat. You got that?"

"Sure, Billy. Thanks."

"Don't thank me. You got nothin' to fear as long as you keep your mouth shut. But you slip up just once, and your ass is dead."

"Can I pack some things?"

"Go ahead. But make it quick."

Connie ran into the bedroom and emerged minutes later with an overnight bag. "I'll never forget this, Billy. I owe you." She glanced at Joey and her eyes softened. She held him in her arms and kissed him hard on the mouth while grinding her pelvis into his groin. Joey returned the embrace and cupped her buttocks one last time.

"Good-bye, Joey. It was fun," she said. Then she left.

The minute she was gone, Joey turned to his brother. "How'd you get me off, Billy?"

"Never mind. You're a dead man if you stay in the States. An open contract will be put out on you if you ever come back. Do you know what that means? You'll never see Mamma or me again."

"But I'm alive. It's a cheap price to pay. Where can I go?"

"Anywhere you want. You got a hundred gees."

"I can't leave," Joey said.

"Why not?"

"I got no passport. No papers."

Billy chuckled. "Little brother, I told you I would take care of everything. Let's go."

"Where?"

"To this place in Brooklyn. The guy makes perfect documents. I got the car outside. Let's get out of here."

Joey embraced his brother. "Thanks, Billy. You really saved my life. I owe you one."

Billy avoided his eyes. "Come on, Joey. We got time for this shit later."

In the car, Billy was silent and avoided looking at Joey. Joey didn't notice his brother's distraction. He was too busy touching the money in the briefcase. *I got it made. One hundred big ones. I can go anywhere I want. I'm really gonna live it up. No more livin' like a shit.*

"You know what I like about money, Billy?" asked Joey. "Its smell. There's nothing like it."

"Is that why you sold us out?"

"Hey, I didn't sell you out for the money. I couldn't take going back to the joint."

"You better keep a low profile, Joey. The Feds will be looking for you."

"I'm not sweating them. How does Mamma feel about all this?"

"It's breaking her up inside. But she understands. She's lost a husband and a brother. At least you're still alive."

"Maybe she can visit me after I get set up."

"Maybe she will." They drove the rest of the way in silence.

Billy stopped in front of Di Mauro's Tailor Shop on Ocean Avenue. "This is it," said Billy.

"What do I do?"

"You talk to the owner. He'll give you passports, visas—whatever you want. But it will cost you fifteen thousand dollars."

"Fifteen grand? That's robbery!"

"So call the cops." Billy laughed and Joey joined him.

The brothers entered the shop and saw an elderly man with Coke-bottle glasses hunched over an old-fashioned sewing machine that operated by a foot pedal. He didn't look up when they entered. Billy stood before him.

"Is Mario home?"

The man looked up, and nodded. He pointed to a gray curtain. As the brothers walked to the rear, the old man left the shop, careful not to look at either Joey or Billy.

Billy brushed the curtain aside and Joey followed.

Angelo smacked Joey in the mouth with a six-inch lead bar, knocking out all of his front teeth. Joey gagged and spat out teeth and blood as he fought to keep his feet. But his arms were pinned to his sides by Rocco and Achille, effectively immobilizing him.

Joey tried to scream, but Angelo stuffed a handkerchief into his mouth. Only muffled sounds emerged. He grabbed a hunk of his nephew's hair and yanked Joey's head back. As Joey choked on his own blood, Angelo stared deep into his eyes.

"Hello, Joey," he said. "Thanks for coming." He turned to Billy. "Where's the money?"

"In the briefcase. He didn't spend a dime."

"Where's the plane ticket?"

"I didn't give it to him. Here it is." Billy reached into his pocket and handed the ticket to his uncle.

"You caused me much pain, Joey. And a lot of grief. My brother is dead because of you. And the family lost a lot of money. You must pay the price."

Joey mumbled a protest that was smothered by the handkerchief.

245

Angelo ignored him. He nodded to Rocco and spoke in Italian. "Make him suffer, Rocco. He's nothing anymore. But kill him before morning. Come, Billy, we have much to discuss."

Angelo put his arm around Billy's shoulder and they walked from the room. Billy never looked back.

CHAPTER 24

I T WAS a great morning for the *Daily News.* Two, count them, *two* "gangland rubouts." Even though the paper treated the murders of Frankie Tartagliano and Joey Castelli as unrelated, they got the first four pages of the paper—plus photos in the centerfold.

Fleming stared in disbelief at the pictures. He saw Joey Castle lying faceup at the entrance to the city garbage dump. Close-ups showed the smears of blood on his face. Helpful arrows showed where two bullets had struck his head. "At close range," the caption said.

Frankie Tartagliano didn't get such major coverage.

But then, his body had only been found in the rear pew at St. Anthony's Church. And his wounds weren't so spectacular.

Fleming had just stepped out of the bathroom, a towel around his shoulders, his cheeks pink from shaving. But when he saw the headlines, all the color drained from his face.

"Shitfuckingoddamn," he breathed. He looked over at Joan's chair. Force of habit. She hadn't been there for weeks—still staying with a younger sister. Fleming shredded the newspaper in his hands. "I've got to get dressed and into the office," he said. "This will be one hell of a circus today."

Fleming's prediction was correct. The morning newspapers had made no connection between the deaths, but by afternoon the television news was beginning to tie them together. Kohler spent the day in his office, switching from channel to channel.

At one point, Kohler called Fleming in. Andy Cavallera's face appeared on the screen, looking very serious. "Yes, I do think the murders are connected," he said. "Both men are under indictment for a major narcotics case." He went on to discuss the case.

Fucking guy sounds like he's running for governor already, Fleming thought. Then he shrugged. *At least he's up-front about it. Well, he'll have a hell of a time repairing this case.*

"This is live," Kohler said. "Cavallera is coming here right after he finishes."

Andy Cavallera was not in a good mood when he came through the door. "You guys have fucked me up royally," he complained. "What's the matter around here?"

"I dunno, Cavallera," Fleming said. "Better check with

your makeup man. Your nose was shiny on the tube just now."

"Look, I don't need your crap after all those reporters," Cavallera said. "I stopped by to see what kind of case we have left." He shook his head. "As far as I can see, all we have left is your word that the Tartaglianos are bag guys."

Fleming nodded. "That's about it. When we lost Frankie, we lost our big name—and our link to the Tartaglianos. Bumpy Morgan was iced, so we have no link to Billy Castelli. And with Joey gone, we don't have an inside man."

"We don't have a fucking case!" Cavallera burst out. "Castelli was supposed to pull it all together. We don't have him, we lose the whole conspiracy case. We lose Angelo Tartagliano!"

Kohler butted in. "We still have . . ."

Cavallera cut him off. "We have a bunch of surveillance reports. Great stories. Beautifully written—some of them may even be true. But they won't convince a jury. We're fucked, gentlemen—and somebody in your Agency did the fucking."

Bile burned in the back of Fleming's throat. *Not somebody. Powers did the job. Toora-Loora Dick got Kohler so drunk he spilled his guts about the case—and doesn't even remember about it.* His stomach muscles tensed. *I ought to open my mouth and fuck Powers right back.*

But Fleming's mouth stayed shut as Cavallera raved on. Maybe it was the years he and Powers had spent as partners. He didn't want to rat on Dick without giving him advance warning. Or maybe it was just the terrifying emptiness he felt in his middle—a void that had grown as the day went on.

Is this how it feels to burn out? Fleming wondered. *I*

don't give a flying fuck about anything. I'm just going through the motions.

Cavallera finally wound down. "Unless you guys get some shit together, our big fucking bust will have nailed one man—Guido Cantalope. Hardly a major figure in organized crime." He stormed out of Kohler's office.

George Kohler turned to Fleming. "He's right, you know. Washington is not going to love this. Where are your big guarantees now, Fleming?"

Fleming shrugged. "Shot to shit. Just like Joey Castelli."

"So what are you going to do about this mess?"

Fleming shrugged again. "I'll get on it right away." He walked out of the office. He had no idea of what to do.

As he passed his desk, however, the phone rang. He picked up the receiver.

"Ed, it's me—Joan."

After all these weeks of having the phone slammed in his ear, he didn't know what to say. It would be so easy to shout—but then he would lose her. He stared at the phone in helpless silence.

Joan's voice shook as she went on. "I just heard the news about your case." She hesitated for a moment. "I thought maybe you'd want some company tonight. What do you say we stay in the city for dinner?"

Fleming had no idea why he picked Puglia's. It was an old Italian restaurant on Hester Street, with high tin ceilings and glasses made murky by generations of finger marks. Joan seemed to enjoy her braciola. Fleming had an American steak, washed down with a pitcher of tepid beer.

It was a weekday night, and the place was quiet. Fleming and Joan had a table to themselves. Nobody was nearby to hear Fleming finally say, "I hate this fucking job."

Joan stared at him. "I never thought I'd hear you say that."

Fleming shrugged. "What have I got to lose? This case was my last chance—a shot at a promotion, an opportunity to *do* something. Well, it's all blown now. The case is in a shambles. We'll never fix it. Angelo is probably laughing at us. And me—I'll just be a street agent, nothing more." He emptied his glass of beer. "Worst of all, I'm no good at it anymore. You've got to be a real prick to work snitches. And I'm losing it."

Joan reached out her hand to him, but Fleming moved his hand away. "I'm feeling sorry for those poor bastards, and that's the end. Remember Larry?"

Joan nodded.

"Well, it's worse with Joey. He was a slug, a weasely little jerk who thought with his balls. The kind where you wash your hands after hitting them. He used to cry— *cry!*—when I squeezed him too hard."

Fleming shook his head. "I felt bad all the time I was turning him. I was glad whenever he got me pissed off, so I could slug him and forget about feeling shitty. Sure, it was all for the case. And when the family got on to him, I tried to warn him. To help him. And it wasn't for the case. It's so stupid. I wanted to save this guy who made my skin crawl. I'm just not thinking straight anymore."

He pushed his steak away, half-eaten. "Larry, Joey, Ross—months of work, day and night stuff. And it's all down the tubes—down the fucking pit." Blindly, he reached for the beer pitcher, sloshing some on the table as he refilled his glass.

"You can't blame yourself, Ed." Joan tried to reach him

with her eyes. But he was staring into his beer. He took a long pull at his glass, then froze when he found her eyes on him.

"I'll bet you tried everything to protect Joey," she said.

"Yeah, everything. Too late." Fleming reached for his glass again, but Joan's hand came down on his wrist.

"I can't believe this is you talking," she said. "I—I know a lot of things didn't turn out the way we hoped—or planned. And maybe I haven't been fair to you . . ."

"You were more than I hoped for. Without you, I'd have burned out two years ago."

"You're not burnt out!" Joan leaned across the table. "You're tired. And alone. We all make mistakes. I made one—running out when I did. But maybe I can fix it. I—I miss you, Ed. I'd like to come home."

Fleming looked at her for a long moment. Then he gave her the ghost of a grin. "You still have your key?"

Joan signaled the waiter. "Could we have our check, please?" she said. Then she turned to Fleming. "Let's get out of here."

They left the restaurant, but Fleming turned in the opposite direction from where they'd left the car. "Let's walk," he said. "Take some air."

He took them on a wandering course through the narrow, quiet streets, until they came to a corner that bustled with activity—lots of people in the streets, all watching one building. Angelotti's Funeral Home.

"Best in the business for hiding bullet holes," Fleming said. "They're waking Joey in there tonight."

Joan stopped. "You're not—"

Fleming looked from her to the door. "I thought about it," he said. "But who would I be kidding? Me?"

Joan felt nervous. She could feel dozens of eyes on them. It made her skin crawl.

"Smile," said Fleming. "We're probably on candid camera. There must be twenty different agencies covering this place." They walked past the funeral home. Then Fleming saw a familiar face—Harold Denton, on surveillance.

Fleming grinned. "Hey, kid," he called. "How's it going?"

Denton was too embarrassed to answer.

Joan and Fleming drove home in silence. As they came through the apartment door, Joan glanced at her watch. "It's late," she said.

Fleming just nodded.

The lights were out, and they were between the sheets. Joan could hear Ed's regular breathing beside her. Regular, but too quick. He was still awake.

"Ed," she said.

He didn't respond.

Joan sat up. "Ed, don't do this."

Silence answered her.

"Ed!" Joan surprised herself as her hands went to the hem of the sweatshirt she'd worn to bed. She pulled it over her head. *If this doesn't get an answer . . .*

She leaned over him, rubbing her naked breasts on his chest.

His reaction startled her. "Ed!" she cried as his arms wrapped around her, trapping her own arms in a circle of muscle. It wasn't a passionate grab. It was more the crushing bear hug of a drowning sailor on a piece of flotsam.

They stayed for a long moment, her lying atop him, his

arms pulling him to her, as if he wanted to become a part of her. His head nestled in the hollow of her shoulder. She could feel the heat of his breath, short, shallow pants against her naked flesh.

Involuntarily, she quivered against him. Her nipples were getting hard. And against her thigh and belly she could feel him stiffening, too.

"Well, now—" she began, but then his lips found hers, his tongue splurging into her mouth, turning her words into a meaningless hum.

With a sudden movement, he rolled over. Joan made protesting noises into his mouth as his body came onto hers. Usually Ed was a gentleman in bed, resting his weight on elbows and knees. They used to joke about it, Ed claiming that eight years of Marine push-ups had been good for something.

But this time he pressed into her, pinning her to the mattress with the full weight of his body, as if he were afraid she'd escape—or disappear. His hands—those big, strong hands that had always stroked her so gently before—roved heavily around her body now. *God, he could leave bruises!* she thought.

She pulled her mouth free from his lips and tongue. "Ed," she gasped, "you're—UH!"

His lips clamped onto hers, to catch an explosion of air gasping from her mouth as his hands found her breasts.

She squirmed under his rough touch. The tips of her breasts were squashed beneath his palms, but when he released her, the nipples seemed to stiffen still harder.

Joan lay limp under him, caught by surprise, tossing her head feebly to free her mouth, naked from the waist up. She still wore her sweatpants.

Ed pushed his knees between hers, spreading her thighs, humping himself against her, right through the material.

Joan's breath blew gustily into his mouth as he moved. She began grinding her hips up to his.

He reared back for a moment, grabbing the drawstring of her pants, loosening them. Then he lay on her again as he wrenched the pants down.

"You're acting like a maniac," she gasped. The muscles in her thighs tightened as she pushed up against him, trying to lift her ass off the mattress, to let her pants slip free.

Their legs kicked together as they pushed the garment down. Her patch of pubic hair scraped along the underside of his prick as she wriggled under him, the sweat-slick flesh of her thighs and belly soft yet taut against his body.

Then her legs were free, wrapping around him, guiding him as he slipped into her warm dampness. He set to with a jarring, harsh rhythm. His intensity almost frightened her. And he still hadn't said a word. His mouth was still against hers, but she could feel his teeth gritted behind his lips. And—could she be imagining it? His face was wet with tears.

Joan had heard the term "in the saddle" before, but now she was experiencing it for the first time. As they bucked together, she felt as if Ed were riding her, riding hard to escape a host of demons pursuing him.

They worked madly together. She came once, twice, then lay limp beneath him as a third orgasm crested within her. With a sound like a choking sob, Ed came, too.

Then he rolled off her, trembling.

Joan stirred, pulling the covers back up, nestling into

Ed. Her head pillowed on his chest and her arm went around him. She shivered as she lay there in the silence.

Even though she was close enough to feel the pounding of his heart beneath her cheek, she felt as if her man were a million miles away.

CHAPTER 25

A FEW DAYS LATER, Fleming stood outside the Church of San Gennaro, watching the show. Limousines, dozens of them, carried family, business associates, and the innumerable floral tributes that always appear at organized-crime funerals. This, being a double-barreled funeral, drew a huge crowd.

Of course, it also drew a huge crowd of funeral watchers, from just about every law-enforcement agency in New York. Six varieties of Feds alone were there. Fleming rested his back against a brick building front, his hands in his pockets, that familiar empty feeling in his gut. The rest of his crew could take names and pictures. He just watched the crowd filing up the brick steps.

San Gennaro's was not a church outstanding for its architectural grandeur. It was an old working-class church, with steep steps and wrought-iron banisters. But it was still the center of the earth for New York's traditional Italians. *They come in from Westchester, Jersey, Brooklyn—back to the old neighborhood. For the feasts, to get married—and to get planted,* he thought.

Watching the crowd enter the church, he took a step or two forward, with the unformed thought of paying his respects to Joey. He stopped before he reached the street. *I must be getting crazy. Pay my respects to what's left of that little creep?*

He stepped back from the edge of the pavement, then stopped. Across the street, at the outskirts of the crowd, stood Dick Powers. *He's got some balls, showing up here,* thought Fleming. *Is he "showing respect"? Or coming to collect his thirty pieces of silver?*

Powers had evidently seen him. He crossed the street, heading directly for him. "Eddie, my boy," he said with a grin. "Nice day for a funeral."

Fleming stared icily, waiting for Powers to step up to the pavement. "You," he said quietly, "are a piece of shit."

Powers stiffened in midstep. His grin slipped. "Now, wait a minute, boyo—"

"And don't give me any of that 'boyo' bullshit," Fleming snapped.

Powers's brogue dropped magically away. "You had some people really worried," he said.

"Yeah. Well, you took care of that."

"Look," Powers said. "They wanted the snitch's head, or

they were going to hand me mine. It was a simple choice. Him or me. And whenever it comes down to that, I'll choose me."

"Thanks," Fleming said. "I'll keep that in mind."

Powers moved closer. "In a way, I did you a favor. Remember that offer I made? Sure, you just blew me away. But you were interested—admit it!"

Fleming nodded.

"A few extra bucks," Powers said. "A few little luxuries . . ."

Fleming remembered a conversation he'd once had with an Internal Affairs guy. "Cops don't become corrupt because of poor pay. The wrong ones are usually detectives or rank bosses, with good salaries. They go on the pad because they want things. Not necessities—food, clothing, shit like that. No, it's the extras. The luxuries."

"But you got bent out of shape when I asked for Joey's name." Powers continued talking. "Well, those people I mentioned. They were really impressed with you. I was talking on the phone . . ."

"To Angelo?" Fleming cut in.

"It doesn't matter. Look, I can make a deal for you. Talk to them and let them tell you the arrangement. What do you say?"

Fleming laughed. "I'd say I'd have to be crazy to trust you, you fucking thief."

Powers actually blushed. "Look, stop dicking around here. There's bucks to be made. Real bucks. They were talking about pounds of money."

Fleming stared at him, taken aback. *Maybe they really would have paid two hundred and fifty grand.* The empty feeling yawned in his gut. *Could I just have been stupid, missing the boat?*

"Set up a meeting," he said abruptly. "I don't trust you. But I'll talk to Angelo. You can be there to protect your interest."

Less than a week later, Fleming was walking toward a dingy social club on Pleasant Avenue. Powers was at his side. "Now remember, this isn't one of the guys at the office, where you just say 'fuck you' if you don't like what they're saying."

"Stop acting like the protocol officer," Fleming finally said. "We're just going to talk, that's all." He gave Powers his wickedest grin. "I promise not to treat him like a street pusher."

Somehow, that didn't leave Powers reassured.

They stepped through the door, into a good-sized room. Chairs and tables had been pushed to the walls, making it look even larger. One table was left out, and one chair—for Angelo Tartagliano. Rocco Mazzi and Achille Aspermonte stood behind him.

Fleming and Angelo locked eyes for a moment. "What's the matter, don't we get chairs?" said Fleming.

"When a man comes to do business for money, he follows the rules of the man with the money," Angelo said.

"That depends," Fleming said. "Maybe he's got something to sell that the man with money wants."

"And what could that be?" Angelo asked.

"Peace of mind."

Angelo shrugged. "I had that before you started involving yourself in my affairs." His voice became steely. "I also had a nephew and a brother."

"Yeah," said Fleming. "You see what a pain in the ass I can be." He glanced over at Powers. "My friend here told me you were ready to pay pounds of money to get me off your back. Let's talk about two hundred and fifty thousand."

"Ah." Angelo put his hands together. "That was when I was faced with a major Federal indictment. Since then, you've lost your main defendant—and your star witness." His eyes changed color as he stared at Fleming. "However, Mr. Fleming, I am impressed by your courage, if not your respect. I could use a man like you. But you would have to understand your place in my organization. And your worth would be nowhere near two hundred and fifty thousand."

Powers spoke up. "Things are different from the way they were a couple of weeks ago. That's what we're here to talk about . . ."

Fleming cut him off. "You still don't get it," he said, looking at Angelo. "You killed off Larry, and you killed off Joey, and you owe something for them. I can still cause you misery, Tartagliano. I can put your ass in jail."

"So the brave policeman puts big, bad Angelo in jail. For how long? A day? How long will that keep you warm?" Angelo stared at Fleming. *They are all the same. He sounds so righteous, but all he is doing is bargaining. It will merely take a little longer to take him in.*

"If it's a day, then it's a day. I can still hope you'll wake up and find a cockroach crawling on your face. I've already talked to the Federal prosecutor," Fleming said. "He'll delay as much as possible."

"For what reason?" asked Angelo.

Fleming gave him an insolent smile. "Well, the official reason will be that I'm trying to turn you."

Powers, Rocco, and Achille held their breath.

But Angelo gave Fleming a thin smile. "Your friend

Powers was right," he said. "You've got guts. Would you consider . . . fifty thousand?"

Powers glared at Fleming. *Take it, you dumb asshole. Take it!*

But when Fleming heard the offer, he felt as if he had just been slapped awake. Now the emptiness inside him began to fill with anger. He had no intention of being owned—of being like Dick Powers.

Fleming rested his fists on the table, leaning over it to look Angelo in the eye. "You cheap guinea prick," he said. "You think I'm some chump you can buy with pocket change, huh? After you've blown your whole setup? I can do better than jail for you. Suppose I gave Vito Panella a phone call. Just one phone call, and you'd be playing a harp."

Eyes glittering, Angelo Tartagliano leaped to his feet.

But Fleming was ready for him. He rammed into the table with his hip, catching Angelo off-balance. Tartagliano flopped facedown onto the table. Fleming's hand clamped heavily onto the nape of Angelo's neck, grinding his face into the wood. His other hand whipped out his pistol, pointing it at Angelo's temple.

Rocco and Achille froze, their guns half-drawn.

"Drop 'em on the floor," said Fleming. "Or I mess up this nice table with your boss's brains."

They stayed where they were until Angelo ordered them in Italian. Then they put their guns on the floor.

"I should have told them to shoot you," Angelo gritted. "But it's bad business to kill a Fed. Others come around and ruin business."

Fleming grinned. "You talk pretty big for a guy with a gun in his ear. Not a good idea."

"This whole meeting was a bad idea," Angelo said.

"Maybe we should forget it ever happened."

"Maybe we should," Fleming agreed. "I'm gonna leave now." He looked over at Rocco and Achille. "Tell your boys to kick their guns away. I don't want any surprises on my way out of here."

Angelo gave the order, and once again, Achille and Rocco obeyed.

"So long," Fleming said, walking out the door.

Rocco and Achille dove for their guns. But Angelo made an impatient gesture. He rose slowly from the table and began to pace the room. One hand was clenched. The other tried to massage away the pain in his neck. "That bastard is crazy," he said.

"He sure is," Powers agreed. He had a hard time hiding a smirk as he watched Angelo's white face pass him. *Eddie-boy certainly showed the head guinea something,* he thought. *And I'm glad I got to see it.*

Angelo whirled around. His knee jerked up, catching the unsuspecting Powers right in the testicles.

Powers let out a choked sob and grabbed himself.

"Take him!" Angelo ordered.

Rocco and Achille each grabbed an arm, forcing Powers to his knees. Angelo kicked him in the gut.

"You will never mention this," Angelo said. "Never. Never. See?" He punctuated each word with a kick to the pit of Powers's stomach. Even in his rage, he was careful in his placement of the kicks. No broken ribs, no long-term injury. Just as much pain as Powers could stand.

One more kick. Then he took a deep breath and stepped back. "Let him go."

Powers sagged to the floor.

Angelo turned to Rocco. "You find Billy. Bring him here." Then he turned to Achille. "You—watch that one."

He sat back down in his chair, and started massaging his neck again.

By the time Billy arrived, Powers had reached the sit-up-and-take-notice stage. Billy glanced at the Federal agent, who sat hunched on the floor, arms pressed to his belly. "What happened?" he asked.

"We talked with that Fleming," Angelo responded. "No good. We can't buy him. And he has just enough brains to be dangerous. We'll have to take care of him. I want you to do the job."

Billy nodded. *He's treating me like a real lieutenant now,* he thought. *But the jobs get more and more difficult.* "I'll need Rocco and Achille," he said.

"I have thought it all out." Angelo pointed at Powers. "He'll help us—lead Fleming to a nice, isolated place. You, Rocco, and Achille will shoot him. Then we can get back to business."

"Hey, I don't know about this," Powers wheezed. "Helping you ice Ed . . ."

"You don't need to know!" Angelo shouted, getting to his feet. He smiled to himself at the way Powers flinched. "You need only to obey. There's no choice here. You're in too deep, and this Fleming knows too much. What if he goes to your Internal Affairs officers?"

Dick Powers nodded, defeated.

"Go, then," Angelo ordered. "You have three days to set this up. Call me. Or I'll get very, very . . . angry at you."

Powers pulled himself up and walked to the door. He moved like an old man.

As soon as the door closed behind the Federal agent, Angelo turned to Billy. "And another thing. You take care of that one, too."

CHAPTER 26

THE SETUP came two days later. Powers had decided on the simplest possible method. He called Fleming early in the evening, at home.

"What do *you* want?" Fleming asked.

"I'm offering you a favor," Powers said. "You haven't had much in the way of busts lately, have you?"

Fleming didn't answer. With the loss of Larry, Joey, and then Ross's informants, arrests had been few and far between.

Powers put his cards on the table. "I got a tip about a deal going down tonight. It'll be all yours."

"And why are you so eager to do me favors? I bet that bossman Angelo wouldn't like that."

"That guinea fuck! I hate him." As far as that went, Powers was telling the truth. "He thinks he owns me. I really enjoyed watching you give the old fart what he deserved." Powers went on, choosing his words carefully. "Besides, I guess I owe you." It was a delicate reference to the fact that Fleming hadn't ratted on him.

He's a slimy prick, but God knows, I need a collar. "What's the deal?" Fleming asked.

"This guy will be waiting to do some business at two A.M. in Long Island City." Powers went into his story. "He'll be in the parking lot under the Flushing line, at Thirty-first Street. We can take him there. Bust him for possession."

"Two A.M., huh?" said Fleming.

"Yeah. Take a nap or something. I want you bright-eyed and bushy-tailed when I come to pick you up."

Fleming's face was studiously bland as he made the date and hung up the phone. Things had been quiet around the house, and he was unwilling to break the fragile peace.

Joan looked up from the couch. Ed had been spending his evenings at home lately, not on the street. This sudden jump into a case filled her with nameless apprehension. "You're going out?" she asked.

"Yeah. A quick, simple bust. It will get Kohler off my ass." He smiled. "I'll be quiet coming in."

"Don't," said Joan. "I want to know when you come back." She paused for a second. "Be careful. Watch your back."

He laughed as he headed down the hall. "I always do." But he stopped by the closet and pulled out his old footlocker. Opening the box, he stared at the contents, frowning in thought. *Something in here might just come in handy . . .*

Queens Boulevard is not the liveliest street in New York at two in the morning. Especially on a weekday. Most especially in the area where Sunnyside fades into Long Island City. In a few hours it would be jammed, commuters lining up to cross the Fifty-ninth Street Bridge. But as Fleming drove down the boulevard, the streets were deserted. A couple of fast-food places made oases of light among the darkened stores. Most of the shops had iron gratings over their windows.

They came up to an old loft building painted white with red ideograms on the front—the press for some Chinese-language newspaper.

"Heads up, Eddie-boy. It's the next block." Powers leaned forward in the passenger seat.

This was the ideal place for a meet. The sixty-year-old elevated train structure was built of concrete on this stretch. It rose in big, ponderous arches, supported by massive, square columns almost five feet on a side. The cavernous space beneath the El was used as parking lots. It was especially gloomy at night—the only illumination provided by the streetlights on the boulevard. On one side rose the blank walls of an industrial building—a waterproofing company. Across the street was an abandoned diner—driven out of business by the fast-food joints farther back.

Fleming drove into the lot. Their quarry was easy to spot—only one car was parked in the place, someone sitting behind the steering wheel.

"Pull in behind him," Powers instructed. Fleming nodded and cut in behind the parked car. His right hand went into his pocket, palming what was in there.

Fleming hit the brakes, neatly boxing the other car in.

Powers was already reaching for the door handle. *I want to be as far away as I can when they waste him,* he thought. But even as he turned, he detected movement. Two figures appeared from behind the concrete pillar across from him. Even in the dimness, he recognized their outlines—Rocco and Achille.

"Oh, fuck, they set me up, too!" Powers said huskily as he rammed into the door, fumbling his gun out. The first shot from his .38 caught the two button men by surprise. It also caught Achille right in the chest. His Beretta clattered to the pavement as he staggered back, literally dead on his feet.

Rocco brought up his bulky Browning 9mm, and let Powers have it as he scrambled from the car. A belly shot—he didn't want this guy to die too quick.

Powers slammed to the ground, his expression almost comical as the round tore into him.

"Eh, balle—dance," Rocco said, moving forward, pumping bullets into Powers's arms and legs, making them jerk. A movement from inside the car brought him back to reality. *This is no time for play. Finish this one.* He put a bullet into Powers's head, then aimed across the front seat of the car. "You—throw your gun out," he ordered.

The advantage of surprise was complete. Fleming hadn't even drawn his gun. Rocco smiled as the Fed awkwardly removed the .38 from his holster and tossed it outside. *This one I can have fun with. Maybe the knife . . .*

"All right. Out of the car now. And keep your hands where I can see them."

Fleming scooted across the seat, hands out, palms down.

Rocco leaned forward. *When he comes out, I smack him with the gun first . . .*

Fleming got out of the car. His right hand came up, fist clenched . . .

Rocco had about a second to be surprised at the spurt of fire that came from between Fleming's fingers. Then the .357 Magnum "super-force" bullet sped from the one-shot palm gun, right into the hole where Rocco's nose used to be. It tore through his brain, the impact so great it sent Rocco into a somersault. His legs swung up straight before him as he spun in the air. The Browning dropped from his nerveless hand.

Holy shit, thought Fleming. *That little sucker packs a punch.* He was thankful the pusher he'd confiscated it from had been too stunned to use his palm gun. *I figured it was just the thing to have along if Powers tried to ice me . . .*

He stepped out of the car, reaching for his .38, when Billy Castelli stepped around the rear fender, aiming his pistol. *The guy in the other car! I forgot about him!*

Billy snapped off a shot with his H & K 9mm.

Ed Fleming felt as if a mule had kicked him in the left thigh. *Shit! I'm hit!* he thought as the shock of the impact set him spinning. The palm gun flew out of his hand. He clenched his teeth against the tearing pain, the burning that radiated from the wound.

Fleming hit the ground hard, wincing as something caught him in the chest. It felt like—a gun?

269

Billy Castelli moved cautiously forward. *Jesus Christ, what did that guy have hidden in his hand? A derringer or something? He really nailed Rocco. But he lost it when I shot him. Too bad he fell behind the car door.*

Squeezing the trigger, he sent a shot into the door, then another one. *Keep his head down,* Billy thought. *I can afford the bullets.* His pistol had a twenty-shot magazine.

Behind the scant cover of the car door, Fleming clawed the gun out from under him. It was Rocco's old cannon, the big Browning. *Hope that sadistic little bastard left a few rounds for me,* he thought. *Gotta get out of here. I'll be a sitting duck.*

His left leg was now a dead weight. The wound still burned. Fleming could feel the warm, sticky wetness of blood making its way down his leg, soaking into his pants. No way would he be able to stand or even crawl. Scrabbling with his right leg, Fleming tried to push himself backwards. Even that small movement sent little pain sparks flickering in front of his eyes. *No. Can't pass out now. Not with that guy coming. Have to get ready . . .*

Fleming transferred the gun to his left hand and pushed up, bracing himself on his right elbow. *Only get one shot as he comes around the door,* he thought. He could hear Billy's shots ricocheting off the door panels.

Billy came around the door, still shooting. His eyes widened in surprise when he saw the gun in Fleming's hand, but he didn't hesitate. He fired almost without aiming.

Fleming's shot rang out right after Billy's—in the same instant Billy's bullet took him in the right shoulder. His elbow collapsed just as he squeezed the trigger. The gun wavered as he fired. He missed Billy's chest, where he'd been aiming.

Instead, he took out the side of Billy's head.

Fleming didn't even see Billy go down. He was lying on his back, breathing in short, gasping pants. Any second, he expected to find Billy appearing over him, aiming for the coup de grace.

But Billy never came.

Sonofabitch, Fleming thought, *I must have got him!* He tried to raise his head, to get a glimpse of Billy. But the world began to swirl around him, so he let his head fall back again. He felt as if someone had nailed him to the ground, running a huge, burning spike through his shoulder. His shirt was fast soaking with blood, too.

Fleming looked at the dingy vaulted ceiling high above him. *Looks like a church,* he thought. *A church with four stiffs in it. Maybe five,* he corrected himself. If he didn't get help soon, he would bleed to death. *Five caskets in the church. Funeral Mass...* He remembered himself as a kid, an altar boy, burning the incense around the coffins. The clink of the censor against its brass chain, the heat of the charcoal within, the sharp stink of the incense, the organ playing something deep and solemn. *Do they still do that kind of funeral now?* he wondered muzzily.

The shrill blast of sirens cut through the organ music in his head for a second. But Fleming didn't care. He was sinking into blackness.

CHAPTER 27

*C*HRIST ALMIGHTY, Fleming thought as he opened his eyes. *What did I do to myself this time?*

His right shoulder and his left leg throbbed, and his chest felt as if it had been on the receiving end of a sledge-hammer. *Right. From landing on that fucking gun.*

The memories of the events under the El came back. *Well, I'm still alive. More or less.* He moved his head, grimacing with annoyance. While he'd been out, someone had shoved a rubber tube up his nose. None too gently.

His eyes began to focus now. He was in a hospital room, obviously, with plenty of bandages on him.

Then he saw Joan, sitting on a chair.

His voice sounded like an old creaking door when he called to her. "Hey. Did I make page one of the *Post?*"

Joan jumped up. She laughed, but there were tears in her eyes. He took her hand. Joan's delicate fingers were lost in his big paw, but he could barely manage a feeble squeeze. "No, you're not famous," she said. "But your play-mates are."

She held up the paper. Fleming could see the big red print of the headline. "GANGBUSTERS!" The photo showed the two parked cars with four bodies around them.

He tried to make out the caption, but the small print kept swimming in front of his eyes. "Can't read," he complained.

Joan read the blurb. "A drug bust turned into a gun battle this morning, as three dope dealers and two Federal agents shot it out in Queens. The dealers and one agent died in the shooting. The other agent was rushed to the hospital, in critical condition."

"No name?" he said.

"They're all inside," she said. "At least you made page three of today's *Post.*"

"Well, aren't you going to read it? I want to know how it all turned out."

Joan shook her head and started reading. It was pure press-release stuff, about the two brave agents, ex-part-ners, who had followed a tip and been attacked. Of course, there was no mention of Powers's extracurricular finan-cial arrangements, or how he'd set Fleming up.

"So, he died with a halo on, even though I bet the guys at the Agency have their suspicions now."

Joan read further about the quantity of cocaine that had been recovered from Billy's car.

"Probably planted afterwards," Fleming said. "He was driving there to shoot me. You can bet your ass his car was clean."

The rest of the story was routine as well, with comments from Andy Cavallera and George Kohler, and a tie-in with the big bust, and the deaths of Frankie and Joey.

"That it?" he asked.

"There's one more late-breaking story here," Joan said. "Angelo Tartagliano was found murdered in his Cadillac, shot by assailants unknown."

A grim smile came to Fleming's face. "So, Don Vito decided to cut his liabilities. Good. That bastard deserved to die." He let his head rest back. It would feel so good to close his eyes . . .

"Ed?" Joan swam into focus again. She was leaning over him. "We've got to talk. It's important."

"You don't have to worry," Fleming said, teasing. "He only got me in the *leg*. If it had been a few inches over, though . . ."

"Stop it!" Joan said. "I was afraid you were going to die when they told me about you."

"Well, I'm going to be pretty fucked up for a while. How do you figure I can use crutches with one shoulder out of commission?"

"That's not important, as long as you get better," she said. "This is about your job. About staying on. I talked to one of the bosses at your Agency . . ."

The door to the room opened, and George Kohler came in. "Ed!" he said. "So, the hero is up and talking." He came over to the bed and stuck out his hand to shake, then realized Fleming's right arm was in a sling. "You done good. Real good. The Tartagliano operation is smashed to shit." He paused for a second. "Too bad about Powers, of course."

"Bullshit," Fleming said. "Powers was on the pad. Angelo owned him. He was the one who gave Joey away. He got his name from you when you were shitfaced drunk. And he set me up. I should have been dead there."

Kohler nodded, as if none of this were news. He did glance anxiously at Joan, though, as the catalog went on.

"Well, Powers is gone now. The less said about him, the better." He paused for a second. "It's *you* I want to talk about. Washington is real pleased with the great job you did . . ."

Fleming wheezed with laughter. "Oh, yeah? Look at the job my 'great job' did on me! I'm flat on my ass, with a fucking tube up my nose." His face grew serious as he looked at Kohler. "I'll tell you right now, I've had enough of the Agency. As soon as I get on my feet again, I'm out. I'll be a dogcatcher, anything. I've had it."

Kohler gave him a nervous smile. "Oh, now, Ed, I know you've been through a lot. You're still banged up. And you certainly don't want to go making major decisions"—he paused delicately—"with a tube up your nose."

He glanced over at Joan, but got no support from that quarter. "I probably shouldn't be saying this," he went on, "but there's some talk from Washington. With Powers gone, we have an open slot in our office for section chief. And you . . ."

Fleming looked over at Joan's tense face. Those fantastic hazel eyes were boring into him. This must have been what she was trying to tell him. He met her gaze, and winked reassuringly.

"George," he said, cutting Kohler off, "you want to know what to do with that gold badge?"

1

3/23/88

M C